Alyssa looked around, desperate to find some sort of weapon she could use. Anything. Hell, at this point, she'd take a rock. Her eyes fell on the knife.

Yes!

She had never thrown a knife before, but it was all she had and she was damn well going to use it. Should she throw it at The Gentleman or the guy who had Jade?

The Gentleman. Always The Gentleman.

NO LONGER PROPERTY OF
ANYTHINK LIBRARIES/
RANGEVIEW LIBRARY DISTRICT

ALSO BY TARA THOMAS

BROKEN PROMISE

TARA THOMAS

St. Martin's Paperbacks

NOTE: If you purchased this book without a cover you should be aware that this book is stolen property. It was reported as "unsold and destroyed" to the publisher, and neither the author nor the publisher has received any payment for this "stripped book."

This is a work of fiction. All of the characters, organizations, and events portrayed in this novel are either products of the author's imagination or are used fictitiously.

BROKEN PROMISE

Copyright © 2018 by Tara Thomas.
Novella of *Twisted End* copyright © 2018 by Tara Thomas.

All rights reserved.

For information address St. Martin's Press, 175 Fifth Avenue, New York, NY 10010.

ISBN: 978-1-250-13798-2

Our books may be purchased in bulk for promotional, educational, or business use. Please contact your local bookseller or the Macmillan Corporate and Premium Sales Department at 1-800-221-7945, ext. 5442, or by e-mail at MacmillanSpecialMarkets@macmillan.com.

Printed in the United States of America

St. Martin's Paperbacks edition / July 2018

St. Martin's Paperbacks are published by St. Martin's Press, 175 Fifth Avenue, New York, NY 10010.

10 9 8 7 6 5 4 3 2 1

TO MY EDITOR, ALEX SEHULSTER,
FOR BELIEVING IN ME.

CHAPTER 1

Though he would deny it if asked, Kipling Benedict felt oddly out of place at his younger brother's vow renewal. He chalked it up to both of his younger brothers now being in committed relationships, but that didn't make him feel any better. In fact, as he stood by Knox and listened as he pledged to love, honor, and cherish his wife, Bea, Kipling actually felt worse.

Worse because he was envious of what his brothers had. Though he could pound his fists into something, it wouldn't change anything. He'd accepted a long time ago that his station in life was to be alone. Having fallen in love hard and fast in college, paired with only being seen for his net worth, left him not wanting to try again. Being alone was so much easier.

However, at times such as this, he became acutely aware of the differences between acceptance and contentment. Because while he may have accepted that he would be alone, he was not content.

"You may kiss your bride," the minister said, dragging him back to the small historic chapel Bea had selected for the renewal.

Kipling clapped as his brother took his wife in his arms

and dipped her low, snagging a kiss while he did so. They both looked so blissfully in love, he couldn't help but smile at the joy and peace seen in the couple. If anyone deserved a happily ever after, they did. They had originally married in secret, but more than that, they'd both narrowly escaped with their lives after a security guard hired to protect Bea turned out to be the thug who had beat her up and left her for dead months earlier.

Kipling had asked Knox a few days ago if he was ready to give up his bachelor status forever since he was going public with his wedding this time. They'd been outside. Tilly sat at a nearby table in the garden and both Keaton and Bea sat with her. From what Kipling was able to pick up on, they were looking at a map and trying to determine the best location for a public vegetable garden. Bea looked up and winked at Knox.

His brother had only replied, "The wedding won't come soon enough for me."

Kipling felt the truth in his words that day, but now he saw it as the happy couple stood up, and laughed, only having eyes for the other.

Kipling felt his mouth curl up into a smile as the couple walked down the aisle, nodding to the small gathering of friends and family in attendance. Kipling's hands froze when he saw who waited by the chapel doors.

Alyssa Adams.

Officer Alyssa Adams.

The corner of his mouth lifted. He hadn't expected her to be here today. It was ridiculous how happy he was to see her. Especially since she made no secret of the fact that she didn't like him, his money, or anything about him. The way Kipling saw it, she presented him with a challenge and he never backed down from a challenge. But it was more than that. It was the way she never backed down from him and how when she sparred verbally with him, it made him feel alive in a way he rarely felt.

He kept his eyes on her as he made his way down the aisle behind his brother. Though he had seen her wear a dress once before at the party announcing Keaton and Tilly's engagement and the new division of Benedict Industries, today she wore a more formal one. It hit above her knee, showing off her long legs and toned calves. He'd always considered himself a leg man. Yes, breasts were great and he had no problem appreciating a woman's backside, but legs . . .

There was just something about a woman's legs. Especially when they looked like Alyssa's. Long and lean and strong. It was so easy to imagine them wrapped around his waist while he angled his hips to—

"Stop it." His youngest brother, Keaton, punched his arm. "Seriously, man. What happened to your poker face?"

They had made it out of the chapel and were waiting for the remaining guests to leave the church so they could all walk to the reception area.

"I don't know what you're talking about," Kipling told Keaton. In truth, he shouldn't be the least bit interested in the police officer. It seemed as if each time he saw her, she only gave him disturbing news about his family. Or worse yet, arrested him. He didn't understand how he could possibly find her attractive, but he did. Not only that, but he wanted her. Badly.

"You don't know what I'm talking about." His youngest brother snorted. "Yeah, right."

Kipling shot him a look that would have stopped another man in his tracks, but that apparently didn't work on younger brothers. No, the look didn't have any sort of impact on Keaton, who kept right on talking.

"You know," Keaton said, nodding toward Alyssa who

was currently chatting with Janie Roberts, her old partner, who would soon become Bea's sister-in-law. "If you wanted, you could, I don't know, ask her out or something."

He thought about playing dumb, pretending he wasn't sure who Keaton was talking about, but he'd never been one to play the fool and he sure as hell wasn't going to start now.

"It's not as simple as that," Kipling told his younger brother. It was a pat answer, but the truth. Looking at Alyssa while she spoke to her friend, he wished things were different. Damn, but he could watch her for hours. Today, there was very little to be seen of the straight-laced investigator she was around him and he found the contrast mesmerizing. She talked with Janie using her entire body. She was so animated and her smile so genuine, he couldn't look away. Not only that, but he'd always seen her with her hair pulled back in a ponytail and today it was free to dance around her shoulders in soft waves. The sunlight made the normal brown a plethora of colors: blond, red, and even hints of black.

Keaton narrowed his eyes and crossed his arms. "Why isn't it that simple?"

"I'm not going to stand here and explain myself to you," Kipling said. "You're going to have to take my word for it."

"If this is about that girl in college . . ." Keaton started, but stopped when Kipling raised his hand.

"Don't go there," Kipling warned his younger brother. "Not now. Not ever."

He would live his life and never complain if no one ever brought up the girl he dated in college. The one he fell hard for. The one he planned to marry. The one who made a fool out of him.

His stomach twisted and he wondered if he'd ever think of her without wanting to throw up. He reminded himself that at least he'd gotten out of the situation and hadn't been stupid enough to elope. She'd actually suggested they do exactly that before they went to his house for Christmas break.

Even then, it appeared as if Keaton was going to argue with him. Fortunately, Tilly, his fiancée, came up to them and looped her arm through Keaton's.

"Come on, you guys," Tilly said. "The photographer wants to do some family shots."

"Why do I have to get my picture taken?" Kipling mumbled while straightening his tie. "It's not my wedding."

But he followed Keaton and Tilly to the front of the chapel anyway, unable to keep himself from looking over his shoulder at Alyssa one last time.

"What's the deal with the oldest Benedict brother?" Janie asked Alyssa as they watched the group move off toward the photographer.

"What makes you think there's a deal?" Alyssa asked instead of answering.

Janie flashed her *I know what you're trying to do* smile. "If I was uncertain as to whether or not there was a deal, that answer just proved there is one."

Alyssa should have known she wouldn't be able to fool Janie. They'd worked together and been friends for too many years for her to think she could pull one over on her. It didn't matter that life would be a lot easier if there wasn't a deal with Kipling; the truth was there was something between the two of them.

Maybe it was nothing but lust. He'd never hid his appreciation for the way she looked. Even when she shot him down and told him off, inside she was secretly thrilled she got a response out of him. The bigger part of her loved that it wasn't only her mind Kipling took notice of. And sure, some small part of herself hated that she'd spent hours in front of the mirror today, trying to decide which dress he'd like, because she told herself she didn't care. But that look of pure animal magnetism he'd given her as he walked out of the chapel?

Worth. Every. Second.

She wasn't about to tell Janie that, though. Not with her already standing there like the cat who just ate the world's biggest canary.

"The deal," Alyssa told her, "is that nothing can ever happen between us. I arrested the man, for crying out loud. Not to mention, it would be a horrible breach of ethics."

But Janie, of course, wasn't going to be defeated that easily. She put a hand on her hip. "You mean like what I did when I started dating Brent?"

That was why Alyssa didn't want to go down the Janie-and-Brent road. Janie had been working undercover at a local gentlemen's club as a bartender, looking into the unsolved mystery of several kidnapped women, many of whom eventually turned out to be murdered.

She'd met Brent there, but unfortunately he had been considered a suspect at the time and her boss had put her on administrative leave after finding out they were involved. Janie felt strongly that Brent wasn't the man they were looking for, but even so, it was at great personal risk that she continued seeing him. Eventually, he'd been cleared by DNA evidence, but Janie had not been able to leave the case alone and was fired when her boss caught her investigating in the club. "I would be remiss if I didn't point out that you were, in fact, fired from that job."

"True, but life has turned out so much better," Janie said without missing a beat. "No offense, but you couldn't pay me enough to work at the Charleston PD again."

She didn't doubt it. Brent had asked Janie to move to Washington, DC, with him as he'd been offered a position in the capital city. The couple now lived in their city penthouse for half of the year and in his multimillion-dollar restored historical home along the Battery in Charleston for the remaining six. Not only that, but they were planning a wedding for the following May. Alyssa was getting ready to say something when Brent came up and interrupted them.

"Ladies." He slid behind Janie and put her arms around her. "Pictures are over. Everyone's heading to the reception."

Since the chapel was centrally located, it was much easier to leave the cars there and walk to the small private ballroom where the small reception was going to be. Already, Alyssa could see Knox and Bea leading the group with the rest of the Benedict family following behind.

"Oh," Janie said. "There's Tilly. I didn't get to speak to her before the ceremony."

Months ago while working undercover, before she got fired, Janie had worked with Tilly and became friends with her. Tilly was now engaged to Keaton Benedict. Honestly, it boggled Alyssa's brain sometimes how interconnected everyone seemed to be. Except her. She felt like an outsider and that realization made her want to leave.

"I think I'll head home," Alyssa said.

"Why?" Janie asked.

"I was only invited because of you and, seriously, what's the point in going?" It all made perfect sense to her, but Janie was standing and shaking her head.

"You're not getting out of it that easy," her friend said. "Come on. People will talk if you leave now."

"And we certainly can't have that," Alyssa mumbled, but allowed herself be led away.

An hour later, she was still trying to plan her escape. Staying had in no way made her feel any less of an outsider. Surely she'd been at the reception long enough to not cause offense if she left. She let her gaze wander to where

Kipling stood, talking with his brothers. It occurred to her at that moment that he didn't have a date. The more she thought about it, the odder it seemed.

He was a good-looking and wealthy man. One whom one would think would have his choice of women to date. Why would he show up alone at his brother's renewal ceremony?

Of course, he picked that moment to turn around and in doing so, saw her staring. Caught off guard, she felt her cheeks flush and turned to watch Brent and Janie dancing. They were discussing something very intently, but laughing every so often. If she had to guess, she'd bet it was about their own wedding. The thought made her smile.

"Dance with me."

She jumped. She'd been so intent on watching the couple on the dance floor, she completely missed hearing Kipling walk up behind her.

Without turning around, she replied, "No, that's okay. I'm fine." Because suddenly the thought of being that close to Kipling and having his arms around her, made her skin flush more.

"It wasn't a question."

She turned around to find him smiling and all but laughing at her. She decided to play along and raised an eyebrow. "Really? Don't you know it's not polite to go up and command a woman to dance with you?"

The hint of a smile teased his lips. "I thought you knew me well enough to know I've never been one to be called polite."

She couldn't think of anything to say back so she stood there, feeling flustered. Damn Kipling Benedict. She should have left after the ceremony and not cared about being offensive.

He took a step closer toward her. "I see you standing here, watching the couples dance, and yet you're not dancing. And I realize you didn't come with a date and I don't have a date." He shrugged. "We might as well have a go."

"No, thank you," she said. "I don't want to be anyone's pity dance."

"Let's get one thing straight, why don't we." He leaned down and spoke in a low voice she knew no one else heard. "I do very many things and I do them for all kinds of reasons, but I never do anything out of pity, especially when it comes to a beautiful woman."

Her brain threatened to short circuit. She blinked. "Why would you . . ." She trailed off as his hand moved to stroke her shoulder.

"We've both tried to ignore it, but we know there's something between us." His voice grew rougher. "Let's give into it just for today. For one dance."

She looked toward the dancing couples, imagining his arms around her, and licked her lips, on the verge of saying *yes*. She shook her head. "It's not appropriate. I'm involved in several cases that have ties to your family."

"It's one dance, Alyssa." While he spoke, he still stroked her shoulder. The touch of his fingers made her want to feel his hands everywhere. "At my brother's wedding. There's nothing wrong with two single people enjoying themselves."

Why did she get the impression he was talking about more than a dance?

She closed her eyes, but doing so did nothing to diminish the way his touch felt. She could get lost in his touch without even thinking twice. To agree to a dance would be one step down a path that offered nothing but heartache and trouble.

"Yes," she said anyway.

His hand slipped off her shoulder and he held it out to her. God, she was actually doing this. She took the offered hand, noting how warm it was and she didn't think she was imagining the strength it contained.

He didn't say anything as he led them to the dance floor. She stared at him, not looking to either side for fear of seeing the other wedding guests' reaction. She didn't realize how stiff and uncomfortable she must look until he whispered, "It's not an execution, you know. A smile wouldn't be remiss."

She smiled, but it felt fake. What didn't feel fake was the way her body reacted when he slipped his arms around her. She lowered her head, hoping to keep to herself the fact that her skin flushed at such close contact with Kipling.

"If I'd known you would feel so good in my arms, I'd have asked you to dance long before now," he said.

She tried to imagine them dancing at any of the previous times they'd been together. The image of them dancing while she arrested him made her chuckle with its ridiculousness.

"There we go," Kipling said. "Now people will think we're having a good time instead of assuming I'm torturing you."

She pulled back to look at him and make a snappy comeback, but instead she found herself caught up in his eyes. They were the most mesmerizing color. A light brown that somehow appeared golden. How had she never noticed his eyes before and why did they seem so familiar?

The corner of his mouth uplifted in a half smile. "Cat got your tongue?"

"What?"

"You looked like you were going to say something, but then you stopped."

Had she? "I don't remember."

"That's not good," he said. "I don't mind rendering you

speechless, but affecting your mental capacity isn't on my agenda."

She'd like to know exactly what was on his agenda concerning her. She bet it was mind-blowing. But what was truly mind-blowing was the way he looked at her with such intensity. It was a bit unnerving and she was starting to understand why Kipling was so good in business. Not a lot of people could stand up to the scrutiny of his gaze. Fortunately, she'd had plenty of experience dealing with intense stares.

"Why are you looking at me like that?" she asked.

"Like what?"

"Like you're looking for something or waiting for me to do something."

"Am I?" he asked in such a way that proved he was, in fact, the most tedious man ever.

She decided not to even bother with a reply. She focused on a blank wall and willed the song to be over soon so she could start to pretend his arms really didn't feel as good as they did and that his body didn't seem oh so right pressed up against hers.

"Actually," he said. "I was wondering if you'd like to have dinner with me?"

She stopped dancing completely. "Are you asking me out? Seriously?"

"For someone who didn't want to cause a scene, you aren't being the most discreet right this second."

She glanced around and saw that they had quite a few eyes watching them. She smiled at them and nodded to Kipling to start moving again.

"Why would you ask me out?" she said.

"You know, I didn't peg you as the type to need an ego boost, but you're smart and attractive." The sincerity of his expression took her breath and she had to look away. "And

I'm willing to bet underneath the layers of sarcasm, you have a delightful personality. I'd like to find out."

"I arrested you."

"And you later released me."

"I have actively investigated your family."

"And you've found no evidence of anything shady," he said, obviously enjoying their exchange way too much.

"You're impossible."

"Now, I wouldn't say that. Difficult? Maybe. But not impossible. Not for you."

"I don't . . . I mean . . . It's not . . ." Why did this man leave her so flustered? "Not a good idea."

Thankfully, she was saved from having to say anything else by the song coming to an end. She pulled out of his embrace, turned, and walked away, while ignoring the way he called after her.

Jade stood across the street from the reception, knowing there was a possibility that anyone leaving the venue might see her. This was the closest she'd been to any of the Benedicts in over a month. Maybe her subconscious wanted them to see her.

She'd hidden her birth certificate in the oven of the house Knox and Bea were renovating. The unassuming scrap of paper that proclaimed for anyone to see that the Benedict clan was more than the three brothers everyone knew about. There was also a daughter no one knew about. Not a legitimate one, of course, but fathered by Franklin Benedict himself. She'd assumed, when she left the birth certificate, that it'd be found by Knox or Bea. But what if they hadn't found it yet? Worse still, what if it'd been found by someone who had no idea what it was and they'd thrown it away?

Or, maybe whoever found it thought it had been left by someone with dubious intentions. She had to admit, they would have correctly guessed her original plans. But, as time had passed and she'd gotten to know them, she'd realized they weren't evil like she'd always been told. And by the time she'd left the birth certificate, she'd only wanted to get to know them better.

It had been a rash move on her part to leave the birth certificate. She always felt a bit socially inept and had no idea how to introduce herself as the found sister that no one knew was missing. Not to mention, there had been doubt on their part about who she was and what she wanted due in part to her initial interaction with Tilly that could not have been seen as anything other than questionable.

But the truth was the next move would be up to her. She'd not only dropped a bomb on the Benedict boys— she still couldn't wrap her mind around the words "her brothers"—but she'd left no way for them to contact her.

It had made sense at the time, but looking back now she saw it for what it was: a way to delay meeting everyone face to face and having them remember, every time they saw her, that their father had been unfaithful to their mother. She hadn't been ready for the looks they would have for her. She still wasn't.

Which was why she was currently standing on the opposite side of the street from the reception, instead of being somewhere safe and away from The Gentleman and his crew. She wondered if Tom was still looking for her. Maybe it was wrong of her to come back to South Carolina. She had actually left the state for a few days, and went down to the northern part of Georgia. But that hadn't lasted long. The call of both South Carolina and her unknown family was too strong for her to stay away for long.

She was going to have to do something different soon, though. She was quickly running out of money. Not to mention food. Although with the ocean nearby that was oftentimes easier to deal with, since she could catch fish.

Sleep was another issue which she hadn't been handling very well. Now that she was back in South Carolina, she needed to get back to her old habits of sleeping for just a few hours, then getting up, and changing places.

She yawned.

She inwardly cursed herself. She was getting soft and forgetting everything The Gentleman had told her. She just needed to toughen up. Maybe a few more days on the street would help.

The only thing that made her uneasy—well, one of the things that made her uneasy—was that she had not seen Tom. He had been after her before she left for Georgia, and she expected him to still be around. He wanted revenge for the beating he'd received for something she'd done, but truthfully, it was The Gentleman he should blame. Regardless, so far, she had seen no sign of him. Though, she would much rather see Tom than The Gentleman.

No, if there was one person she wanted to stay away from, it was The Gentleman. She was probably a fool for coming back to the state of South Carolina with that man still looking for her. But to not come back would be to let him win, because she knew he would never stop looking for her.

The plan was to somehow approach the Benedicts and work out together how to approach The Gentleman and bring him down.

She could almost imagine it. In fact, she was so caught up in the fantasy of her newfound family embracing her with open arms, and the downfall of The Gentleman, she didn't hear the footsteps behind her until it was too late.

Strong arms came around her. She inhaled the scent of evil. And then she heard it speak.

"Welcome back. I'm going to make you wish you stayed away."

She tried to struggle but he was too strong. She felt a pinprick in her neck. The last thing she remembered before darkness overtook her, was Knox and Bea coming out of the reception hall. Standing in the sunlight and kissing.

CHAPTER 2

The Monday following the vow renewal, Kipling stopped by a locally owned coffee shop on his way to the Benedict Industries office near the waterfront. He wasn't a regular patron, but he'd left the house without his normal cup and since he had to walk past the shop to get to where he was going, he decided to swing by.

He opened the door, not surprised to find the place nearly filled to capacity. What did surprise him was the woman patiently waiting to place her order at the end of the line.

Officer Alyssa Adams.

He still remembered how good she felt in his arms while they danced. Her body soft and responsive to his. The way her hips swayed against his for those brief precious moments she'd let her guard down.

Of course he couldn't forget how she'd turned him down when he'd asked her to dinner. He wanted to think her refusal bothered him more than just a case of wounded pride. Granted, he wasn't accustomed to being turned down. That came with the territory of being who he was.

No, it was different than that. Wounded pride wouldn't explain why all his fantasies since the day she walked through the doors of Benedict House involved her and her alone. It couldn't explain why no other woman seemed even remotely interesting. Nor could it explain why he craved to get in another verbal battle of wits with her. Coming from anyone else, it would be annoying, but from her, it was damn hot.

She still hadn't seen him. He walked up behind her and whispered in her ear, "If it isn't Cinderella. Are you even supposed to be out this time of day? Aren't you afraid you'll turn into a pumpkin?"

She turned around, but it wasn't her normal *I can do better than that* gaze on her face. She looked pale and vulnerable. It took everything in him not to take her in his arms and beg her to tell him what was wrong so he could fix it.

"Alyssa?" he chose to ask instead. "Are you okay?"

Surely it couldn't have been his teasing. She'd never seemed bothered with it before.

"Yes, I'm fine," she said, waving her hand, even though it was obvious she was not fine.

"Ma'am?" the barista asked.

Alyssa turned away to order her drink. On a whim, he stepped up beside her. "I'll have the same thing."

Alyssa reached for her purse, but Kipling cut her off by handing the cashier his credit card. "Put them both on here."

"You don't—" Alyssa started, but Kipling shook his head.

"Stop," he said, using the tone of voice that people didn't question because he didn't want to spend what time they had arguing. Not with her so upset. Even still, he was shocked when she didn't say anything further. Her lips were pressed tightly together. She was a bit pissed, but he'd take that over the look she had when she turned around. "Come and have a seat with me. You're obviously upset about something."

"And you think you can help?" She cocked an eyebrow at him.

"Maybe not, but I'm a good listener."

She didn't look like she believed him, but she didn't argue and she followed him to a table in the back. He pulled her chair out, not missing her brief look of surprise at the action.

"Thank you," she said, and took a sip of her coffee.

When he'd taken his seat across from her, he spoke softly, "Tell me what's going on."

She didn't seem too thrilled to do so, but she wrapped both hands around her paper cup and looked into her coffee. "It's the anniversary of my sister's death."

Her confession knocked the wind out of him. He hadn't expected that. "I'm so sorry." He shook his head, unable to even imagine losing a sibling. "How long?"

"I was fifteen."

He was surprised it'd been that long, given how upset she looked. "Losing a sibling is unfathomable to me. It must have been extremely hard as a teenager."

"Yes." She looked up and met his eyes. "Especially since she was murdered."

Alyssa saw his face contort as understanding dawned.

"My God, Alyssa," he said, horror still on his face. "That's horrible."

She wasn't surprised he had said the "I'm sorry" everyone else said when they heard the news. She'd never understood why everyone also thought they should apologize. It wasn't as if they'd done anything to cause her death. "It was a long time ago and I was still young when it happened."

"Maybe so," he said. "But it's still impacting you."

She couldn't deny that. "Yes, but it's so much more. It's this case, the missing women, the murdered women. All of it. It's all starting to get to me like it never has before. I see my sister in the women in this case and I can't help but feel as if I've let them all down. I know that's not rational, but that's how I feel. I became a cop to help and I'm not doing a very good job." She sighed. "I'm just tired. Can I say that? I'm tired."

He smiled tentatively and though she'd always thought of him as attractive, with that easy smile he wore now . . . trouble and heartache. And she'd had plenty of both. Enough to last for three lifetimes.

"Of course you can admit to being tired. You're only human." He crossed his heart. "Though I promise to keep that last part to myself. I won't tell anyone you're actually a mere mortal."

She enjoyed his teasing and found it actually made her feel a little better. She allowed herself a small smile. "Thanks, I appreciate that."

"Tell me about your sister," he said and though it wasn't a topic she discussed very often or with many people, she felt herself opening up to him.

"She was ten years older than me. I was an oops baby." She'd always known her parents had only wanted one child. And really, it didn't take that much thinking to figure it out. A pair of forty-somethings with an almost teenager and a newborn? "When I was little, Allison looked after me sometimes more than Mom did, mostly because Mom was too busy with her new husband to spend time with me. Allison was beautiful and funny and I wanted to be just like her."

"How so?" he asked.

She smiled, remembering. "I would hang out in her room while she got ready to go out on a date. Like I said, she was beautiful and I can't recall a weekend when she didn't go out. I was mesmerized watching her put on makeup. All the brushes and bottles. Mom would never let me wear makeup, even for fun. Though I'm pretty certain that was my stepfather's hangup and not hers. Anyway, right before she'd finish with her makeup, she'd lean back and say something wasn't right and then she'd put some lipgloss on me and declare everything was perfect. She made me feel special."

"She sounds like a wonderful sister."

"She was and everything was prefect until she graduated."

"What happened then?"

"Shortly after she graduated from high school, she came home saying she'd met a man. Not a boy. A man. And she was eighteen. I thought she made him up because she never brought him to meet us like she'd done with other guys she went out with. Mom and Dad didn't talk about it much, not around me anyway, but I could tell they weren't happy with the situation."

While she talked, Kipling listened to every word. She'd always pictured him as the lackadaisical type and she'd never talked with him without him saying something sarcastic every other word. To have him ask questions and look so intent made her want to open up and tell him things she'd never told anyone.

"Then she went away. I asked Mom and Dad where she was, but Dad wouldn't say and Mom just cried. The only thing Mom ever said was that Allison was one of those people who had to learn things the hard way. She never explained what she meant."

Across the table, Kipling was still listening patiently, but she bet he was wondering what any of that had to do with her sister being murdered.

"She came back five years later. I remember that better because I was fifteen. Dad told me to wait in my room and I was so upset that he wouldn't let me talk to her or even see her. To this day I don't know what was said, but I know there was a lot of yelling. At least, there was from Dad. Then the front door slammed."

Alyssa remembered running to the upstairs window that overlooked the front of the house. All she saw was her sister's back as she ran down the street. She felt a tear run down her cheek as she remembered how her sister never once looked back.

"I went downstairs, but before I could say anything, Dad stopped me and said her name wasn't to be spoken in our house anymore. Mom never stood up to him like I thought she should. She just went along with whatever he said. Less than a week later, Allison was dead. Her body was found in a shelter. Her throat cut. There's never been an arrest."

"Jesus, Alyssa." His face had lost all color. "You mean they never found who did it or why?"

"No." She gave him a weak smile. "But it all works out the way it's supposed to, right?"

"It's hard for me to see how that's the case here," he said.

"My sister is the reason I became a cop. I joined the force after college. After her death, I became obsessed with getting criminals off the streets."

"I think that's very admirable," he said softly.

Her face heated as she met his eyes and saw the sincerity in them. "It's not that big of a deal."

"We'll have to disagree on that," he said and before she had a chance to reply, asked, "Have you looked into your sister's case?"

"Once or twice. Just to see if anything new's turned up. It never has." She bit the corner of her lip.

"There's more you aren't telling me," he said, and she supposed she should be surprised he picked up on that fact, but he was a very successful businessman so it stood to reason he would read people easily.

"They brought her things by later. I remember being glad they did it during the day so Dad wouldn't know. Mom put it all in the attic and one day, when I was alone, I looked through it all. There was an envelope in her stuff. Whatever was inside was never found. I don't know if someone took it or if she threw it away somewhere." She took a deep breath and decided. It was about time she told someone. "The envelope was addressed to her, but with no date. For the return, all it said was 'Finition Noire.'"

She paused, waiting for him to make the connection. As she expected, it didn't take long.

"Finition Noire," he spoke it out loud as if testing the words and as soon as they left his lips, his eyes grew wide. "That's the name of the fake company that was on the spreadsheets Knox and Bea found and gave to you."

"Yes," was all she said. She knew those spreadsheets well. They had originally been in Tilly's possession since she got them from her mom. The thought had been that perhaps they contained some information that could be used to clear her father's name.

Instead, Alyssa and her team had found evidence pointing them to relook at the plane crash that took the lives of both Kipling's parents. They eventually discovered it hadn't been an accident, but a murder. They weren't sure who had orchestrated it, but Finition Noire played some part in the puzzle.

His eyes narrowed. "So why is that name in both your sister's case and ours?"

"I don't know. I'm looking into it."

"Do you think that's wise?"

She lifted an eyebrow. "As opposed to not looking into it?"

"Don't play me for a fool."

"That's not what I'm doing," she couldn't help but say.

"I'm serious, Alyssa." That he didn't come back with a snappy comment told her more than if he'd elaborated.

"What?" she asked.

"I agree that someone needs to look into this. I question if you're the right person to do it." He spoke the words softly as if by doing so he would be able to lessen the blow. He failed miserably, but she wasn't going to tell him.

"Why would I not be the right person?"

He didn't answer for several long seconds, but stared at her with those intense eyes of his. When he finally did speak, his voice was low. "Don't be obtuse, you're smarter than that. You're too emotionally involved in your sister's case and you know it. You should hand everything over to someone else."

She knew that, of course, or at least her mind did. Convincing her heart, however, was a different thing altogether. How could anyone else want her sister's case solved more than she did? And how would anyone else possibly work harder than she would to finally get to the bottom of Finition Noire?

"It's not happening," she told him.

"Does your supervisor know about the connection?" he asked.

Hell no. She wasn't stupid. If he knew, Martin would take her off the case, no questions asked. But she'd be damned if she'd tell Kipling that. "I don't see how you have any right to know the particulars of an ongoing investigation."

Kipling gave a curt nod as if that was the response he expected. "I'll take that as a no."

"I really don't care what you take it as. It's the truth." She wouldn't put it past him to call Martin up and tell him, but she wasn't going to beg him not to, either. "I know how it looks."

He leaned forward and she found herself doing the same. He looked altogether like the no-nonsense business-man that he was and she felt for those who found them-selves opposite him in the boardroom. Even more so, she hated herself for being attracted to him. Seriously, here she was sitting across from a man who had the potential to ruin her career and all she could think about was how good his arms had felt around her when they danced.

"I don't think you do know how it looks," he said. "You're the one sitting here talking about how tired you are, how the cases are getting to you like never before, and how you feel guilty. I'm worried about you, emotionally. It's not good to live in the past."

He could have said little else that would have shocked her more. "I'm fine."

"No you're not and before you decide to argue with me, I'm just calling it like I see it."

She resisted the temptation to flip him off and say *See this,* but it was hard. "No," she said instead. "You're call-ing it like you *think* you see it. You forget that you're emo-tionally involved in the case, too."

A look of satisfaction covered his face. "So you admit you're emotionally involved."

"My sister was murdered, I think that automatically qualifies for emotional involvement."

"My point exactly," he said with a smug grin.

She didn't know how to respond. He had her mind going in so many different directions, she wasn't sure how to continue. She finally settled by saying, "You would do the same thing for your sister. Can you honestly tell me that you'd step aside?"

"That's a moot point because, one, we're not talking about me and, two, I'm not a police officer."

She knew he was right. She'd been thinking of telling Martin everything and to step down from the case for weeks. But every time she had a chance, she didn't do it. She was Allison's sister, for crying out loud; there was no way anyone else could put as much into the case as she did. She'd even convinced herself that it was fate that she wound up on the Benedict case, because if she hadn't, the connection of both cases due to Finition Noire would have never been made.

And she'd be damned if Kipling Benedict was going to step in and mess everything up.

"We're finished here." She pushed back from the table, catching Kipling off guard. "Thank you very much for your offer to sit down. I'm so glad I accepted because I feel much better now," she said, her voice dripping with sarcasm.

Kipling lifted his coffee cup in a mock salute. "Anytime you need someone to ride your ass, I'm your man."

A sudden image of her on her back with Kipling between her legs popped into her head, freezing her in place. *Oh, dear sweet Lord,* she thought as her face heated.

"You have a horrible poker face." Kipling grinned. "But I'm your man for that, too,"

"You are . . ." she started, but her mind blanked.

"Your every dirty fantasy come to life? The man you dream about when you're in bed alone? An amazing sex god?" He leaned back in his chair and her eyes couldn't move from how broad his shoulders and chest looked.

She couldn't help but picture what he'd look like without the suit. "You wish," she replied, hoping her voice and expression didn't betray her thoughts.

"I never denied it."

That he calmly acknowledged he'd fantasized about her made her heart race. Far too late, she realized she had no snappy comeback. In fact, she had no comeback at all. Without saying a word, she spun on her heel and walked away.

But at the last minute, she looked back over her shoulder. "You'll never know what it's like to lose a sister."

Kipling watched Alyssa's retreat, but not with the mirth he'd portrayed to her. What the ever loving fuck had gotten into him that he'd flirt with a woman he'd been mad as hell with mere seconds before? What was it about Officer Adams that had him want to beat his head against a wall and rip every stitch of clothing off her body in equal measure?

He'd hoped that by dancing with her he'd get her out of his system. Though now that he had time to think about it, it made no sense that in holding her for a dance, he'd no longer yearn to hold her. No, his plan hadn't worked. It'd failed miserably. Instead of being satisfied with the fact that her embrace held nothing, he'd found out the opposite was true. Holding her for one dance had only increased his desire to hold her again and again. Preferably naked.

He'd joked with her about him being her every dirty fantasy when in fact, she had quickly become his. Even his subconscious agreed. At night he dreamed of a sultry police officer who loved to give in bed just as hard as she gave out of bed and whose sexual drive matched his own.

"Excuse me, sir," a waitress interrupted. "Can I get some of this out of your way?"

He jerked back to reality, thankful of the napkin in his lap. He nodded and then checked his phone for messages. Nothing that couldn't wait for his return to the office. He remained at the table for a few more minutes, taking the final sips of his coffee before leaving the shop.

From there, it was a short walk to the harbor side offices of Benedict Industries. Keaton and Tilly were working off-site today and Knox and Bea were still out on their second honeymoon, so Kipling was looking forward to a relatively quiet and uneventful day.

He needed a slow and uneventful day so he could think about what to do with Alyssa. How to move forward with her. To not only get to know her better, but to continue to connect with her on an emotional level like he had earlier this morning. He chuckled as he unlocked the door and stepped inside. He knew exactly what he wanted to do with Alyssa. Unfortunately, he had a feeling after their coffee chat, the odds of that ever happening were somewhere between slim and none, leaning heavily toward the none.

He'd been surprised she'd opened up about her sister. She didn't appear to him as one who shared that type of information lightly. More than likely, it only happened because she was emotional due to today being the anniversary of her sister's death.

He tried to imagine losing one of his brothers in such a violent way and he couldn't. The very thought made his chest hurt. Alyssa had been so much younger when she lost her sister. He had a new respect and appreciation for her. Though neither one voided the fact that she really shouldn't be on the case in his opinion.

Sitting at his desk, he sighed, unsure of what, if anything, he should say or do about that. He wanted to trust her when she said it wouldn't impact her adversely, but how could he be sure? From everything he saw, Alyssa was whip smart and not the type to let emotions get in her way. But having a family member murdered and to have that case go unsolved for years and years, to have it dictate what you did for a living?

He drummed his fingers on the top of his desk. He just didn't know.

His desk phone rang and he welcomed the opportunity to think and talk about something else.

"Kipling Benedict," he answered.

"Mr. Benedict," the person on the other end of the phone said in a voice so low, Kipling had to strain his ears to hear.

"I know you're a very busy man, so I'll keep this short and to the point. I have your sister. She's alive for now. If you want to keep her that way, you'll follow the instructions that I'll be sending your way soon."

Before Kipling could reply, the line went dead. He stared at the handset for several long minutes, his heart pounding madly. He forced himself to think rationally. No one could have possibly kidnapped Jade. Hadn't Keaton sworn up and down that she was half ninja? She was such a fierce, adept fighter. Sure she had been thin and rundown looking the last time he saw her, but she was smart.

He tapped his pen on his desk, trying to think of what else could explain the call. In his head, he heard Alyssa snap at him that he'd never know what it was like to lose a sister. *Alyssa.* He snorted and dialed the phone number he'd memorized, but never used.

"Officer Adams," Alyssa answered just as quick and efficient as he'd suspected she would.

"Well played, Adams." He relaxed, leaning back in his chair. "You almost had me for a minute."

"I would say *thank you,* Benedict, but I have no idea what you're talking about."

"I find lying to be a most unattractive quality in a woman."

"I know you find this hard to believe, but I'm not trying to attract you. Even if I was, I still don't know what you're talking about."

Right. Like he believed either of those to be true. Of course, he really hadn't expected her to admit to setting up the phone call. At least, not right away. He could wait. "If that's the way you want to play it for now, I'll go along with you. But be sure to tell whoever you got to make the phone call that he has the sinister villain voice nailed. I actually thought he had my sister for a minute."

"Kipling," she said, sounding a bit worried. "What are you talking about? You don't have a sister."

He realized his oversight as soon as the words left his mouth. He felt clammy, sick, and couldn't speak as the truth hit him. Alyssa didn't know.

Except he did. A half-sister that he and his brothers had only recently found out about. Kaja, or Jade, as she preferred to be called. Kipling had only met her once and he hadn't been overly kind to her. But to be fair, at the time he hadn't known they were related and he'd thought she'd been breaking into his house.

"Kipling?" Alyssa asked again.

He cleared his throat and managed to find his voice. "Officer Adams, would it be possible for you to come by the office near the harbor? I believe I need to report a kidnapping."

CHAPTER 3

Alyssa hurried to her unmarked car, her mind working overtime trying to make sense of Kipling's phone call. Nothing within the last five minutes had made any sense. The only thing she was certain of was the fear Kipling couldn't hide in his voice.

It had been that fear that made her hang up the phone and get to her car so quickly. She wasn't even sure he realized what his voice sounded like, but it shocked her to her core.

As she drove to his office, she ran over what she knew, while trying to ignore her trembling hands. Kipling had received a phone call from someone with a sinsiter voice. That person had mentioned a sister, and a kidnapping. For some reason the combination of the two hit a nerve inside him and he'd asked her to stop by. She had worked numerous kidnapping cases in her career and never before had she experienced this feeling of foreboding. It actually reminded her of when she found out her sister was dead.

And that scared the hell out of her.

She pulled into a public parking lot near the building that housed the harbor offices of Benedict Industries, still not able to grasp what was happening. Hopefully Kipling would make more sense in person than he had on the phone.

She stepped into the office to find him pacing in the front room. He turned toward her and his harrowing expression froze her in her tracks.

"Kipling?" she asked.

"Thanks for coming so quickly."

"Tell me what's going on."

He hesitated for a moment and that surprised her. But given his reaction, she suspected whatever he had to tell her would cost him something. He waved her toward his office.

"Let's go sit down," he said. "I'm not expecting anyone, but given recent circumstances, I'd prefer we be as private as possible."

She followed him to the large office in the back and sat down on the small love seat he had in a sitting area off to the side. He followed, sitting down across from her, and dropping his head into his hands. He took a deep breath and looked up.

"God," he said. "Where to start?"

She couldn't help him, so she remained silent and waited for him to continue.

"We've recently discovered that our father wasn't . . . damn . . ."—he grimaced—"he cheated on our mom."

Alyssa would have liked to have said she was surprised, but the truth was, she'd seen too much to be shocked that a wealthy man—hell, any man—cheated on his wife.

"But beyond that," Kipling said. "He fathered a child. A daughter. We don't know who the woman is he had an affair with and there's a suspicion that she's dead." He closed his eyes. "The daughter is Jade."

Her mouth fell open in shock. "Jade? You mean Jade, Jade?" Her head told her it had to be another Jade. Surely it couldn't be the Jade she'd assumed was a criminal trying to break into Benedict House only to discover that not only was she Bea's client, but she'd helped Keaton rescue Tilly by showing him a secret passage he hadn't know existed. The youngest Benedict brother had also been impressed by the numerous knives she had strapped to her body.

He gave a smile that wasn't really a smile. "Yes, the little ninja. And to answer your next question, no, we didn't know the night she spent at the house that she was our sister. Though we have a feeling she's known who we were this entire time."

Jade was their sister? Her mind kept repeating the question. The little street urchin? It didn't seem possible. Tilly also claimed to have seen Jade before, but in a homeless shelter and according to Tilly, Jade might have had a hand in the disappearance of one of the residents. She shook her head. Nothing Kipling said made sense.

"We were just as shocked as you look," he said.

"You have a sister," she said.

"A half-sister, but yes."

Suddenly, she remembered why she was sitting across from him in the first place. "Someone's kidnapped her."

"It appears that way."

But there was more and her mind worked frantically trying to sort it out. "Whoever has her knows who she is. And unless I'm missing something huge, I don't see how that's possible."

"That's what I've been thinking," Kipling said. "And that's important, because only a handful of people know the truth. That I'm aware of, anyway."

"But you yourself just said that Jade's known all along who she is. She could have told anyone and those people could have told people. You can't assume there are only a few people who know."

"I think it unlikely to be the case. If she was in the habit of telling people, don't you think she would have told us before now? After all, we're her family."

She leaned forward so she could ensure herself that she had his undivided attention. "You might be able to disregard the unlikely in your business, Mr. Benedict, but when it comes to what I do, ignoring the unlikely is liable to lead you into trouble. Also, don't forget the last time any of us saw her, she was living on the streets and a good number of those present, yourself included, made no secret about the fact that they thought she was a criminal. Can you blame her for not telling you?"

He didn't say anything. He just looked at her in that studious way that made her feel like an anomaly.

"What?" she finally asked.

He grinned and it appeared that he'd almost returned to normal. At least on the outside anyway. His color wasn't nearly as pale and he no longer looked scared to death. "Sitting here, talking to you, listening to the way you reason and argue with me, on top of knowing what a good police officer you are?" He shook his head. "I actually have hope that we'll find her."

She cocked an eyebrow. "I'm obviously missing something here because I don't have a clue as to what you're talking about."

He stood up and she didn't like the feeling of him looming over her like that, so she stood up herself. He reached out a hand and it occurred to her that he'd anticipated she'd stand as well. She took his offered hand.

"I'd like to offer you a proposition," he said.

Her hand slipped out of his. "What?" She had no idea what sort of proposition he was offering, but she feared if they touched, she wouldn't be as professional as she needed to be.

"Look at your mind going straight to the gutter." He made a tsking noise. "It's not that type of proposition. Though if you'd like to discuss that kind later . . . ?"

"Shut up." She crossed her arms across her chest,

because no matter how infuriating he could be, his close proximity paired with the images of *that kind*, had her body craving things it had no business craving. "Tell me."

He assessed her once more, perhaps to see if she was serious. She leveled her gaze at him to prove she was.

He nodded, as if understanding. "I won't tell your supervisor about your personal connection with the case and in exchange, you allow me to work with you. No secrets. You know something, you tell me."

Other than him keeping quiet about her connection, it sounded like a horrible deal. He would get complete access to the case, but other than his silence, what did he bring to the table?

"I know you're a powerful businessman and that you're incredibly successful, but let's face it." She waved her hand around the room. "You're a shipping expert. How are you going to advance the case? I'm sure I don't have to remind you that every family member of every missing person wants them found, and yet, we don't invite them to work with us."

"Surely you aren't that naïve." She tried to take a step backward, but hit the love seat.

He was so close, she felt the heat radiate off his body and she couldn't stop thinking about his touch or how his body would feel against hers. Or above hers . . .

He chuckled. "Someone's thinking naughty thoughts again, aren't they?" he asked in a low seductive voice that sent shivers up her spine. "Whatever am I going to do with you?"

She had a top ten list ready in response to that question, but she pushed all thoughts of it aside and when she spoke, she hoped her voice didn't tremble. "How about we start with you answering the question?"

"Okay," he said. "But I thought that much was obvious. Yes, I'm a shipping expert and that has made me wealthy.

Very wealthy. Obscenely wealthy. That means I can fund your investigation into Finition Noire and I can do much better than the Charleston PD."

She was crazy to even think about it.

Wasn't she?

She told herself she wasn't going to risk her career for money. Especially *his* money. She'd arrested him once, for crying out loud. But the more she thought about it, the more she liked the idea.

She would have to quit the force. Not that quitting made it right to do what she was thinking about doing. But maybe, just maybe, with the availability of funds, she'd be able to do more on the case. It definitely wouldn't hurt. And hadn't she been thinking about leaving the force anyway?

God, she was so tempted.

"You're thinking about it, aren't you?" he asked.

"You know I am."

"Do it, Alyssa," he said in that same seductive voice. "You know we'll be good together."

Why did she get the feeling he wasn't talking about the cases?

"Would we?" she challenged him. "I have the feeling we'd get on each other's nerves."

He laughed softly. "Of course we would. That's what's going to make this so interesting."

"I need to think about it," she said. Preferably somewhere that he wasn't so he wouldn't be able to influence her decision. Or at least that's what she told herself. The truth was, she knew she'd more than likely already made up her mind. She just didn't want him to know.

"Offer stands until tomorrow at noon," he said.

She raised an eyebrow. "That's not very much time."

"You've already decided and you know it. You want to make me sweat." His cocky grin was back. "Something you should know about me before you agree to work with me is that I very rarely sweat about anything."

"You're an ass." She pushed him aside and walked to the door of his office. She turned around before walking out. "It may not be over this, but I guarantee I'll make you sweat about something."

"I'm counting on it," he said while wearing a look that somehow managed to be playful and yet still carried a hint of wicked intent.

The Gentleman gave a grunt in acknowledgment as Officer Alyssa Adams dropped a few coins into the cup he had beside him. Dressing up like a homeless man wasn't his favorite way to gather information, but he had to reluctantly admit that it typically ended up being fruitful. Not only was he able to observe his prey relatively unnoticed, but he'd been playing this part for long enough that he could question those who were actually homeless, as well.

Most people did everything they could to avoid the homeless. Because they wanted the homeless to be invisible, they became that way. Other than being able to say, yes, she'd walked past a homeless man, he doubted Alyssa would be able to remember anything substantial about him. And for now, that was the way he wanted it.

He'd pretty much left Officer Adams alone, she'd inadvertently done him a favor by eliminating a thorn in his side some months ago. He couldn't help but chuckle remembering how Officer Adams looked when she found out it was her lover who was also the killer and kidnapper she'd been hunting. He'd been grateful, so he let her investigate while keeping an eye on her to ensure she didn't get too close. Thus far she hadn't, but he was going to have to keep a closer eye on her. He'd always known he'd have to eliminate her. Maybe he should move the timeline up.

He wasn't sure why she was spending so much time

with Kipling Benedict, but it needed to stop or else she would find she'd reached the end of his gratefulness. Perhaps she needed a warning, a little lesson in why she should stay away from the Benedicts.

It was all up to him now. He was finished letting others take care of things. This was too important to fuck up again. Which meant he had to do it.

First, though, he had to make sure his troublesome ward wasn't getting into anything she shouldn't. He'd left her tied up, but he'd trained her and trained her well. He wouldn't put it past her to attempt escape.

CHAPTER 4

Jade wondered if she closed her eyes and pretended she was back at Knox and Bea's house, she could actually convince herself that she was there. She'd stayed there earlier in the summer and it had been one the best times in her life. She'd been able to do whatever she wanted. Eat whenever and whatever she wanted. And the absolute best part was her ability to sleep for however long she wanted.

But the truth was, absolutely anywhere would be better than where she currently was, tied to a chair at this table of terror she only knew from the other side. On his good days, The Gentleman called it his interrogation table. On his bad days, he didn't bother with a name. A name wasn't needed when its function was easily determined by observing.

She'd give it him, though, he certainly knew what he was doing. "The mind is the best weapon there is," The Gentleman taught her at a young age. She knew he was right when she was seven and she knew he was right today when she was too old to have a guardian, but found herself at this damn table anyway.

Once again he was proving his superiority as well as

how he was using her mind against her. Surely he knew that in leaving her here she would remember every time she'd sat here before but in a different capacity. The times when he went easy on the person being interrogated and only broke fingers. All the way to the times when he went harder and cut them off completely.

Something banged down the hall and she jumped, immediately hating herself for doing so. She wasn't sure where he was, but she knew he was watching and she'd just given away more than she should. She was weak, so very weak and now he knew and he'd use it against her.

From down the hall came the sound of footsteps. It sounded like he had his boots on. The leather ones with the metal toes. The thought of them made her shiver. She thought that was bad, until he started to whistle and she felt sick to her stomach.

It was too late to try and visualize anything. Sweat dripped down her back. He was here and it wouldn't be much longer until he was in the room. And while she wasn't sure what he was going to ask, she knew there was one thing she could count on.

He was going to hurt her.

Kipling left his office shortly after Alyssa did. He knew he wouldn't be able to concentrate on anything following the phone call and pursuant conversation with Alyssa. He walked slowly back to the house. Without Alyssa nearby to tease, his thoughts went back to Jade.

He remembered the day Knox found the birth certificate in the oven of the house he'd bought for him and Bea to renovate. He'd thought Knox was playing a joke on him at first. Jade was their sister? The young woman the family couldn't decide if she was out to get them, misunderstood, or disturbed? It didn't seem possible.

But then he'd looked at the birth certificate and it seemed real enough. Knox had gone a step further and called the Department of Vital Records to verify its legitimacy. He'd hung up the phone looking pale and said simply, "It's legit."

With those two little words, it was as if he'd been punched in the stomach. He had a sister, a little sister, and he'd all but thrown her out of the house. Looking back at that day now, it was obvious she needed help and he'd done nothing, NOTHING, to help. Now she was in danger and he had to rescue her.

He cringed every time he thought about that night. He tried to tell himself that, based on the information he had, his actions were justifiable. But that didn't make him feel better, because he knew he'd acted like a horse's ass to her.

It came as a surprise to no one other than Bea that Jade had slipped out of the house in the middle of the night, leaving through the secret passage that was so secret, neither he nor his brothers had known of its existence until she'd told Keaton. After that, no one had heard from her, other than the birth certificate. Knox got online and exhausted his extensive search capabilities, but every lead he chased turned out to be a dead end. He'd wanted to find her guardian, if nothing else, but the files pertaining to her whereabouts after her mother died were nowhere to be found.

Kipling couldn't help but think the guardian was related to her current situation. It just seemed odd that they couldn't find any information on the man, or woman. He ran a hand through his hair, knowing he had to call Knox and have him and Bea come home early. Maybe with Alyssa's help they could find something new and finally get to the bottom of this.

He arrived home to find Tilly and Keaton working in the office. He must've looked bad, as they both looked up and suddenly had concerned expressions when he walked in.

"What?" Kipling asked.

"You look horrible," Keaton said. "What happened?"

So much for his little flirtation with Alyssa helping him look better. He sighed. "I got a call at the office; they said Jade had been kidnapped. If I want to see her alive again, I'll follow all the instructions that they'll be sending." He hadn't planned on spitting it out like that, but it just happened that way.

"Shit, are you serious?" Keaton asked.

"That's a bit odd, don't you think?" Tilly asked. Both brothers looked at her. She continued, "Odd that they would call you to tell you that Jade was kidnapped, I mean."

"They actually said that my sister had been kidnapped," Kipling clarified.

Tilly nodded. "That's even odder. How many people know you have a sister and that Jade's it?"

"It doesn't matter who knows," Keaton said. "If Jade found herself in trouble, all she'd have to do is tell whoever nabbed her that she was a Benedict and to call Kipling. They might not believe her, but the potential that she was right and could be worth millions would be worth taking a chance and calling."

"That's a good point." Kipling hadn't thought of that. "Unfortunately, it just made our search bigger. I'd hoped we could narrow our list of suspects down to only those people who knew, but if it was someone unrelated to this whole mess, that list is huge. I think it's also important to note that whoever it was didn't ask for ransom money."

"I don't even know how to start looking," Keaton said.

"I called Knox and he and Bea are coming home early." Kipling hated they had to cut their honeymoon short, but he'd had no choice. "I'm going to have him relook at a few things. And you two should know that I've asked Alyssa Adams to help us."

"She's a police officer, isn't that her job?" Keaton asked.

"I asked her to join us in an unofficial capacity." Kipling was prepared to field more questions, but instead all that happened was a look passed between Keaton and Tilly. "I have no way of knowing if she'll agree or not."

Tilly shook her head. "She won't. She'll think doing so is unethical."

Kipling hated it, but had to admit she was probably right.

"I can't believe you asked her that," Tilly said.

Keaton gave her a funny look. "Really? I can."

Thankfully, the doorbell rang and he was spared further funny glances from the couple. He met their longtime housekeeper Lena in the hallway and told her he'd get the door. He opened it to find Alyssa on the other side.

He couldn't help it. He broke out into what he knew was a huge grin. "I must say, Officer Adams, I didn't expect you to decide that quickly."

"If I remember correctly, you told me I'd already decided." She shrugged. "Since you told me I couldn't make you sweat, I figured why expend the energy?"

He leaned in as if telling her a secret. "I never said you couldn't make me sweat, I said I very rarely sweat over anything. I can think of several things we could do that would lead to sweating on my part."

"A condition of me working with you is that you have to stop with the not-so-subtle sexual innuendo. As much as it is to spar with you, we need to keep this professional."

Damn, he liked her. "It's August in Charleston, Alyssa. All I have to do is walk outside to sweat. You're the one making everything sexual."

"If you let her come inside so you could close the door,

no one would have to sweat," Keaton said from the hall-way.

"Now I know which Benedict brother got the brains." Alyssa swept her way inside, past Kipling, like he wasn't even there. "Hello, Keaton. Tilly."

They both said hello to her and then Tilly led them all into the kitchen where she'd made a cake earlier in the morning.

"I'd planned on having it for after lunch," she said, slicing everyone a piece. "But it works just as well as a pre-lunch snack as well."

"Even better if you ask me," Keaton said. "Cut me a bigger piece than that."

"I'll take a small one, thanks," Alyssa said.

They all took their cake and sat around the kitchen table. Kipling waited for Alyssa to sit down and then took the seat beside her. Not that she noticed, she was too wrapped up in Tilly's cake.

"This is divine," Alyssa said, digging into her slice.

"You should have gotten a bigger slice." Keaton held up his plate.

Alyssa laughed. "I really should have."

Kipling realized that was the first time he'd heard her laugh and he felt strangely jealous that he wasn't the one who made her do it.

Across the table, Keaton had finished the monstrous slice Tilly had given him and was watching Alyssa care-fully.

"So," his younger brother said. "You're going to work with us?"

Alyssa wiped her mouth. "Yes, I came over to tell your brother I'm going to resign from the police department. I'm not going to tell them why."

Another one of those looks passed between Keaton and Tilly. Kipling did his best not to roll his eyes.

"Decided to come over to the dark side?" Keaton teased.

"Something like that." Alyssa finished her cake and put her fork down. "I was wondering as I drove over here, when did you find out about Jade?"

"She left her birth certificate in the house Knox and Bea are renovating," Keaton said. "They found it not long after he was released from the hospital."

"But before that, he had the birth certificate mailed to him." Kipling looked at Alyssa. "It had the child listed as Jane Doe, so we didn't know it was Jade at that point."

"We also thought she was dead," Keaton added.

"That's very odd," Alyssa said, thinking out loud. "Why would you think that?"

"We also had what we thought was her death certificate," Keaton said. "But Bea was able to determine it was a fake."

"And," Kipling added. "She found that the date of the fake death certificate was very close to the time Tilly's father was fired for supposed espionage."

Keaton placed his hand over Tilly's. "But we think Tilly's dad was set up. It never seemed right that he would do something like that and we've been looking over all the old records to try and prove it."

Something else struck Kipling at that moment and he couldn't believe he'd never put it together before. "Bea was looking into those records when she was attacked the first time."

Alyssa whipped a notebook out of her purse. "Wait a minute," she said. "I have to write this down. I want to make sure I don't forget any of this."

Kipling watched as she wrote and didn't miss her frown. "What?" he asked.

"I've got: Tilly's dad, Jade, your parents' deaths, and the attacks and threats on Tilly and Bea. Bea was attacked shortly after she started looking into Tilly's dad and he was fired around the date on the death certificate." The frown hadn't left her face. "I'm missing something. I know I am."

"We all are," Kipling agreed.

"What do you know about Jade's mother?" Alyssa asked.

Kipling shook his head. "Nothing."

"Who was Jade's guardian?" Alyssa asked.

"That's another thing we don't know," Kipling said. "Knox has been trying to find out, but so far hasn't had any luck."

"He's a hacker. He did some work in the Middle East for the government during the summer, while he was in college," Keaton added and Kipling shot him a dirty look. "Sorry, man, but if she's going to be working with us, she should know."

"Part of the problem," Kipling picked up, hoping Alyssa would ignore the hacking part, at least for now. "Is that we aren't sure we have her real name. She gave us Kaja Jade Mann, but there doesn't seem to be a record of such a person."

Alyssa gave him a snarky smile. "And your hacker brother hasn't been able to find anything out?"

Kipling did his best not to show any sort of response. "No, apparently he needs a complete name."

Alyssa didn't react in any way to his statement, other than to tap her pen against the pad of paper again. If anyone else had been doing that, it would have annoyed Kipling, but for some reason, seeing her do it made it hot somehow. Of course it seemed like everything she did he found hot.

The tapping stopped abruptly. "I know." Alyssa reached into her purse and pulled something out. "Where did Jade sleep and which bathroom did she use when she was here?"

Kipling raised an eyebrow.

She sighed. "I'm looking for hair."

"You won't find it on the sheets she used and Lena will take it as an insult if you suggest as much."

"Let me see the bathroom she used then. Maybe there's some hair left in a brush or something."

Kipling nodded. "Come with me. I'll take you."

He led her down the hall into the room Jade had used the one time she stayed at Benedict House. There was a connecting bathroom she'd have used as well. Kipling knew Lena would have changed the sheets, but there was a possibility if Jade didn't have a brush she may have used the one in the bathroom.

Alyssa went straight for the drawers in the bathroom and smiled when she found the hairbrush. "There's hair in it. Has anyone else used this brush?"

Kipling shook his head. "The last person to stay in that room before Jade was a distant cousin from England. I'm not even sure the brush was in the bathroom then. I know Lena restocked the bathroom after he left. That's probably when she got it."

Alyssa collected several strands of hair and placed them in what Kipling now saw was an evidence envelope.

"What exactly are you doing?" he asked.

"I'm going to submit this hair to the lab," Alyssa said.

"For DNA?" Kipling had to admit it was a good idea and one he hadn't thought of before.

"Mitochondrial DNA," she clarified.

"What's the difference?"

"Mitochondrial DNA is what we typically use in kidnapping cases. It's not the entire genotype, however, and it's not unique. It's passed down through the maternal line, so for example, my mitochondrial DNA is exactly like my sister's and is exactly like my mother's."

"How will this help find Jade?"

"For one, if any maternal family member of hers is

in the database, we'll find it and that might help us find her."

That was good enough in his book. "How long will it take to get results?"

She got that glimmer of excitement in eyes. The one he loved so much. "Don't worry about it. I know people."

CHAPTER 5

A week after both agreeing to work with Kipling and after turning in her resignation, Alyssa stood in her room, brushing out her hair. Because she wore it in a ponytail all day, she loved nothing more than when she was able to take it down. In fact, it was one of her most favorite parts of her day. She flipped her head over and ran her brush through the tangles until the strands were smooth and crackled. Once she put the brush down, she ran her fingers through her hair, scratching her scalp so that it felt so good, she almost groaned.

She still couldn't believe she told Kipling all that information about her sister, but it had felt so good to talk to someone. She'd never even told Janie about her sister. Why had it been so easy to tell Kipling? More than that, why was it impossible to get the man out of her hair? And did she want to?

Stupid question. No. She didn't want Kipling out of her hair. The exact opposite, in fact—she *wanted* him in her hair. With her head still flipped over, she ran her fingers through her hair again, and pretended they were his. Would he be gentle or rough? In her fantasy he would be both. He'd start gentle and the more aroused he became, the rougher he'd get.

And because it was her fantasy, the closer he got to his release, the tighter he'd fist her hair. She buried her fingers in her hair and pulled. That wasn't enough, so she grabbed two tight fistfuls and gave them a good, solid yank.

And let go with a sigh.

It was nowhere close to being as good when she did it herself. How long had it been since she'd had rough, hair-pulling sex? Definitely before Mac. He never wanted to do anything of the sort.

Why would you want your hair pulled? Mac had treated her like a freak and by the time he died, she believed she was one. She knew nothing about Kipling's life. Had no idea what he was like as a lover, but she'd bet her house on the fact that he'd never make her or anyone else feel like she was a freak because she liked having her hair pulled. Maybe he secretly wanted to pull hair.

"You might as well forget it," she told herself. "Want to or not, he's so far out of your league it's not even funny. Just deal with it and go on."

She brushed her hair all over one last time and then put her hairbrush down. Laid out the outfit she planned to wear the next day and tried to decide if she wanted to go jogging today. She snorted. She never *wanted* to jog. She did it because she had to. She pulled out a sports bra and put it on the bed when a floorboard creaked from the front part of her house.

She froze.

It wasn't unheard of for her house to creak. After all, all houses did. But she knew the noises her house made and that wasn't one of them. Her heart began to pound. Was someone in her house?

She strained her ears, trying to listen for anything that

sounded out the ordinary. But all she heard was her own heart beat and her breathing. She held completely still, although why she wasn't sure. If anyone was in the house, they knew she was, too.

She stayed that way for several long minutes, trying to be completely still and closing her eyes in order to pick up on anything out of the ordinary. She looked across the room at her weapon. Too far away to reach without moving and because she knew her house so well, she knew there was no way to get to it without walking across the squeaky floorboards in her bedroom.

There.

Was that another squeak? The silence in her room was so complete it was actually loud. She kept thinking she heard things and wasn't sure whether they were real or not. It was not unlike a game of chicken, assuming there was somebody in the house, with each of them trying to wait out the other to see who would make the first move.

She finally decided that whoever was in the house, knew she was as well and that whatever happened next, she wanted to be armed. She made a step toward the gun, determined to get to it before whoever else in the house made it to her. She eased her foot around the squeaky floorboard and gently pressed down on it.

Right as the floor moaned underneath her foot, she heard the clicking of the front door and she froze again. Had someone entered or had they left?

Deciding she wasn't going to wait any longer, she ran across the room, grabbed her gun and headed toward the front of the house. Through the window, she saw a nondescript black car pull out of her driveway. There was no license plate on the car.

She took a deep breath. She was fairly certain that whoever was in the house had left, but she wasn't going to rest until she knew for certain. Gun in her hand, she decided to go through each room.

Nothing was out of place until she reached the kitchen. In the middle of her table, placed where she couldn't miss it, was a perfect black rose.

"Mr. Kipling?" Lena poked her head into his office.

Kipling looked up from the contract he'd been reading and pushed back from his desk. "Did I miss dinner again? I'm so sorry. I seriously don't know how you put up with my worthless self."

"No, sir. Dinner still has a while to cook yet." Lena gave him a big grin. "It's that Ms. Adams who was here last week. She's back."

"Officer Adams?" He looked behind her to see if she had followed Lena.

"I told her to wait in the foyer. I wasn't sure where you wanted to talk with her."

Kipling narrowed his eyes at the much-too-helpful Lena. As expected, she continued. "I thought you might like to invite her to dinner. I cooked plenty and that woman could use some good home cooking."

"I'll ask her if she's interested." He walked swiftly to the foyer. It wasn't like Alyssa to come by this time of the evening. He worried that something had happened. She stood facing away from him and when she turned around, his heart sank. Not only because of the look of fear she had in her eyes, but because of what she held. A black rose.

"Kipling," she said. "I'm sorry. I didn't mean to ruin your evening."

He held a hand up. "Don't apologize. Ever. For coming by my house when you need to." He nodded toward the rose. "Where did you get that?"

"It was left in my house."

"Inside your house?"

"Yes, I was upstairs and I thought I heard something downstairs. I crossed the room to get my gun, but whoever it was ran outside before I could get to them. This was sitting on the kitchen table."

He needed to calm down before he blew a gasket. "Come in here and sit down." He led her to the living room and took a seat across from her. "Someone was in your house the same time you were?"

She tried to put on a brave face, but he saw the fear hidden in her eyes. "Yes, but I had a gun."

He leaned forward, resting his hands on his knees. "Alyssa, I don't give a damn if you had a whole arsenal. Someone was in your house. You're in law enforcement, I can't imagine your place is easy to get into. How did that happen? Have you given that any thought?"

"I have, but I don't have any ideas." She looked dejected admitting it to him and he knew her well enough to know how much she hated that.

"I'm willing to bet you don't have a spare key under your doormat."

She narrowed her eyes. "Seriously?"

He held his hands up. "I'm simply thinking of the easiest way to break into your place."

"Think harder."

"Any neighbors or friends with a key?"

"Just Janie and . . ." Suddenly, her eyes grew big.

"What?" he asked after she didn't say anything.

"Just a thought." She drummed her fingers on the arm of the couch. "Mac had the keys to my house. After I . . . after he . . . died . . ." She closed her eyes. Kipling remembered how he'd teased her once before about her ex who ended up being a murderer. At the time, he hadn't thought about how it'd affect her. He could have punched himself.

Damn, he was an ass. He knew now that Mac had kidnapped Janie. Janie was fine now, but still . . .

He reached out his hand and they were close enough that he could just brush her knee. Just to let her know he was with her. Not that he understood, because there was no way he could, but as a silent show of support. At least, that's how he hoped it came across. Maybe it worked; she didn't jerk away.

No, if anything, her body seemed to relax a bit. Maybe he was only seeing what he wanted to, but it truly appeared as if his touch calmed her. He was filled with the sudden urge to gather her in his arms so he could protect her.

"Take a deep breath and tell me," he whispered, somehow feeling that this was an important step in their relationship. Outside of that time shortly after they'd met, she'd never mentioned Mac.

Her eyes were open as she took several deep breaths. She gave him a weak smile. "Sorry, it's not easy for me talk about this."

"I imagine not." He squeezed her knee and sat back, giving her space.

"Mac had a key," she said. "I don't know what happened to it. After."

"We have to assume that it somehow fell into the wrong hands and that they knew it was to your house." And if they got in once, they could get in again.

"I'll call tomorrow and have my locks changed." She sighed and ran her fingers through her hair.

Kipling tried not to pay attention to her hair, but it was easier said than done. Especially since she normally wore it up and this was one of the few times he'd seen her with it down. He told himself to focus on the issue at hand and not how soft he imagined her hair would be or what it would smell like.

Focus. "If you would like, you're more than welcome to stay here."

"Thank you, but no," she replied in a clipped voice.

Her lips were pressed into a thin line and he didn't have a damn clue what he'd done or said to elicit such a response. "Based on your reply, I get the feeling I should apologize for something, but I'm at a loss as to what."

"I'm not Tilly or Bea," she said. "I'm not your girlfriend or your wife, so no, I'm not staying here. I'll get a hotel room tonight. They'll come out and replace my locks tomorrow and everything will go back to normal."

"Then I apologize if my offer came across as anything other than one friend reaching out to another." He crossed his arms and leveled his gaze. "I assume it is safe to call us friends, or is that pushing the envelope as well?"

She didn't shrink from his stare. "'Friends' is fine."

"Although I have to be honest with you. I'm not sure I want to be your friend. What I'd like to be is a bit more intimate than mere friends."

Her cheeks flushed with a hint of color and she refused to meet his gaze. But before she had the chance to reply, Keaton and Tilly's voices filled the room and then they both appeared. Tilly entered the room first, though Keaton was right behind her. She was all smiles as she spoke to her fiancé. "I told you it was Alyssa's car." She turned to Alyssa and at once seemed to be aware that she'd walked in on something. "Should we leave?"

Kipling stood up. "No, of course not. We were just chatting. Nothing important. Alyssa," he said, "come have dinner with us. You'll upset Lena if you don't stay."

She frowned. "I don't know. I should probably go make sure I can get a room somewhere."

"Have dinner with us," Kipling said. "And if I have to call everyone I know in Charleston to ensure you have a place to sleep tonight, I will."

Alyssa didn't look convinced, but she followed him out of the room.

"What was all that about?" Kipling heard Keaton ask Tilly.

"I think we did interrupt something," Tilly said in a loud whisper.

Alyssa was happy to see Bea and Knox already in the dining room when they entered. It wasn't that she disliked Keaton and Tilly, but Knox and Bea were more sedate than the younger couple. More her own temperament.

Bea looked up from her conversation with Knox as they all entered, but her smile faded at the sight of Alyssa. Knox reacted immediately, sitting up straighter and looking around, trying to find what had scared his wife.

Bea pointed to the rose Alyssa had in her hand. "Where . . . where did you get that?"

Alyssa didn't miss the *what in the hell* look Knox shot Kipling. Kipling's only reaction was to step closer to her and put a hand at the small of her back. Her body relaxed almost immediately.

"Alyssa found the rose inside her house this evening," he said, pulling her chair out for her and seeing that she was settled before taking his own seat. "If you remember, it was a rose like that one that led to my unfortunate arrest some months ago."

It was a day Alyssa would never forget. The body of a dancer from a local gentlemen's club had been found and since several people had seen her talking to Kipling not long before she died, Alyssa and her partner stopped by Benedict House to question him. They were getting nowhere until Alyssa pulled out a black rose.

Kipling asked her when she took it out of his car, but the rose had been found on the dancer's body. To this day,

Alyssa wasn't sure which one of them were more surprised when she arrested him.

Bea still hadn't regained all of her color. "There were some of them in an arrangement at my father's service. I remember thinking they were the creepiest flowers I'd ever seen." She shivered. "Still do."

"We always assumed, later," Knox said, continuing to keep a careful eye on the woman at his side, "that it was Tom who had arranged for the flowers and the note."

Alyssa froze. "There was a note?"

"I've been roasting this chicken all afternoon," Lena said, entering the dining room and carrying a tray that looked as if it weighed more than she did. Alyssa stood to help her, wondering why no one else was. She glanced down at Kipling by her side. Seriously? He was just going sit there? She lifted an eyebrow, but Kipling shook his head and motioned for her to sit down.

"Yes, Ms. Alyssa," Lena said. "Listen to Mr. Kipling and sit back down in your seat. I've been serving this family for more years than you've been alive and no one else is going to do so until I'm cold and dead and in my grave."

Alyssa felt her cheeks grow hot. "Sorry, Lena."

Lena put the tray down and placed her hand on top of Alyssa's. "Don't you worry one little bit about it. Now, if you find yourself over here one day and you'd like to join me in the kitchen, I'd be happy for the company." Lena took a step back and put her hands on her hips. "Like I was saying, that chicken has been roasting all afternoon and I don't want to hear one word about those threats or anything else unpleasant. Hear me? It'll mess up your digestion."

No one said anything until Lena left.

"Wow, Alyssa," Bea said. "Lena didn't invite me into the kitchen until we were back from our honeymoon. She must like you."

Across from her, Knox and Keaton exchanged a look. Kipling must have noticed as well. He cleared his throat and asked Keaton a question about the charity division he had recently started at Benedict Industries.

After dinner, they all gathered in the living room. Bea and Knox had excused themselves before everyone else finished, but they were waiting for them. Bea had something in her hand she gave to Alyssa.

"That's the note that was on the black roses at my father's service," she said.

It was much too late to attempt to get prints off of the note, and Alyssa wasn't sure it would have mattered anyway. "Interesting that whoever this is keeps using black roses."

"They aren't black," Kipling said.

"What?" Alyssa held the flower in question up. "It looks black to me."

Kipling shook his head. "It's a very deep crimson. I did a little bit of research when I found a similar one on my desk."

"Interesting." Alyssa twirled the rose. "It still looks black to me."

"Just because they look that way, doesn't mean they are." Kipling took the rose from her. "Also, these are so rare, they're almost extinct. And they are only grown in Turkey."

Knox gave a low whistle and slipped his arm around Bea. "That's a rather extravagant threat, wouldn't you say? Why spend so much money?"

"Unless you really want to make a statement," Alyssa said.

"Is there any way Tom could have afforded anything close to what I assume those cost?" Bea asked. "If not, it seems to lend credibility to our idea of there being someone who is not only the mastermind, but also has fairly deep pockets."

"Which once more narrows the field of potential suspects for us," Alyssa said.

"I can pull a list of nurseries in Turkey that export those roses," Knox said to her. "I'll have it to you in the morning."

"Thank you. I'll start making phone calls while my locks are being changed." Alyssa glanced at her watch. "Speaking of, I need to head out so I can find a hotel room."

"I'll go with you and see that you get settled," Kipling said. "Since you're being stubborn and won't stay here."

"I'll be fine on my own. I don't need you to follow me."

"I know that," Kipling said in a low voice. "I want to go for me, so I can make sure you're safe."

She didn't roll her eyes the way she wanted to, instead, she told herself that he was only looking out for her best interest, and if she argued, it wouldn't do any good. He would come anyway. And, though she'd never admit it to him, it was sweet.

"Let's go," she said.

Kipling looked momentarily stunned that she didn't argue, but he collected himself quickly, and followed her outside to get the cars. "You know where you're staying?"

She named a middle-of-the-road hotel that wasn't a roach motel, but that she suspected was nowhere near the opulence of anyplace he'd typically stay.

"Lead the way," he said.

She waited for him to get in his car and then drove to the hotel she hoped to stay for the night. It wasn't far from Benedict House and for that she was glad. If something else were to come up or happen, God forbid, he would be able to get to her easily.

He didn't get out of his car after parking in the *Check In Only* spot next to her. He was talking on the phone to someone, and her stomach twisted, but she wasn't sure why. She decided not to get out until he did.

Three minutes later, he waved for her. She couldn't help

but notice as he got out to meet her just beside the front door, that he was frowning. That wasn't what bothered her the most, though. What set her on high alert was the *too careful to be casual* way he looked around the parking lot.

She did the same thing, trying to determine if anything looked out of the ordinary. "What?" she finally asked.

Based on his expression, he was upset, or angry. And she couldn't say with great certainty, but it seemed possible that there was a hint of fear, or at least worry there as well.

"Knox called," he said.

Her stomach twisted tighter because there was only one reason for Knox to call while they were on the way to the hotel instead of simply waiting for Kipling to make it back home.

"So soon?" she asked.

"Yes."

"That was fast."

He nodded. "As it turns out, there is only one business in the US that has imported those roses recently."

"Who?" she asked, even though deep inside she knew what the answer would be.

"Finition Noire."

She forced herself to breathe normally.

In. Out. In. Out.

"Are you okay?" he asked after about three more breaths.

She wasn't ready to talk yet, so she kept breathing in and out. At the same time, trying to determine why it seemed like everything she did was somehow connected to the Benedicts.

"Alyssa," he said, more forcefully the second time. "Are you okay?"

She peeked at him with one eye and he wondered why he kept asking her if she was okay when it was clearly obvious that she was not.

"No," she said. "Let me take a few more deep breaths and then we'll reassess."

Kipling glanced around the parking lot again. He wasn't sure why, but something felt off. Almost as if they were being watched, but he didn't see how that was possible.

Unless . . .

He looked to his side where Alyssa was still taking deep breaths. He didn't want to stress her out any more, but he didn't want her out here in the open if there was a potential she could be harmed.

Her eyes opened and all traces of fear were gone. In its place was an unwavering resolve. "We need to go."

"Why?"

Her eyes swept the parking lot. "I called the hotel earlier this afternoon, before I drove to Benedict House, just to tell them I might come by tonight and to make sure they weren't booked. But I never said for certain. Something doesn't feel right."

Since he had the same feeling, he couldn't agree more. He held out a hand. "Give me your keys. I'll call and have Knox come and get your car."

She stuck her hand in her pocket and handed him her keys. He collected Alyssa's bag from her car, settled her into the front seat, and within seconds they were headed south.

She was silent, but not for long. They weren't too far out of the city when a glance to his side showed him that her resolve was still in place. She amazed him with the way she handled everything.

"Where are we going?" she asked, catching the glance.

"Just a little way outside of the city where no one would expect us to be."

"You keep saying 'we' . . . aren't you going back home?"

She'd asked the question with no emotion or any way at all for him to guess what she'd like his answer to be. He decided to answer with the same type of tone. "Not anymore."

"I should give you my credit card number." She bent down and reached for her purse, but he put a hand on her thigh to stop her.

"No," he said. "This is on me. Remember? My contribution to the case."

"That was supposed to be things other than travel."

"I don't remember that stipulation."

"I just added it."

The fact that she was in a mood to argue with him was a good thing he decided. He smiled. "It doesn't work that way."

"I'll let it slide this time."

"That's awful magnanimous of you."

"Don't get used to it."

"Right. I'll make a note of that." He couldn't hide the grin that the brief exchange left on his face.

Her phone rang and she reached for it. "It's the lab."

"It's almost seven. Why would anyone be calling this late?"

"I sent an e-mail earlier to see if it was possible to expedite Jade's hair." She answered the phone. "Hello?"

There was nothing but silence for a minute. Whatever she was told, it couldn't have been good news. Not with the look of pure rage that grew with every second.

"What do you mean you have no record of the sample? I had a confirmation email that you received it." There was a pause as whoever was on the other end spoke. "I suggest you look again because if you can't find it, I'll come to the lab myself and find it." Another pause. "I don't want to hear that it *may have* been anything. Call me back when you have something concrete." She ended the conversation with a curse.

"They lost Jade's hair?" Kipling asked.

"They don't know what the hell they've done to her hair. It's not in the system, but the woman I talked to said she remembers it and thought they'd finished testing."

He was floored by the incompetence her words suggested. "Is that normal for them? To lose something like that?"

"No. It's completely out of character. Which makes it even more maddening. Why that sample?"

"I want to say it's purely coincidental, but I don't think either of us believes that." The bigger question was, what were they going to do about it? Kipling got the feeling that something or someone more powerful than they realized was at play. And that worried him. "We need to be very cautious about what we say to whom."

Alyssa nodded offhandedly. "I'm trying to think of who I trust the most that has contacts in the lab." She appeared to be scrolling through her phone contacts and muttered under her breath, "I just don't know. I'm at the point where I don't feel like I can trust anyone."

"Don't look at it like that. There are plenty of people you can trust. Right now you're having to be overly cautious about what you say and to whom. It won't be like this forever."

"It just seems like it," she mumbled.

They drove the rest of the way in silence. Alyssa scrolled through her phone, looking for someone to contact about the situation at the lab. He wasn't going far out of the city, so it didn't take long to make it to the hotel he had in mind.

Several minutes later, he pulled into the driveway of the hotel and retrieved Alyssa's bag. Of course, he didn't have much other than the clothes he had on, but he'd deal with that later.

They walked together to the front desk and approached a woman who was much too perky for the time of day and in light of everything that had happened the last few hours.

"Yes, sir," she said before they'd even made it to the desk. "How can I help you?"

Kipling waited until he stood in front of her before answering. "We need two interconnecting suites and at least one them needs to have a large table. Put us down for a week, but I might end up extending."

Five minutes later, Kipling decided he didn't mind perky if it came with results like the front desk had arranged. The two suites were prefect. One had a conference table and the other a small kitchen.

But a glance at Alyssa showed her frowning.

"What?" Kipling asked.

"A week, maybe longer?" The frown deepened. "Why?"

"Everything we turn up points to whatever happened to your sister somehow being connected to whatever or whoever is threatening my family now. When I look at what happened to Tilly and Bea, I can picture something just as dangerous, if not more, happening to you."

She didn't let him finish. "You're forgetting that Knox and Bea were married and Keaton and Tilly were not only dating, but also had an entire history of childhood memories together."

"I'm not forgetting anything, Alyssa. Whether you like it or not, you and I have been paired together."

"Because we danced at your brother's wedding?"

He walked across the room to stand in front of her, purposely getting inside her personal space, but not touching her. She was a tall woman, but he was taller and standing like he was, she had no choice but to look up at him. "Tell me you don't feel the connection between us. Tell me your heart isn't racing right this very second." He ran a finger down her cheek. "Tell me you aren't affected in any way by my touch. That your body doesn't long for more. Tell me that, Alyssa, and I'll walk out of here and never bother you again."

She kept her eyes on him. "You know I can't do that."

He had no intention of gloating over her acquiescence. But he did want to kiss her, and badly. Standing like he was in front of her, he could feel her breathing in and out. He could smell her, and he wanted nothing more than to taste her.

But he wasn't going to. At least not at that moment. So with a heavy sigh, he forced himself to take a step backward and put some distance between them. "I'll do whatever it takes to keep you and my family safe. And if that means keeping a few hotel rooms for a week or so, that's what I'll do. Are you tired?"

For just a second, he sensed rather than saw her put her guard down. For that brief moment it was as if he connected with the real Alyssa. Just a glimpse, but it was enough. Enough for him to know that he would do anything to see more of that side of her. "Not in any way, shape, or form."

"Me, either." He nodded to the suite with the kitchen. "I'm going to go take what few things I have into the other room. Why don't you do the same in here and we'll meet at your table in thirty minutes?"

"What's the plan?"

"I'm going to call Knox and fill him in on what we're doing and make sure he's uploaded everything he has on Finition Noire to a secure and private server I have access to."

She cocked an eyebrow up. "Because you just happen to take your laptop wherever you go?"

He knew she had hers, but then again, she'd been planning to spend the night away. "No," he admitted. "But I never go anywhere without my tablet."

"If I didn't know better, I'd think you planned this."
"I would never do anything to intentionally scare you."
"I know that," she replied softly.
He simply smiled and said, "Back here in thirty?"

CHAPTER 6

Alyssa groaned and pushed away from the table with a glance at her watch. "Ugh. We've been sitting here going through these records for three hours. I need a break."

She'd taken a quick shower earlier before they'd reconvened at the table. Kipling had somehow managed to change clothes. She wasn't sure if he just happened to keep extra in his car, along with his tablet, or if he'd called someone and had them sent over. She knew he'd had food delivered, because for the last few hours, they'd been snacking on delicious cheese cubes and crackers that tasted far too good to have come from a hotel vending machine.

She also needed a stretch, she decided, and stood, lifting her hands high in the air and then marching in place. She looked Kipling's way, expecting him to be watching her ass or something, but no, he was standing and stretching as well. He mimicked her moves and she couldn't help but appreciate the way his muscles moved under his shirt when he lifted his arms in the air.

Their gazes locked together and, for a second, something deliciously sinful passed between them. Very slowly, he brought his arms back to his side. She remembered how his arms had felt wrapped around her at the wedding. How safe they were. And strong.

"There's a bottle of wine in the other room, if you'd like a glass," he said, breaking the spell. "I know I could go for one."

"That sounds wonderful."

They walked silently into the living area of his suite, and she sat down on the couch while Kipling gathered the glasses, the bottle, and a corkscrew.

"It's a red," he said. "I hope that's alright."

"It's wine. There's no way it could be wrong." Besides, she gave the label a quick look as he uncorked the bottle. She wasn't a wine expert by any stretch, but doubted it was a vintage normally stocked by the hotel.

He gave a little laugh as he poured two glasses. "Don't be so sure, I've had plenty of awful wine in my time."

"I had wine out of a box a few years ago." She scooted over, giving him room to sit down beside her. "It wasn't as bad as I thought it would be."

He grimaced. "Why would you drink wine from a box?"

"Someone at the office gave it to Mac." She peeked at him to see if there was any judgment in his expression and found nothing. "The wine was way before . . ." She trailed off, not wanting to finish her sentence. "I'm sorry, I always feel like I shouldn't talk about him."

"How long were you two together?" he asked.

"Three years." She closed her eyes. Like she always did when Mac crossed her mind, she wondered how she could have been so blind.

Kipling gave a low whistle. "That's not an insignificant period of time."

"I know. I should have seen he was off long before I did."

"Why would you?"

She didn't understand his question. Or more to the point, she didn't see the reason for the question. She opened her eyes and shot him a *just what are you talking about* look.

"Hear me out," he said, and he sounded so genuine, she found herself agreeing.

"He basically led a double life that you knew nothing about or had no reason to suspect. I also think it's safe to assume he went to great lengths to keep it that way."

She had no trouble agreeing to that much.

"So what, in your opinion, was the clue you should have seen?" he asked.

She'd asked herself that too many times to count. Had played back in her mind every interaction he had with Janie after she'd started receiving the threats. There was nothing that stood out as off or out of place.

"I don't know," she finally admitted. "But surely there was something. I knew he had gambling debt, but a lot of people do and they don't kidnap or kill. I must have missed something."

"Why?"

"Because he was so evil, he had no business being around people. That kind of evil should be easy to spot."

"Should be. That doesn't mean it is," he spoke softly, keeping his eyes on her as if he could somehow look into her soul and speak right to it. "Besides, isn't that what makes evil even more horrific? Its ability to masquerade as normal?"

She took a deep breath. "Somewhere deep inside, I know you're right. But that knowledge doesn't alleviate my guilt."

"The guilt you feel is personal, no one else holds you accountable for what he did. But you have to forgive yourself and move on. You're too good of a person to be alone forever because someone you had no control over did something horrible."

Neither of them spoke for a long moment, until she broke the silence again. "You're a tantalizing catch . . . why hasn't someone taken you off the market?"

"You ask that as if to imply I'm willing to be taken off the market."

"Aren't you? I mean you're probably considered American royalty. Isn't it your job to produce an heir or two?" she asked in a joking, lighthearted manner. Yes, she wanted to know, but couldn't they discuss something with a touch of levity? Sometimes it felt like everything they discussed was shrouded in darkness and shadows.

He laughed. The abrupt change in the conversational tone had worked. "I suppose it is, but fortunately, I have two younger brothers and one is married and the other engaged. I don't think producing an heir or two will be problematic for either couple."

"Leaving you as the perpetual bachelor?"

"I did want to settle down once," he talked with a faraway look and an expression that was heartbreakingly transparent. "I was a freshman in college and fell madly in love. I know it sounds too young, but I'd never felt that way before her or after."

Something in his voice made her heart hurt, and she wanted nothing more than to track this woman down and ask her what the hell she'd done to Kipling. "What happened?"

"I thought I was in love and when she started asking for money, I gave and gave because I felt like it was my duty to take care of her. Hell, I brought her home to meet my family. They tried to warn me and I refused to listen. Eventually, though, it became too much. When I stopped paying her bills, she got ugly. Talk mostly. But the gossip eventually made its way here. When I went home the next weekend, Dad called me into his office as soon as I arrived. Our family lawyer, Derrick, was there, and he and Dad discussed filing a libel suit. I begged him not to that. The way I saw it, it was only talk and a suit would totally devastate her: financially, socially, you name it. I couldn't do that to her. Derrick ended up sending her a letter and everything stopped after that."

Alyssa nodded. "Let me guess. She told you that if you loved her you'd do it. That's what all the best manipulators say. It doesn't even matter what 'it' is. They're just using it to mess with your mind. Their only real goal is to get you to do what they want you to do. It has nothing to do with love. Real love doesn't make ultimatums or demand proof."

"What was his 'it'?" Kipling asked with the relief of someone who'd just found a kindred spirit. "What did he want you to do?"

She could still hear Mac's voice; still recalled his roundabout way of talking to her. "He wanted me to leave the police force."

Kipling whistled low. "Wow."

"He never came out and said it. He was much too passive-aggressive for that. But it was clear." She closed her eyes in an attempt to shut out the pain and anger at what Mac had told Janie when he'd kidnapped her months ago, on the night he died. Janie had been tied up and had wondered aloud how deeply Alyssa had been involved in Mac's plans.

Janie hadn't wanted to tell her at first, but Alyssa insisted.

"She's much too weak to be involved," he'd told Janie. *"Like all women. She couldn't handle it. Women are good for one thing and it's not what they have between their ears."*

"Yup," Janie said. *"I'm beginning to see why she always put off marrying you. That's disgusting. Tell me, is she aware of your view on womanhood?"*

"Of course not. I'm not an idiot. I was planning to wait until our honeymoon before telling her she had to quit the police force."

She shivered. "Something in me knew not to marry him. At least I did something right."

"You've done a lot of things right," Kipling assured her. "I can't believe he felt that way knowing how good you are at your job and knowing about your sister."

She jerked her head up. "That's because he didn't know about my sister."

"That you had one or that she was murdered?"

"Either. He didn't know I had a sister, much less that she was killed."

Kipling didn't say anything even though the question stayed there in the room with them: *You told me about your sister and not your boyfriend of three years?*

He ran his hand through his hair. "I don't know about you, but my situation fucked me up. To this day, I rarely allow myself to see or go out with the same woman twice."

She raised an eyebrow.

"Present company excluded," he clarified.

"Why is that?"

"Damned if I know."

"Probably because we're not going out."

"I don't think that's it. I must feel safe around you." His eyes grew dark. "Though why that is, I'm not sure. *Safe* is definitely not the first word I think of when I'm around you. Not from the very first time I saw you." He shifted closer to her. "It was that day in Tilly's apartment. Do you remember? You were there with your partner."

He was so close, she could feel the heat from his body and every so often she would catch a hint of the soap he washed with. Cedar with a hint of pine and something else she couldn't quite put her finger on. God, he smelled so good. She had the sudden urge to taste him.

"Don't let me stop you," he said.

"Damn it, did I say that out loud?" she asked. "It must be the wine. I'm usually in better control of myself."

"Note to self," he said. "Keep wine away from Alyssa."

She snorted. "Most guys would pour me more."

"I've seen far too many men take inappropriate liberties with women. I refuse to do so."

There was still a touch of sadness in his voice when he spoke, and she wished she knew how to make that sadness go away. She lifted a hand and lightly brushed his jaw, felt the stubble under her fingers. "You're one of the good guys, Kipling Benedict. You can fool some people, but you can't fool me. Under that gruff, take-no-prisoners exterior you show the world is a noble gentleman."

He turned his face to softly brush his lips across the palm of her hand. "I'm happy you think so. Once upon a time, I may have believed you, but now I'm not so sure."

The spot on her hand where he had kissed felt electrified and she fought the overwhelming urge to ask him to do it again. She focused on what he'd said. "That's okay. You don't have to believe me right now. It's the truth and you can't hide the truth, no matter if it's good or bad. You'll see it for yourself before too long."

"Thank you. Listening to you, I almost believe it myself."

She cocked an eyebrow at him and dropped her hand. It was clear he wasn't going to kiss it again. "Why are you being so nice to me?"

He actually smiled and it looked real this time. "What an odd question. Would you prefer I be boorish and rude?"

"What I'd prefer is for you to kiss me. And not on the hand this time."

A huge grin covered his face and she groaned.

"I can't believe I said that out loud." And whether it was the wine or that she was just damn tired of denying what she wanted, she said, "But I can't deny the truth of it."

He nodded. "Then the way I see it," he said. "I can either pretend like I didn't hear you or . . ." He scooted closer to her, maddeningly close, but not touching.

"Or?" she asked, shifting the last of the remaining distance between them, so close she felt certain he could see her shirt move with the pounding of her heart. So close to the side of his leg pressed against hers, and yet, it still wasn't close enough.

He slowly raised his hand, all the while looking into her eyes, until he gently cupped her face. He stroked her cheek and she shivered in response. "Or this."

Her eyes drifted closed as his lips came toward hers, and when they brushed hers so softly, she feared she imagined it. She put her arms around him and drew him in for a longer kiss.

The moment their lips touched for the second time, Kipling groaned low in his throat and tightened his embrace on her. She feared he'd be hesitant, that maybe he hadn't wanted to kiss her, but any such thought was soon swept away as his lips crushed hers.

His fingers fisted in her hair, holding her to him as he parted her lips and his tongue brushed hers. His other hand drifted to her waist, locking her in place. It was an altogether possessive and controlling move and she wanted more. She ran her fingers down his back, ensuring that he felt her nails. His groan assured her he not only felt them, but he liked it. He deepened the kiss and shifted, allowing her to brush against his erection.

The sharp knock on the door made them both jump. She thought about telling him not to answer it, but he was already standing up.

"Damn it all to hell," he muttered as he strode over to it. "What?" he asked, throwing the door open.

A uniformed man stood outside with a room service tray. "Room service," the man said, stepping inside and placing the tray on a nearby table.

"Wait a minute," Kipling said. "I didn't order room service. Did you?" He looked at Alyssa.

Her heart began to pound. "No."

She mentally calculated where her gun was and how long it'd take her to get it. She'd had it on when they arrived, but had taken it off before her shower. Which meant it was now sitting useless in her room. She could have cursed her stupidity.

Kipling jerked the order from the server. "This says room 1845. We're room 1945." He looked over to her and nodded. It was all okay, he was saying silently. Just a misunderstanding.

That being the case, she still wasn't able to stop trembling even after the deliveryman apologized profusely and left. She walked with shaky legs into her adjourning room and strapped on her weapon, making sure it was loaded. They had been fortunate this time and she wasn't going to be caught unprepared again.

She was seriously losing her touch. She'd been refusing to think about it, but now that it looked as if they might possibly find out who was responsible for her sister's murder, she wondered if she was going to do what she had scarcely let herself imagine.

Quit the police department for good. When she'd quit to help Kipling, she'd always intended to go back.

But what if she didn't?

It was a dream she only let herself contemplate at night, when she was all alone. That time when reality was shrouded in darkness and anything seemed possible. Those few precious moments when she danced between alertness and dreams, when she would allow herself to drift.

She'd always loved history, though she'd never given serious thought to what she'd do with a history degree. How could she when she'd decided at such a young age to become a cop? But at night, she'd allow herself to imagine the possibilities.

She could be a history teacher. Or do research. Maybe work in a museum. Or maybe she'd go even further and get a degree in archaeology. Go abroad. She would usually chuckle as she thought about becoming the next Indiana Jones.

But as she stood in the room, it hit her. After they solved the case, she wouldn't have a reason to be around Kipling anymore. She looked to her side and her heart sank. No matter how passionately he'd kissed her only moments before, she would always have her sister's death hanging over her. And even if she wanted to quit the force for good, she doubted she could. How else would she be able to help all those women and their families?

And as for Indiana Jones, though he always had a romance, it never seemed to work out. Either way it turned out, history or police, at the end of the day, she would still be alone.

Kipling hadn't followed her into her room. She supposed he was giving her privacy. On one hand, it was probably a good thing the room service had been mistakenly delivered to his room because if it hadn't, she wasn't sure she'd have been able to pull away from him. Even now his presence in the next room seemed to pull at her.

Jade slowly opened her eyes to ensure she was alone. She breathed a sigh of relief that she was. At least for now. But that was the only good thing. She was still bound in a cell-like place she nicknamed Unknown.

She knew she was in serious trouble. For one, she was unable to get a read on The Gentleman. That had never been an issue before. He'd always been transparent in his emotions toward her, no matter what they were about. If he was angry, she knew that. And she stayed away from him. If he was planning revenge, or some other kind of coup, she would stay in the room and help him. If he was happy, she would pour the wine and join him.

Unfortunately, he was wearing a mask around her. She had no idea what to think. Not that she needed to be able to read his expression to know that she was in trouble. That much was obvious from the way he had tied her up.

Not only that, but she had no idea where they were. She thought she had known all the places where he would take people. Hell, she'd been to most of them. But the place she found herself at now was unlike any other she'd ever been to before with him. Every so often, the wind would blow a certain direction and she could smell the sea.

That in and of itself made no sense to her. The Gentleman didn't own any beach property. She knew this for a fact because he let her keep his books. Unless, which seemed likely, he only gave her access to a few of them.

Right now she was in a very dark and damp shelter; perhaps she was even underground. For the moment, she was also alone. She had no way to keep time, but she thought he'd been gone for at least three hours. Which meant he would be returning soon.

As if she'd spoken him into existence, a door behind her opened. She knew it was him, but he didn't say anything until he got closer.

"Your eldest brother is an idiot," he said.

It was probably for the best to not reply to him. She kept her thoughts to herself.

The Gentleman, of course, was undeterred. "He has taken his girlfriend, that worthless police officer, out of the city, to a nearby hotel. Like I can't find them."

Kipling was dating Alyssa? She had always pictured him with a boring high-society chick, but the thought of him with Alyssa made her smile.

But as curious as she was about Kipling's relationship with the police officer, it would have to wait. There were far more important things to find out.

"Thus far," The Gentleman said, "he doesn't seem overly concerned about you. He seems to have his hands full keeping the police officer out of trouble. But he's not as smart as he thinks he is. I've just bugged his room."

He sat down in front of her, and took his phone out of his pocket. "I didn't place the bug myself, of course, too much risk of being recognized." He sighed. "I've recently run into David. He was looking for work and, even though I said I wouldn't bring anyone else on, I hired him. Hopefully, he doesn't turn out to be a disappointment like you."

Her mouth grew dry. David? She hadn't thought about him in ages. When she was around ten, he started hanging around, until The Gentleman ran him off. He had been a street kid, an orphan influenced by a bad man, just like her. They'd understood each other, been friends long ago. If she had thought of him lately or wondered how he was doing, she would not have wanted him to hook up with The Gentleman.

The Gentleman seemed to be scrolling through his phone apps. "Here it is," he said, finding what he was looking for. "Now the real test."

He made a few adjustments on his phone, and before too long there was static. A few adjustments more, and she heard Kipling's voice.

"Alyssa," he was saying. "Wait."

From further away came the sound of the police officer. "I'm sorry, Kipling. I shouldn't have gotten distracted like that. It put us both in a bad spot."

"If you're expecting me to apologize, I'm not going do it."

"Why would I expect you to apologize for something I asked for?"

Kipling didn't respond and after a few seconds, they heard Alyssa again. "Look, it's been a very busy day. A very trying day. I'm going to go to bed and try to get some sleep. You should do the same and we'll get back to this tomorrow."

There was only silence then and after a while The Gentleman put his phone down. "Sounds as though we missed something between the two of them. Too bad, I think I'd have liked to hear whatever they were doing."

The Gentleman got up and walked around the small space where she was being kept. Checking to ensure everything was secure and there was no way she could escape. Although why he bothered she wasn't sure. It wasn't like she could go anywhere since he'd tied her up, making sure he told her as he did that this was one knot she'd never untie and, damn him to hell, it appeared he was right. She'd tried her best to do just that the night before, eventually falling asleep, pissed off and unsuccessful.

"Stop looking at me like I'm an idiot, girl," he said. "I'm not about to do anything that would allow you to get away from me again. Especially considering what it took to get you back this last time."

She decided not to acknowledge that with a response, either.

"You better hope that brother of yours decides quickly to turn his attention back to you instead of that police detective. Your time is limited. And if he doesn't get his head back in the game again, it'll be a lot more limited than you believe it might be. In my perfect world, all three of your siblings would come running and I could take them out all at the same time. But I'm fine with only killing Kipling for now. Once he's gone, the other two will be easy to take out."

CHAPTER 7

The next day Alyssa and Kipling worked separately. They didn't leave the hotel rooms, but they kept the door between their suites open so they were within eyesight of each other. For his part, Kipling seemed to want to ignore, and not talk about, the kiss they shared the night before.

Alyssa eventually told herself she was being ridiculous. Even if Kipling seemed inclined to discuss it, what was there to say other than they shouldn't do it again? The kiss had been eye-opening in more than one way. She still couldn't get over how out of character it was for her to have forgotten her gun.

Suppose she and Kipling were dating, she honestly couldn't see herself lasting very long with somebody who caused her to forget what she must be doing. It just wasn't a good thing. Not to mention it was unsafe. If she was smart, she'd stop thinking about him, period.

But still, he got to her in little ways. How he'd pour her more coffee if he was getting himself some. The way he'd adjust the thermostat when he saw she was cold. He was exactly what she'd pegged him as the night before—a gentleman. Frankly, he was a lot easier to deal with when he was just an obnoxious rich guy she could ignore. Or arrest.

But now, especially with them sharing the suites, he was always underfoot, always nearby. She could never *not* think about him. And though she tried not to let her thoughts go to the carnal, it didn't always work.

Shortly after lunch, an e-mail appeared in her inbox that had her calling Kipling to come to her quickly. He made it to her side in less than five seconds.

"Everything okay?" he asked.

She turned to face him, blocking his view of the computer. "Yes, I just wanted you to be here before I did anything else."

He tried to look over her shoulder. "Did you find something?"

"That's yet to be seen, but I got an e-mail from the lab this morning saying they hadn't misplaced the results, they had just been delayed and the results would be entered today." She sighed. "Finally."

"You have them? Thank goodness. I was beginning to think we'd never get them."

"I don't have them quite yet." She turned back around to face her laptop. "I was getting ready to log on to the portal and bring them up. But I wanted you to be here to see."

He pulled a chair over to where they were and sat down. "Go for it." While she was logging in, he asked, "Tell me again what you tested and what we potentially could see."

"From Jade's hair, we tested mitochondrial DNA. It's less specific because all the females in a family will have the exact same expression. So, if Jade's biological mother, sister, grandmother, or aunt is in the system, we'll find them. In this case, we're throwing our net wide in hopes of finding out more about Jade. Especially since we already know who her father is."

"Makes sense," Kipling said as she pulled up the home screen.

Alyssa typed in her username and password and held her breath as she waited for her account page to load. She hadn't used this lab too many times in the past and hoped that word of her leaving her job hadn't made it to the private lab the police department sometimes used for testing. Most of the time, she didn't use mitochondrial DNA. Her account showed the handful of cases and tests she'd ordered in the past and, most importantly, it had Jade's test file marked as completed and a hyperlink that would lead to the test results.

"Does that mean there was a match?" Kipling asked. "Or would they still use a hyperlink to tell us there was no match found?"

"Good question," Alyssa said. She'd clicked on the hyperlink, but instead of getting results, she was taken to another account verification page. "Are you kidding me with this?" she asked no one in particular.

"What?" Kipling asked. "Does it normally not do that?"

"It's never done it to me before." She went through her security questions to verify who she was before the system allowed her to continue. "Very interesting. I don't know if it's a new layer of security or if it's because the results are sensitive."

She hadn't thought about that angle. What if Jade's mother wasn't dead, but was a celebrity? Knowing what she did of Benedict Senior, she could see it happening.

It became such a tempting possibility in her mind that she was still thinking about it and pondering who the celebrity could be as the results populated her screen.

"What does it say?" Kipling asked.

She read the report summary. It didn't make any sense

at all, so she read it a second time. The second read through was worse than the first. She refreshed her screen. Although her body must have been processing the results faster than her brain because her hand trembled in shock.

"Alyssa?" Kipling asked again.

She clicked on the report. The summary must be wrong, that was all there was to it.

"Damn it," Kipling nearly growled. "Tell me what's wrong. I've never seen you like this before."

She couldn't talk to him yet. She had to know. If she was going to tell him what the results indicated, she had to believe two-hundred percent that there could be no mistake. Taking a deep breath, she read through the words on the screen. From the first sentence that started with the date of the sample to the last sentence that simply stated, "Results verified by repeat analysis."

Satisfied, at least intellectually, she turned to Kipling. He sat completely still, his expression showed he knew something bad was getting ready to happen, but there was a lingering hint of hope that he was wrong. He wasn't, though, and she was going to be the one who smashed that hope to pieces before his eyes.

She took a deep breath. "Jade's sample hit on three profiles in the nationwide database."

"Really?" he asked, and there was that damn hope again. More pronounced this time. "Three? That's really good news, isn't it?"

Damn, but it was hard to talk to him while she sat in front of him. The best thing she could do was spit it out. All at once. "The three matching profiles are me, my sister, and my mother."

He sat frozen for several long seconds.

"You?" he finally asked in a hoarse voice. "Why are you a match?"

"Jade is either my half-sister or my niece. I'm inclined

to go with my niece because the timing fits and I'm fairly certain I'd remember my mom being pregnant. I don't believe any teenager can be so self-absorbed as to not notice that."

"Your sister?" he asked.

"Yes."

He hung his head and buried his hands in his hair. All at once, he sat up, eyes blazing, but she wasn't sure with what exactly. "Your murdered sister."

"Sir?" The Gentleman's butler knocked on the door.

The Gentleman stood panting as he looked over the pile of glass, water, and leather that had once been on his desk. Somewhere in the background Alyssa and Kipling kept talking, but he wasn't paying them any attention.

"Go away!" he yelled at his butler.

"But, sir—"

"Go. Away."

His wife had given him a rare fifteenth-century Ming vase for their anniversary ten years ago. The antique blue-and-white porcelain made a satisfying smash as his fist connected with it and it shattered to the floor.

The butler didn't knock or say anything else.

How had he missed the fact that Allison and Alyssa were sisters? How? They didn't even have the same last name.

He'd been a fool. A fool. All those times he'd let Alyssa go because he could always take her out later. After Mac had died and he'd decided not to kill her just yet because she'd done him a favor by being part of the team that took him out, unintentional though it had been on her part, and because he'd always been focused on the Benedicts.

He may have been a fool then, but those days were gone. He couldn't wait to hear if Alyssa would sound just as pathetic begging for her life as her sister had in the seconds before he slit her throat.

"Now we know what the connection is between our families," Kipling said.

"We know your father slept with my sister when she was barely eighteen," Alyssa countered. "And we know he got her pregnant. It still doesn't make sense. We don't know where she went for five years or why she came back. We don't know who killed her or why. We still don't know who Jade's guardian is. And we still don't have a clue who or what Finition Noire is. We don't know anything."

"I disagree. We actually know a bit more than that," Kipling said, risking her wrath, and not surprisingly at his words, she glared at him. "Listen to me. I believe we now have a good understanding as to why your stepfather kicked her out the house. He found out that she was pregnant. And I would be willing to bet that is the same reason he kicked her out again when she returned five years later."

Kipling still couldn't believe it. How was it possible that his father had slept with such a young girl? That he got her pregnant, and then did nothing to support her or his child? He wouldn't have thought his father to be so cold, so uncaring, but there it was.

Alyssa stood up; she seemed to have aged in the last few minutes. "I have to get out of here. Walk. Do something. I don't care what, I have to get out of this hotel room."

"I'll go with you," Kipling said.

"You don't have to."

"I know I don't, but I want to. And I don't want you to be by yourself. It's not safe."

He was surprised when she didn't argue with him. Instead, she calmly walked to the door and waited for him to get ready to walk outside with her. Of course once they were outside, he saw what her plan was. She took off walking quickly, not looking behind to make sure he followed her, or talking to him at all.

He knew she had received quite a shock today. Hell, he did, too.

After walking about four blocks, she finally turned. "I wish one of them were here," she said. "I don't care which one. I'd ask them what the hell they thought they were doing. And if they had any idea how much they're messing up everybody because of their actions. I want to ask Allison if it was worth it." Tears filled her eyes. "And then it hits me, I can't, because she's dead. And regardless of what she would say, it wasn't worth it at all."

He moved toward, her unsure of how she would read, but knowing he had to do something. He placed a tentative hand on her shoulder, and when she didn't flinch or try to move away, he placed one on the other. She took a step toward him and he enveloped her in his arms. For several minutes, he held her, and though he meant to give her comfort, she gave him the same.

"Let's go back to the hotel, and regroup." He kept an arm around her shoulder and gently turned her back to the hotel. "We need to plan our next steps."

She didn't say anything, and silently, they walked back to the hotel together.

CHAPTER 8

Alyssa knew as soon as she walked into her suite that someone had been in her room. It wasn't housekeeping. Kipling had placed the *DO NOT DISTURB* signs on their doors before they went for their walk, and her bed was still unmade and her towels unchanged.

In fact, there was nothing she could point to as proof. Rather, it was a feeling in her gut. Those who had never experienced it would likely not understand, but after years of working on the police force, she'd learned to listen to it.

She took her weapon and carefully looked over everything, searching for any minute detail to back up her feeling. Nothing was out of place until she reached the work area. In the middle of the conference table, a kitchen knife had been shoved into the tabletop, pinning a picture to the surface. She gasped when she saw what was.

The crime-scene photo of her sister's body.

To the side was a note, typed, "Your sister couldn't stay away from Benedict men, either. You'd better learn or else you'll meet the same fate."

She didn't realize she was shaking until she tried to take a step forward and almost fell. She reached for the knife,

then stopped herself. It was unlikely the culprit left finger-
prints, but on the off chance they hadn't wiped the knife
handle, she was going to dust it for prints.

"Kipling," she called. "Come here, please."

She blocked out the picture of her sister's broken body
as best as she could and tried to concentrate on the note.
There was something she had the feeling she needed to pay
attention to, outside of the words on the note.

Kipling's footsteps sounded, getting louder as he came
closer. "Alyssa?"

She didn't answer. All of her focus was concentrated on
the note. There was something there. What was it she was
missing?

"Alyssa? Are you okay?" Kipling asked and within the
next three seconds he had made it to where she waited.

She could lie and tell him everything was okay and
she was fine, but the truth was, she needed to trust someone. She closed her eyes and whispered, "No."

He walked to her and put his arms around her; until he
did, she wasn't aware that she was cold or trembling. But
it took mere seconds for her to feel warm and for the
trembling to stop. She didn't even know if Kipling knew
or realized the effect his touch had on her.

As it was, he took one look at her, pushed the hair back
from her forehead, and asked, "What happened?"

Silently, she pointed at the table. Because she couldn't
bear to look at the picture again, she kept her focus on
Kipling's face. As such, she watched as shock turned to
anger.

"What the hell is this?" he said. When he looked up,
his face was more controlled.

Alyssa collapsed into a nearby chair. "That's my sister.
Or was."

He looked down at the picture once more, and cursed
under his breath. "Who did this?"

She assumed he meant the picture and the knife, since they both knew she had no idea who had murdered her sister. "I don't know. I think they were here while we went out." She shivered just thinking about it. God, that had been close. And following along that line, she purposed she wasn't going to keep doing this. The time had come to take these bastards down once and for all.

There were too many emotions going through Kipling's body at the moment. Rage. Shock. Disgust. Fear.

"How did they know?" he asked. "Seriously. How? I mean, we just found out. And unless I'm mistaken, those reports are confidential. Right?"

She nodded, but her attention seemed to be elsewhere and was no longer focused on him or the knife in the middle of the table.

"Alyssa?" he asked as she walked away from the table.

She looked at him only to hold her finger to her mouth. He raised an eyebrow. She wanted him to be quiet? What was her deal? Who could they possibly be disturbing?

It hit him as she moved around the room, running her hand under the various surfaces. He told himself it was only a precaution and one they should have taken before now. But when she stopped in front of the table the deliveryman had used the night before when he placed the room service tray down, he knew it was more than a mere formality. She looked resigned, sighed deeply, and pointed to a bug.

Fucking hell. Kipling frantically tried to remember everything they had discussed. So damn much.

They needed to get out of here and quickly. The only thing was, he wasn't sure where they could go. Alyssa was one step ahead of him, pulling papers together and packing them up. She motioned with her fingers for him to go get his stuff.

"I'm hungry already," she said, like it was most natural thing in the world. He was once more struck by her calmness and how she always acted so cool under pressure. "Do you think you could eat dinner early?"

"I don't see why not. I'd love a big ol' rack of ribs." He grinned at the last part, knowing Alyssa didn't eat pork. She stuck her tongue out at him.

"Fine," she said. "You can have ribs and I'll get something else."

They continued their fake argument as they went around the room, throwing their clothes and toiletries in whatever bag that was the closest. By the time they'd decided where they were going to go for dinner, they were packed.

From the conversation they had, no one would guess that they had walked out of the two suites with no intention of ever returning. By silent agreement, neither one of them said anything until they made it to Kipling's car. Alyssa did a quick check, looking for both GPS devices and bugs, but finding neither.

"We lucked up," she said as they climbed into his car. "They weren't expecting you, so nothing of yours is bugged. We have to be more careful from now on. I can't believe I didn't think to look for bugs after that bogus deliveryman last night."

She almost added she didn't know where her head had been, but she knew the answer to that one. It had been on Kipling and his kiss.

"Anyway, I think that'll keep them off our trail for a little bit," Alyssa said as Kipling sped away from the hotel as quickly as he could without drawing attention to himself. "We need a place to stay that whoever is looking for us won't find easily."

"I'd been thinking along those lines," Kipling said, "and I think I have just the place."

"Where?" Alyssa asked, as if she didn't quite believe he'd have the perfect location at his fingertips.

"We own a beach place, down in Edisto," he said. "It's in my mother's maiden name, so someone would have to look hard and dig deep to find it."

"It does sound perfect. But why is it still in your mother's maiden name?"

"My grandparents, my mother's parents, were never thrilled with my mom marrying my dad. You have to understand, at least from their point of view, Franklin Benedict wasn't to be trusted. You think my brothers and I are given a hard time by the newspapers? Apparently, compared to my father, we all three qualify for sainthood."

"Surely after they got married, they didn't think the worst of him."

Kipling grimaced. He wasn't one to typically share dirty family secrets, but Alyssa's sister had not only slept with his father, but had also borne him a child. But more than that, he wanted to share things about his family with her. He wanted her in that circle, "The thing is," he told her. "I was born six months after their wedding and I was almost nine pounds."

"Oh, man," Alyssa said.

"Right? There was no way they could pass me off as early." He shrugged. "I'm not sure if that was their plan or not. Either way, my mom's parents never got along with my dad."

"Are they still around?"

"They are, but they're in France and they only make it stateside about once every three years. They say the air in France keeps them young and they're both almost ninety. Who am I to argue with that?"

"They sound like they're quite the pair."

Kipling couldn't help but smile. "They are. I do wish I

was able to see them more. I swear, they're busier than most people half their age. My grandmother has the ear of a few fashion designers. Last time we saw her, she had just given her opinion on fashion accessories for the mature woman. There was a purse strap she said was going to revolutionize the industry."

He chuckled. "I remember her exasperation that her three grandsons had no idea how impressive the strap had been. She'd mumbled something about testosterone and went to find Lena, who could better appreciate her brilliance."

He glanced to his side, expecting to see Alyssa grin at the story, but instead he found himself unable to read her expression. "Are you okay?"

"Her purse," she said. "My sister's purse. That's what's missing in the crime-scene photo."

"What do you mean missing?"

"Her purse was in the box of things the police brought over, but it wasn't in the crime-scene photo."

"Tell me what I'm missing, Alyssa," he said. "Tell me why the purse should have been in the photo."

She took a deep breath. "She never went anywhere without that purse and in the photo, she was dressed to go out. The purse should have been by her side, but it wasn't. I remember seeing that purse in the box when they brought it to Mom. I couldn't believe she was carrying it five years later."

She didn't say anything after that and Kipling glanced to his side. "What?"

"I can't believe I didn't realize it sooner. I got her that purse for her birthday. I was in scouts and I added a secret compartment. Oh my God. I'd forgotten about that. She used to joke that she could keep the secrets of the whole world in there. What she normally kept in there were things she didn't want Mom to see. Notes from boys, that sort of thing."

"Is it possible whoever found the purse also discovered the secret compartment, and later returned it?"

"Of course," she said. "Whatever Allison had hidden in the purse, if anything, I'm sure is gone by now."

He had pulled into the driveway of the beach house, but instead of heading to the main house, he took a small side drive and came to a stop at a much smaller property.

Kipling turned to her. "On the off chance that some-one knows about this property, we added this cottage after we bought it and even fewer people know about it."

Her half-hearted nod and faraway expression told him that her body was with him, but her mind was still think-ing about a purse. He recalled that she was very thorough and would never leave any clue unexamined.

"Alyssa?" he asked softly, placing a hand on top of hers. "I agree with you. We need to get that purse and make sure there's nothing in it."

She looked at him in surprise. "But I didn't say any-thing."

"Not with your mouth, you didn't." It took all his strength not to brush her lips with his own. "I vote we get settled inside and you look at the picture again and I'm going to call Knox."

"To see if he can find out anything about the purse?"

He shook his head. "To find out who became Jade's guardian after your sister's death."

CHAPTER 9

They walked into the cottage and Kipling pointed to the outside patio where he suggested she could sit and look over the photo if she wanted, while he would ensure the house was ready for occupancy. It didn't take her long to review the photo, just long enough to verify that the purse was the only item she had a question about.

She leaned back in the wicker rocker and watched as Kipling set about making sure the house would meet their needs for the next few days. Again it struck her how this giant of business and industry was just as comfortable setting up the cottage as he was running negotiations.

Her stomach rumbled, reminding her how long it'd been since they ate. She got up and wandered into the kitchen to see if she could find something to fix for dinner. She found what she was looking for right as Kipling came up behind her.

"Did you find anything?" he asked. "I was going to take a shower, but it can wait."

She shooed him out of the kitchen. "You. Out. Go get a shower. I can handle dinner."

Once he was out of the kitchen, she pulled the frozen shrimp she'd found and grabbed the grits she'd discovered in the pantry. She didn't cook a lot, but considered shrimp and grits one of her specialties. Within minutes, she had the shrimp thawing and the sauce cooking. By the time Kipling rejoined her, everything was coming along nicely.

"If that's shrimp and grits I smell," he said, coming up behind her so he could peek over her shoulder, "I'm yours forever."

"You may want to wait until you've tasted it."

"Nah," he said. "I can tell by the smell that it's going to be great."

She didn't say anything, but turned around to face him, expecting to raise an eyebrow. However, she was not expecting him to be standing quite so close and when she turned around; she found him in her personal space and swore she could feel the heat from his body. She forgot everything she was going to say and do.

"Yes?" he asked, a hint of laughter in his voice.

"I had to do the grits a different way. They might not be good." She didn't know why she told him that, other than it was the truth.

She ducked around him and grabbed the two plates she'd set out earlier. Kipling took the plates from her with an "Allow me," and carried them to the small table on the patio.

Flustered and hating herself for feeling that way, she snatched up the napkins and forks and followed. She didn't know why she felt so out of sorts, but when she made it out to the patio and found him holding one of the chairs out for her, the out-of-sort feeling slipped away. At the sight of his easy smile and breezy confidence, she couldn't help but feel the same.

"I hope this table will do, ma'am," he said with all seriousness as if he was indeed working in an upscale restaurant and not at his own family's patio. "I'm afraid we're rather busy tonight and this is all we have available." His composure slipped on that last sentence and he coughed in what she assumed was an attempt to cover up a chuckle.

Playing along, she slipped into the offered seat with a sigh. "I suppose I'm not in any position to complain since I didn't have the courtesy to call ahead."

He nodded and turned away, doing something she couldn't see. When he turned back around, it appeared he had a wine bottle in his hand that he held out as if expecting her to inspect it.

"Ma'am?" he asked.

He still had that playful grin on his face and she couldn't imagine why. He took a step closer and she saw it wasn't a wine bottle at all, but rather a plain glass decanter. She swallowed a laugh.

"South Carolina. Low county. Current year flat," he said, his grin getting bigger. "It's our best reserve yet. I thought that with what happened the last time I gave you wine, water might be the best choice tonight."

She didn't try to swallow her laugh this time; she let it out, waving at his seat across from her as she did so. "Please," she said, between laughs. "Sit down."

He finally relented, taking the seat across from her with a sigh. "I could never work in the service industry."

She raised an eyebrow. "Was I really that bad? I thought I was most polite."

"It's not you," he assured her. "I was just thinking about how it could be." He poured himself a glass of water and sat back to take a long sip. "I don't think I would last one night. I'd more than likely have to punch somebody out. Or maybe cuss them out? Either way, it wouldn't be pretty and I would probably end up getting myself fired."

"All that aside, I think you did a fine job out here on your parents' patio. In fact, I thought I might set up a reservation for tomorrow night." She twirled her wineglass that contained water. "I thought the service was exemplary."

"If you think dinner service is good, you should see this place at breakfast."

There was nothing inherently suggestive about his statement. After all, they had shared several breakfasts together over the last few days and none had been remotely uncomfortable. So why was it her face heated at his statement and her heart raced?

Because there were hours to go until breakfast and the heated look he gave her led her to believe he had several suggestions on how they could spend them. Quite a change from what she thought he'd feel as recently as a month ago when she couldn't picture him with a police officer.

But no sooner had that thought popped into her mind than she chastised herself for being so rude and disrespectful to Kipling in her thoughts. She had not once—not before they wound up together like they currently were or in the last few days when she was with him almost twenty-four seven—ever seen him hold himself above anyone or look down on anyone.

Kipling Benedict was not a snob. If anyone was being judgmental about class, or his bank-account amount, it was her. And that thought made her feel very small. Was she really so petty that she wouldn't want Kipling because he was wealthy?

She heard his voice from the not-so-distant past, on one of the first times they'd met.

"For the record, I'm not just wealthy. I'm insanely wealthy. And guess what? News flash. Everyone is for sale. Even you. All I have to do is find your price." His voice dropped a notch. *"Would you like for me to try? Rumor has it I'm very thorough when it comes to something I want to buy."*

She realized his words now for what they truly were—a

defense mechanism designed to keep him from getting hurt. If he could make the world think he was nothing more than a playboy, then no one would bother to get to know him. And that way, he would never get hurt.

He sat across the table from her, serving them both hearty scoops of grits followed by the shrimp she'd made to go over it. He caught her looking and smiled, but it wasn't until he frowned that she realized she hadn't returned it.

"Are you okay?" he asked, and she knew she had been a fool.

Who had hurt him so much that he no longer wanted anyone to get close to him? It had to be that girl from college. It was a good thing Alyssa wasn't around in those days; she'd have taught that piece of trash a thing or two.

"Alyssa?" he asked, this time with concern in his voice because she realized she'd never replied.

"I'm good," she said.

"Are you sure? You looked confused there a few seconds ago."

"That was nothing. Just me hoping dinner doesn't suck." She picked up her fork. "Eat up."

"I don't believe you for a minute," he told her. Though normally, if she didn't want to tell him, no amount of badgering would get her to change her mind, he decided to try. "Tell me."

She put her fork down with a sigh. "If you must know, I was thinking about that girl from college and how I wished I knew who she was, because I'd love to tell her a thing or two. Can we change topics now?"

Even though her response touched him, he did as she asked and changed the topic completely, launching instead into stories of his childhood when the Benedict clan came to their beach property. Even then it took some time for her to realize that he didn't want to try a bait and switch. All he planned to do was talk about the past and occasionally tell something frightfully embarrassing about his brothers.

He told her about a sea turtle Keaton wanted to take home to Benedict House and how his brother had concocted a story about the turtle coming up to the beach house while everyone else but he was asleep. Keaton would let him in and they'd drink orange soda and eat Lena's chocolate chip cookies.

Kipling leaned in close. "Lena told him that if she woke up and found that some sea turtle had tracked sand in all over the floor she'd cleaned, and on top of that he was being fed cookies? She'd never make them again. Knox jumped up and said no turtle was going to eat his cookies. He was going to go to the beach and capture that turtle and make soup out of it."

Alyssa laughed softly. The first time she'd done so all evening. "How did Keaton take that?"

It hit him that with her family situation being what it was, she probably didn't have many stories to share about her sister. "Alyssa, I'm so sorry." He shook his head. "I never meant . . . I mean, I go on and on all the time, and it never occurred to me to stop and think that you . . ."

He looked up, expecting to see her upset or possibly sad, but instead the reverse was true. She looked serene, for lack of a better word. The late-evening light touched her hair in a way that almost made her look like she glowed. Or at least made her look otherworldly. He wasn't sure he'd ever be able to perfectly describe how she looked, but the effect was stunning. She was stunning. All at once, he found his mouth so dry, he couldn't speak.

Seemingly unaware of the effect she had on him, she ever so gently placed her hand on top of his. "You're worried about telling me about you and your brothers growing up because you know I don't have anything similar to share about my sister?"

He winced slightly and put down the glass of water he'd taken a sip from. "It made more sense in my head than it did to hear you say it out loud."

She didn't move her hand, and he swore he felt her touch echo throughout his body. "I can only imagine that the way you grew up, with two brothers, makes my childhood look very boring and bleak. But I had fun; there were some good times, too."

"I didn't mean to imply otherwise."

"I know that."

She still hadn't moved her hand. A quick glance at the table told him she had finished her dinner.

"Ah," he said. "I knew you were mistaken about something."

His only response from her was an arched eyebrow. He loved how she used that perfectly sculpted brow to convey any number of sentiments. In the past, she'd lifted it at him in annoyance, in disbelief, and like now, in question. He imagined that same brow had been lifted a time or two at work as well and he suddenly wanted to see her in her element.

"You're killing me with the eyebrow," he said.

"I'm waiting for you to tell me what I was mistaken about."

"The grits," he said. "You said you thought that they would be awful, but they aren't. They're wonderful."

She glanced at his plate. His empty plate. "Or perhaps," she said, "you're just a typical male, and will eat anything that is put in front of you."

He didn't answer for a few seconds, instead choosing to look at her and gaze into her eyes. When he finally answered, his voice was low and she had to lean forward to hear him. "Do you really think I'm a typical guy?"

This close to her, he could see she was trembling. It wasn't cold, and she wasn't frightened. That left one thing. Other than the one kiss they had shared, they had ignored this thing between them for the most part. That was going to end tonight.

"Do you, Alyssa?" he asked again. She tried to jerk her hand back, but he wouldn't let her. He didn't hold on to it tightly, but gently. And when she stopped trying to pull away, he brought it to his lips and kissed it.

"Do you?" he asked again.

"No."

No. That word said in answer to any other question at a point like this would've stopped him. But said in response to the question he'd asked, it made him move forward more.

"Thank you," he said. "I have to admit I'd be rather put out if you were to think I was typical. For the record, I don't think there's anything typical about you, either."

"Kipling," she said. "What are we doing?"

"At the moment, the only thing we're doing is talking. We're two people who just finished a delightful meal and we're sitting at the dinner table enjoying each other's company."

"That isn't what I meant."

He knew she was going to say that. It made a part of him deep inside feel very pleased with himself that he was able to predict her so well. "In that case, you must have asked the wrong question. Perhaps what you should have asked was *'What are we going to do?'*"

He might be pleased with his ability to guess what she was going to say next, but the laugh she gave at that moment told him she knew him just as well. "What?" he asked, though he had a feeling he didn't need to ask.

"As soon as I said that, I knew what you were going to say," she said.

"What am I getting ready to say now, Alyssa?"

But she didn't reply and dipped her head instead. Trying to hide the color that his question brought to her cheeks, he assumed.

"I don't know," she said.

He stood and she looked up, but if she thought he was getting ready to leave the patio, she was sorely mistaken. He held his hand out to her and she took it, getting to her feet.

He decided to be silent and wait for her to say something. When she lifted her head and looked at him with her intense eyes, he could no longer be quiet. "I want you, Alyssa."

There was no surprise in her eyes. She knew how he felt.

"I know," she said, and he appreciated that she appeared neither embarrassed nor coy. She was matter-of-fact about the entire thing. He had no idea it would be so refreshing for a woman to act that way.

"I know," she repeated. "And by now, you must know that I want you, too."

"Yes," he said, giving her the same straightforwardness that she had given him.

"The thing is, I'm not sure what I want to do about it."

He brought her hand to his lips and kissed her fingertips. "I sure as hell know what I want to do about it. Come to bed with me, Alyssa."

She closed her eyes. "I don't know."

He brought her hand to his lips again, but this time kissed her open palm and hiding his smile when she sucked in a breath and her eyes flew open. "You do know."

Now that her eyes were open, he saw they were dark with desire. "Yes," she admitted.

"Tell me what's making you hesitate."

"So you can tell me why I shouldn't feel that way?"

"So I can understand."

She took a deep breath and seemed to steel herself. "I'm afraid I'm going to like it too much."

"I would hope so," he couldn't stop himself from saying. "Otherwise, I'd consider myself a horrible failure."

"And," she continued as if he hadn't said anything, "when that does in fact happen, I'm not sure I want to know it can be so good, if I can't be with you."

"Why won't you be able to be with me?"

She tried to turn her head, but he took his free hand and held her in place, forcing her to meet his gaze.

"Tell me why you wouldn't be able to be with me," he stated again.

"Don't make me say it."

"I'm afraid you're going to have to. I don't have any idea where you're going with this line of thinking."

"I'm a police officer. You're a Benedict."

He dropped her hand. "Damn it, Alyssa. Are we back to that? Really?"

"Listen to me. You keep saying it doesn't matter, but it does. Bea is an attorney, her brother is one of the wealthiest men in the state. And sure, Tilly was working as a waitress in a gentlemen's club, but she was *born* wealthy. She's part of that lifestyle."

"I don't know what I can say or do to make you understand I don't give a rat's ass about your net worth."

"You say that now, but one day it will matter." She held up her hand when he tried to speak. "Let me finish. I know you don't think it'll ever matter, but it will. Maybe not this month or even this year, but one day you'll see that you need a woman who can understand and fit into your world. A woman at ease with everything it holds. More importantly, you need a woman who won't be forever tainted by the choices of men she dated."

She was bringing Mac into this? Suddenly he couldn't

104   TARA THOMAS

stand to hear it anymore. He dropped her hand. "If that's
how you really feel about me, it looks like we're done here."
He put on the frostiest expression he had. The one he always used when he needed to be a cold-hearted bastard.
"I have to thank you for ensuring we didn't go any further.
What a colossal mistake that would have been. Now if
you'll excuse me, I think I'll go for a walk. I'm too
agitated to remain indoors at the moment. Don't worry
about the dishes, I'll take care of them when I get back.
And don't wait up. I don't know how long I'll be out."

Alyssa watched as he turned and walked away. Not once
did he look back at her. But then again, she didn't call out
to him, either. She knew if she did, she'd take back everything she'd just said because even if what she said was true,
she didn't care. She wanted him. Wanted to be with him.
And damn the consequences.

She took the dishes back inside the house, refusing to
look down the hall where the bedrooms were. If she hadn't
been such a complete and utter ass, they'd be headed down
that hall right now, on the way to his bedroom.

"I royally fucked that up," she said to no one.

The question was why? She thought about it as she
washed the dishes and put them away. While she cleaned
the pots she'd cooked with and set the patio table to rights.

When everything was in the exact location and in the
same shape she'd found it, she ventured to the bedroom
he'd put her stuff in and prepared to take a shower.

She had one shot to fix this mess. She wasn't going to
screw it up.

It was two hours later before she heard the front door
open. Darkness had fallen and except for the one low lamp
light she'd cut on in the living room, everything inside the
house was dark. If he went by looks alone, he'd assume
she took his advice and went to bed.

She loosened the belt around the robe she had on, preparing for him to make his way to where she was. Closing her eyes, she took a deep breath, and seconds later, she heard his steps enter the living room.

She knew exactly when he saw her because his breath hitched and he spoke, though in a lower voice than she'd thought he'd use.

"I thought I told you not to wait up," he said.

She stood up. "There are a few things I need to say."

"That's great. Unfortunately, those are things I have no interest in hearing."

He took a step toward the hall, but she moved faster and blocked his way.

"I was wrong," she said.

"I know you were."

He wasn't going to make any part of this easy on her, not that she expected him to, nor did she particularly want him to. He wouldn't believe her if she didn't fight for it.

"I was also scared."

He may have expected the first few things she said, but he had not planned on her to say that. His body tensed. "Scared of me?"

"No, of course not. Not you."

He seemed to realize he was stuck then. Since he'd questioned her on what she said, he could no longer plead disinterest. And she knew him well enough to know he would never be so impolite as to simply walk away. But that didn't mean he'd ask her another question.

Therefore, she took it upon herself to answer what he wouldn't ask. "I'm scared of what I feel for you. I'm scared because it's the most real and most intense thing I've ever felt and I'm afraid that if you knew exactly how much I felt, it'd scare you off and you'd want nothing to do with me. But the minute you walked out tonight, I knew I'd rather scare you with the truth than run you off with a lie."

He still didn't say anything. And nothing about him, not his stance, or body language, or expression gave any insight into what he was feeling or thinking. Even less could she even guess if he'd be open to what she planned next.

Telling herself this was it and he would either welcome her or reject her, but either way, she owed them both the opportunity for him to do one of them, she lifted her head. "What I'd like to do is have a do-over." Still, silence from him. Calling upon every bit of strength she could find in her body, she looked him in the eyes, and repeated part of the conversation where everything had gone wrong earlier. "Surely by now, you know I want you, too."

He only stood there and looked at her. The seconds went by, feeling like hours, and he only stood there. She told herself she was not going to cry. She'd known it was a risk when she decided to wait for him. She'd been brave enough to roll the dice, now she had to prove she was brave enough to loose.

She dropped her head and took a step back, dejected, but telling herself she couldn't cry until she was alone.

"Yes."

He spoke it so low, she thought it was only in her head when she took another step back and he said it again.

"Yes, I know you want me, too."

She allowed herself to look up and gone was his blank expression and in its place was longing and desire and need. For her.

"And God knows I want you, Alyssa." It was all he had time to say because as soon as he'd started talking, they both started walking toward the other, and when he said her name, they were already in each other's arms.

She lifted her head at the same time he lowered his and at the touch of his lips on hers, she knew she'd redo all the uncertainty of the last few minutes time and time again to experience the heaven that she found in his arms and in his kiss.

He pulled back only long enough to ask, "Bed?" And for her to reply, "God, yes," and then he took her face in his hands and kissed her again.

They somehow made their way to his room in what had to be the most clumsy, disjointed walk ever. Both of them trying to undress and yet, unwilling to separate from the other to do so completely. They finally made it, though, and when they did, they had managed to get most of their clothing off.

Or rather, she had managed to get hers off, since she only had a robe on. Kipling still had his T-shirt and boxer briefs. She reached for them, but he shook his head.

"Why not?" she asked.

"Because this," he said, placing his hands on her shoulders and walking her backward until her legs bumped the bed. "Since you're already naked, and I'm going to kiss you all over."

"I don't think I agreed to those rules," she said, just to see what he'd do.

"Give me five minutes and you'll agree to just about anything I suggest."

"Four," she countered with a playful grin, because really, he could take as long as he pleased to do anything he wanted and she wouldn't care.

"Alyssa, if I stop at four, the only thing that's going to happen is your begging for more."

She almost laughed and said that was why she went into law, because she sucked at negotiation, but before she managed to get the first word out, he'd lifted her onto the bed and placed her on her back. His mouth was on her neck and moving lower, and the only things she could manage to think were "Yes" and "Please don't stop."

Or at least those were the words in her head; she actually

spoke them and they sounded more like a moan. Kipling didn't seem to notice that she'd lost the ability to make coherent words. He was too busy exploring the skin of her breasts and learning how she tasted.

He'd made a joke once about being both a sex god and her every fantasy come to life. Under him, on his bed, with his lips and hands and mouth and tongue doing things that no other lover ever had and making her body experience sensation she hadn't known was possible, she agreed with him.

She eventually managed to work her body in such a way that he was under her. She ran her hands over his chest, loving the feel of him beneath her fingertips, but irritated that his shirt was still partially on.

"This is why I wanted you completely naked," she said, fumbling with his shirt and coming to the conclusion that she wasn't very coordinated when she was extremely aroused.

"Rip it off," he said through clenched teeth.

"What?"

"I want to see you rip it off me." Even in the darkness, the moon gave enough light for her to see his eyes blazing with desire. "Now, Alyssa. Show me how much you want me. Be wild for once. Be wild for me."

That was all he had to say and the only motivation she needed in order to act. She took the rejection she'd feared, the uncertainty she'd experienced, and meshed them together with the desire she could no longer deny, the need she felt, and the compulsion to do as he requested because she was wild for him and she wanted the world to know.

She took the shirt in her hands, took a deep breath, and with a yell and a pull, the shirt came off. She held it airborne just long enough for him to see before she dropped it off the side of the bed.

"Damn, Alyssa," he said. "I think that was the hottest thing I've ever seen in my life."

"You haven't seen anything yet," she promised, not waiting for him to reply, but taking his boxer briefs and pulling them down in one smooth motion. Before he could speak, she engulfed his length in her mouth.

Though she didn't doubt her ability to give a decent blowjob, she was pleased Kipling seemed to be enjoying it, as evidenced by the way his hands fisted the sheets at his side. She would have preferred his hands to be in her hair, but she told herself you couldn't have everything.

But Kipling was much more astute than she gave him credit for. He must have sensed her hesitation or picked up on some other movement she didn't recall making, because he lifted his head.

"Alyssa, are you okay?" he asked.

After what had transpired between them earlier, she wasn't about to lie to him now. "I like having my hair pulled and I saw you holding the sheets. I thought, if you wanted to . . ."

"I do, but I didn't want to presume you would."

He didn't have to say anything more, she went back to what she'd been doing moments before and it wasn't too long until his hands found their way to exactly where she wanted them. She hummed in pleasure around him as he tightened his fists and pulled.

"Yeah," he said, and his own voice was laced with pleasure. "I knew you'd like it dirty. Such a dirty girl for me, aren't you?"

She didn't know how he expected her to answer with him in her mouth. But he kept on whispering and most of it was so low, she couldn't make it out, so she decided not to worry about it.

It didn't take long until his breathing became choppy

and the muscles in his stomach began to tighten. His hands became more urgent as he tried to pull her away.

"Alyssa, please. Not like this. I want to be inside you."

It was his "please," combined with the hair pulling, that made her stop. "I'd have been perfectly happy to continue, you know," she told him, "for future reference."

"Future reference?" he questioned, flipping her over and coming up on her body so he was level with her eyes. "I'll keep that in mind. Right now, I have more pressing matters to attend to."

"You do?" she asked. "What would those be?"

"Well," he said, clearly getting into his playful nature, which she loved. "I'm going to start here"—he nibbled on her neck—"and work my way here"—he brushed her torso—"before ending somewhere along here." He stroked her thigh.

As soon as he touched her thigh, she froze.

"What?" he asked, obviously picking up on her change in demeanor.

"Please, please, please tell me you have a condom."

He propped himself up on his elbow so he looked down on her, while drawing figure eights along her belly. "Alyssa, I've wanted you for months. Do you think there is even the slightest chance of me not being prepared?"

She wanted to tell him that he didn't actually answer the question, but before she could get the words out, he spoke first.

"I not only have a condom, I have an entire box."

She ran her hand across his chest. "You must have been a boy scout when you were younger. Since you're so well prepared."

"Hell, no," he said with a look of mock outrage. "I got kicked out my first year."

She loved how he joked along with her, but then he brought his lips down on hers and within seconds she wasn't able to focus on anything other than him and his touch and what it made her feel. He wasn't a gentle lover, and for that she was grateful. She appreciated a man who wasn't afraid to touch her. One who didn't act as though she was made of glass.

She didn't have to worry about that with Kipling. His hands were knowledgeable and he somehow knew just how and where to touch her to drive her wild. Most of the men she'd been with before rushed through foreplay, but not Kipling. He took his time. In his arms, she felt like a newly discovered masterpiece. Not only because he was so thorough, but because he seemed so full of joy, for lack of a better word, to be the one doing the exploring.

After, when every other man she'd been with would roll over and sleep, once he disposed of the condom, he took her in his arms, pulled her to his chest, and told her how beautiful she was while drawing who-knows-what across her back.

He made her feel incredible and while she'd always enjoyed sex, it seemed *more* with Kipling. By the time their eyelids started to grow tired, she knew she was in major trouble. Kipling had effectively stolen a bit of her heart and she knew it'd always stay with him.

CHAPTER 10

The next morning, Alyssa expected there to be tension between her and Kipling and she was surprised when he casually kissed her good morning. They were still in bed and enjoying being lazy for a few minutes.

He stroked her back. "Do you still think today's a good day to visit your parents?"

She snorted. "No day is a good day to see those two, but yes. Might as well do it today."

"Anything in particular I should know?" he asked.

She wondered how different things would be if she was meeting his parents for the first time and felt an unexpected jolt of sadness that she would never have the chance. She stretched against him. "To be honest, I haven't seen them in years and the last time I did, things were tense." She felt a little bad admitting that to him. After all, at least her parents, or her mom anyway, was still alive. "How about I make us some coffee?"

"Only if you want," he said, but she was halfway out of bed.

"I don't think we should tell them all the details. That it's Jade and your connection. I say we leave it very high level."

He nodded. "That's completely your call. I'll go along with whatever you think best. What time is best to go?"

"I think sometime late this morning." She slipped a shirt on and didn't miss the pinkish red blooms on her torso, left there as a result of Kipling's lavish kisses and explorations the night before. Every time she looked at them, she knew she'd remember some new part of the night before and it'd warm her heart.

Kipling's eyes grew wide as he took in the marks on her body. "Alyssa," he said, his voice heavy with emotion. "I'm so sorry. I didn't mean to be that rough."

She held up her hand. "Don't you dare apologize about anything that happened last night. If I didn't like you rough, I would have told you about it last night. Understand?"

"Yes, ma'am," he said, and actually smiled.

"Now, I was thinking we head to my parents' house around eleven and we don't call beforehand. I believe the element of surprise will work in our favor." At his questioning glance, she added. "I'm not saying they'll lie, but something doesn't feel right about them whenever they talk about my sister."

"Again. It's completely your call. You know them best."

She actually didn't feel like she knew them at all.

"The only question I have now is, we don't need to leave until ten and it's just after eight now." His eyes danced with the mischief she'd noted the night before. "Whatever are we going to do until then?"

She'd just put her shirt on and though it felt foolish, she walked over to stand in front of him. "Well, I have an idea or two." While she spoke, she drew her shirt over her head.

"Mmm," he said, slipping his hands under her bra strap and arousing the same feeling he had the night before. Except this time, the feelings were even more intense because she knew exactly what was in store for her when they walked back into his bedroom.

Alyssa was uncharacteristically quiet on the way to her parents' house. At first, he thought it was because she was apprehensive about meeting with them. From what he'd inferred, they didn't have a close relationship. But as he continued glancing at her every so often, he realized she was reading the same handwritten note over and over.

"Interesting read?" he finally asked her.

"I think it's a clue."

"How's that?"

"It's a note your sister left Bea that time she set off the alarm at Benedict House. Listen to this:

I'm sorry I had to take off without saying good-bye. Maybe one day, I'll be able to explain. I really hope I can. If not, thank you for being so kind to me. If I ever had a sister, I'd want her to be like you.

"Now, at face value, it could be exactly that—a lonely orphaned girl wishing she had a sister. But, if we go with the assumption that Jade knows she's actually a Benedict, then she also knows that Bea is her sister."

Kipling nodded. "Interesting."

"Next, she talks about Tom and how Bea should be careful around him, which, looking back, I think we can all say was an understatement. But listen to this last part:

My name is Kaja Jade, but Mann isn't my last name. I'm sorry I can't give it to you yet, but if I have any hope of surviving, I have to go where no one knows me from Adam.

As you have probably guessed, my guardian is

no gentleman. My mother died before I was five and he took me in. I don't remember much about my mother, but I remember she loved me and she could sing like an angel."

He had to admit, she had a point. "Taken as a whole, it does sound a bit strange."

"Right," she said. "'My guardian is no gentleman?' What does that even mean? And why word it that way?"

"I don't know, but I'm getting ready to move heaven and earth to find out."

He was still thinking about the strange note when they pulled up to her childhood home a few minutes before eleven. They sat for several seconds, neither one of them saying anything.

"The lights are on," he finally said.

She just nodded. He tried to imagine what it was like in that house, when she was growing up. How it felt knowing that her sister had been murdered, and that she wasn't supposed to breathe her name again. How hard that must have been for someone who loved her sister.

Knowing that, what did it say about her mother, that she let her husband dictate what she did with her child? That she allowed him to determine if she even spoke about her? There were no words of encouragement he could think of to make Alyssa feel better. All he could do was place his hand on her knee and given it a gentle squeeze. *I'm here if you need me.*

Alyssa looked up at him and he knew that was what she needed. "Thank you," she whispered softly.

Not only were the lights on in the house, but there was a car parked in the driveway. He wasn't sure how many cars they had, but at least the evidence pointed toward somebody being at home. They walked to the front door, he remained a step behind her. This was her family and she had to be the one to make the first move.

He saw the curtains move in the front room seconds before they heard footsteps approaching the door. Before too long, an older version of Alyssa was at the door and was looking at them.

"Good heavens," was all she said; her face a deadly chalky white. As if she'd just seen a ghost.

"Who is that, Mildred?" could be heard from a second room.

It didn't appear that Mildred was going to answer him. She stood there in shock, looking at both her daughter and him.

"Mildred?" came the voice again.

When she didn't answer that time, they heard more footsteps approaching. From his spot at the doorway, Kipling saw a large giant of a man appear. He looked huge. With muscles that would make one believe he could snap man in half like a twig. The other man looked at him, looked at Alyssa and then back to him. His lips curled into a snarl. But Kipling was used to working with his share of giants, both in and out of the boardroom. And he wasn't about to let this man intimidate him. He looked at Alyssa and was glad to see she wasn't going to back down either. She took a step forward, but the man held out his hand to stop her.

"Oh no, not again," he said. "Hell no. Get out of my house. Got off my street. Don't ever come back."

Beside him, Alyssa's mother wailed, "No!"

"Mildred," he said. "Can't you see the same thing is happening again? It is the same thing. I won't have it, they can leave now."

Finally, Alyssa spoke up. "What do you mean the same thing?"

"Go away," he said, and slammed the door in front of them.

"Asshole," Alyssa mumbled under her breath.

Kipling took a deep breath and took a step back from the closed door. "Well," he said. "That was certainly interesting. When was last time you saw them?"

Alyssa rubbed her head. "It's been years."

Kipling bit back the remarks he wanted to say badly. He would bite his tongue for now because this was Alyssa's family.

She banged on the door. "It doesn't work that way. We're not going anywhere."

There was only silence on the other side of the door.

She lowered her voice, "If I knew the neighbors wouldn't call the police, I'd shoot the damn door off its hinges."

"As much as I'd like to see that," Kipling admitted. "I agree. Not the best course of action here."

"Mom." Alyssa knocked on the door. "Mom, please. You know I wouldn't be here if it wasn't important. I'm close to solving this case. Help me."

They looked at each other at the sound of raised voices from inside the house. The sound escalated until it suddenly stopped. The door creaked opened, just a little, but wide enough for them to see the red eyes and wet cheeks of Alyssa's mother.

"Mom." She pushed the door open further and wrapped her arms around her mom when the older woman started crying. Kipling heard the low mummers of mother and daughter talking as they walked further into the house and took a step forward to join them.

He was stopped by Alyssa's stepdad. "You're not welcome in my house."

Kipling glanced at the man before him to make sure he was serious and for all appearances, from his crossed arms to the near constant frown, showed he was.

Kipling took a step backward. "Listen to me," he said. "Someone has threatened Alyssa's life and I take that sort of thing very seriously. I don't care what you have against her. I don't care what you have against me. Neither of those matter as long as that threat exists. And for as long as it does, I'm going to be right by her side to make sure she's okay. I don't care if you like it or if you agree with it. This has nothing to do with you. It has nothing to do with your murdered stepdaughter. It has everything to do with keeping Alyssa safe. Do you understand?'"

Everything was strangely silent when he finished speaking his mind to Mr. Adams. He no longer heard Alyssa and her mother talking, either. Without saying a word, her stepfather moved to the side, allowing him to pass. He walked into the hallway, where he saw Alyssa and her mother.

"Mrs. Adams," he said, holding his hand out to her. "Kipling Benedict. Nice to meet you." The poor woman didn't seem to know whether to talk to him or not. She looked from him to her husband to her daughter and back again to Kipling.

She shook his hand, but didn't reciprocate his sentiment. She sighed. "What can we do for you? I'm assuming you didn't come by just to see how we were doing."

Alyssa hadn't been lying when she said there was still tension between her and her parents. Not only that, but her mother looked cold and distant. Her expression was flat when she spoke, "I suggest we all go sit down."

Kipling turned around to head in the direction Mrs. Adams indicated and almost ran into the Neanderthal, holding a newspaper.

"There." He shoved the paper at Alyssa. "Look at that, look at you, and tell me what you think."

At first, Kipling thought he was looking at a picture of himself, but as he kept looking, it became obvious that it was his father. Even with that revelation, however, he couldn't take his eyes off his father. Kipling couldn't remember him being that happy or smiling so brightly. And the woman at his side was not his wife of almost twenty years. But rather, it was a woman who looked all too much like Alyssa.

She must have noticed the same thing, at the same time, because she gasped.

"Striking resemblance, yes?" her father asked, but didn't wait for an answer. "I thought so, too. So if you think you're going to sit here in my house, like your sister and your sorry excuse for a father, you can think again."

"It's not like that," Alyssa said quietly. Kipling wanted to touch her, to simply place his hand on the lower part of her back, to give her some sort of strength, some sort of secret sign to let her know that he was with her. But his actions would not go unnoticed by her stepfather, and he didn't think it would make anything better.

In the end, Alyssa finally pushed past her stepfather to continue on her way into the other room. They all followed her, first Kipling, then her mother, with her stepfather trailing behind them. Kipling just had a chance to take the briefest glance around the room. For all intents and purposes, it was a typical middle-class house in the typical middle-class neighborhood. They all sat down on the living room's couch and love seat.

"What was that I overheard you say about Alyssa being threatened?" Alyssa's mother asked.

"There's been some recent activity in the case. New evidence has been brought to light," Alyssa said. "And whoever killed my sister . . ." She looked at her stepfather briefly, letting him know she wouldn't say her name. "We believe he's still alive and might be after me."

"How is he involved?" her stepfather asked, with a nod toward Kipling.

Kipling raised his eyebrow at Alyssa. *Do we tell him?* She shook her head no.

Kipling cleared his throat. "I have a family member we fear has been kidnapped. Based on some of the similarities, we think she may have been taken by the same man in your case. We need to find her and put whoever is behind this away for good. We don't want her to meet the same end that your stepdaughter did."

Certainly her stepfather should understand that. Of course he wouldn't want anybody to meet the same fate as his stepdaughter. But as it turned out, her stepfather wasn't like normal people.

"She deserved what she got," he said. "Being a whore for your daddy."

Kipling closed his eyes. If he stood any chance of swallowing the rage building inside him and not unleashing it on Mr. Adams, he needed not to look at the man for a few seconds. A few deep breaths and he felt calm enough to continue.

He leaned forward. "Sir," he said, far more evenly than he felt. "Your stepdaughter was killed in a vicious and violent attack. Nobody, I repeat nobody, no matter what they have done, deserves to have their life end that way."

Mr. Adams didn't say anything, he just nodded and sunk back into his chair with his arms crossed. But the look he gave Kipling was of pure hatred.

Mrs. Adams, on the other hand, looked visibly distressed. She looked at both of them, seeming to ignore her husband on purpose. "What can we do for you? Do you need to see something?"

"What we'd really like is to see her room," Alyssa told her mother. "Along with the items the police gave you."

"Of course," her mother said. "Everything's still in there." She took a side glance at her husband. He didn't look any happier. "I believe your stepfather and I will go out for lunch. We'll leave the key here in case you finish and need to leave before we get back. Just lock up and put the key under the mat." The understanding and unsaid meaning, of course, was that they would leave before they got back.

"How long do you think you'll be gone?" Kipling asked.

"Probably about three hours," she said. "We have some shopping to do as well."

Mr. Adams looked less than thrilled to be shopping or going out, much less leaving his house empty except for Alyssa and a Benedict. But he got up and followed his wife out the door.

Kipling didn't think it was his imagination that he could hear him yelling as they left in the car.

Alyssa watched her parents drive away with a mixture of anger, shock, and embarrassment. She couldn't believe the way they treated Kipling. "I'm so sorry," she said. "I had no idea they were going to be like that."

Kipling shook his head. "There's no need to apologize for them not liking me. There are plenty of people who can't stand me. At least your parents have a reason."

"But you didn't do anything to them," she said.

"It's not me personally," he said. "It's my dad."

"It's not right. You shouldn't be judged on what your parents did," she said.

"Unfortunately, a lot of us are. And in this case, one can see why your parents aren't happy to see me."

His words sounded sincere, but she wondered if he was being truthful or if her parents' actions upset him more than he was letting on.

"Which room is hers?" he asked. They had made it to the hallway.

Preparing herself for what lay ahead, she straightened her shoulders and led him into her sister's room. She stopped in the doorway, taking deep breaths. She always felt her sister's presence so heavily in this room.

"It's okay." He stepped behind her, placing his hands on her shoulders. "I'm right here with you."

His touch did more than all the deep breathing she'd done on her own, and she stepped further into the room. As expected, her mother had not changed anything since her sister's death. Everything was exactly the way it had been the day she walked out, other than having been dusted every so often. She bet her stepfather hated that.

It had been years since she'd been in this room. The last time, when she stood in this exact spot, she still felt her sister. She no longer could and not only that, but her memory seemed to be fading as well. She couldn't decide if that was good or bad. But she told herself not to think about it because no matter what the answer ended up being, either way, she'd cry.

What she needed to do was to remove her personal bias. To be the policewoman she'd claimed to be when Kipling first asked her if she was too personally involved.

He stood off to the side, watching her, but not with doubts in his eyes.

"I can do this," she told him.

"I know you can."

She held out her hand. "Let me see the crime-scene photo."

He took the picture out of the folder he carried and handed it to her. Though she had verified the night before that the purse wasn't in the photo, she wanted to check one more time to make sure she wasn't overlooking anything.

Not seeing anything in the photo, she looked at Kipling. "Ready to look in the box?'

He nodded solemnly. "Need me to get it? Is it in here?"

"Top shelf of the closet."

She watched him as he went to retrieve the box and

wondered how he would react if it were his brothers who had been kidnapped or killed.

But one of his own, had been kidnapped, and most likely by the same man who killed her sister.

"We're going to get him," she said when he returned with the box. "I'm sorry. I make such stupid promises sometimes."

"In that case, put me down as stupid right along with you, because I believe we're going to get him, too."

Kipling looked around, obviously trying to find a place to put the box. The only piece of furniture with any space free was the bed. He didn't seem to mind, walking instead to the middle of the room and having a seat on the rug. Alyssa joined him.

"Do you want open it?" he asked.

"No, you go ahead," she said. Truth be told, always before, she had been the one to open the box. She wanted to see if she noticed anything different with someone else opening the box.

Kipling took the top off and looked at her. "I know it's okay to touch the stuff inside, but I still feel like I shouldn't be doing it."

She nodded, knowing exactly how he felt and watched as he one by one took the items out of the box. There wasn't much and by far the largest item was the purse. She reached for it, but he said, "Wait."

"What?"

"Where is the Finition Noire envelope?" He shuffled through the remaining items in the box. "I don't see it here."

"I took it with me the last time." She shrugged. "Call me crazy, but I could see it getting lost or stolen."

"Makes sense."

"I mean, it's all already been looked over. It's not like I was stealing evidence or anything."

"Alyssa," he said. "You don't have to explain yourself to me. You're the expert here. I'm not going to question you." He held the purse up. "I'll let you do the honors."

"Humor me," she said. "Look it over and see if you can find the hidden compartment."

He gave her a look that told her he didn't think he'd have any trouble at all finding it. It was a basic clutch with a small strap and while most of the girls in her troop opted to put the hidden pocket along the inner lining, she thought it was hidden better by putting it in the folder flap. While she knew that the killer had more than likely found the compartment, she wanted to see if she could fool Kipling at least. Or maybe she was delaying the inevitable.

She watched him as he looked over and through the purse. It was so hard to believe he was the same man who drove her up a wall after they first met. How wrong she'd been about him then. At the time, she thought he was a spoiled playboy who only cared about money and women. Now she knew she couldn't have been more wrong.

He was fiercely protective of his family, she'd seen that up close. Before she'd arrested him, she'd looked into his business dealings and discovered a man who was tough, but fair. Even those who had been opposite him at the negotiation table spoke highly of him.

The papers loved to paint him as an egotistical philanderer, but she knew that more times than not, he'd rather spend his evenings at home. Besides, in the entire time she'd known him, she'd never seen or heard of him even taking a woman out to dinner, much less participating in anything anywhere near debauchery.

Kipling looked up from the purse. "Okay, I admit it. You've stumped me. Where is it?"

She was surprised he hadn't located it and for the first time held out real hope that maybe whatever Allison had put in there, if anything, was still there.

She took the purse and shifted it in her hands, then flipped it over and exposed the hidden seam.

Kipling smiled. "I'm impressed."

"Thank you, but what will truly be impressive is if we find anything inside."

"Open it."

She didn't have to be told twice. Within seconds she had the compartment open. She took a deep breath and glanced at Kipling. He gave her a big smile of encouragement. Reaching into the space she'd made that was a little larger than a business-sized envelope, she honestly didn't expect to feel anything and she froze when her fingers brushed paper.

"Alyssa?" Kipling asked.

"I feel something."

He looked as shocked as she felt. "What is it? Take it out."

Silently, she grabbed the papers and pulled them out. Someone, her sister she suspected, had them bound together with a rubber band.

"Oh my goodness," she said. "It's more than a sheet two."

Excitement bubbled up in her stomach, but as she unfolded the documents, she felt something else. It was hope and she hadn't experienced hope in a long time. And it felt good.

Looking through the stack of papers, the first thing that caught her eye was a handwritten note. She hadn't seen her sister's handwriting in a long time, and seeing it for the first time after so many years brought tears to her eyes.

"The note first?" she asked Kipling.

"I think so," he said. "Are you okay?"

Obviously, he knew what a toll it took on her to see her sister's handwriting. "Yes," she said. "I'm more okay than

I have been in a long time. I feel like we're getting some-where."

"I agree."

She picked up the note, and read out loud the first part:

This is my letter to the world;
That never wrote to me.

She looked up, unable to keep her eyes from filing with tears again. "She loved Emily Dickinson."

I know that sounds horribly melodramatic, but it's the truth as far as I see it, especially since I've been an unwed teenaged mother. However, this could be one of the last things I do, so I think I'm entitled to act a bit melodramatic.

I don't know who's reading this. But I kind of hope it's Alyssa. Whoever you are, I'm probably now dead. I have only one thing to ask. Please, if it is at all possible, please don't let him get Jade. She is all that is good and right with the world and he will de-stroy her. Please, please, please keep her away from him.

I've always heard to start at the beginning and while that's good advice, I'm not really sure where the beginning is. I'll start at when I came back. Why did I? For one, I thought Franklin might be inter-ested in seeing his daughter. Apparently, he was not. He wouldn't even see me, much less Jade. I don't know why I was surprised. I told him when I called that I knew I should have gone by his house first. He got very angry and said he didn't want to see me or his daughter again.

And then, because I'm a glutton for punishment, I went home. They wouldn't let me see Alyssa and then I was told neither I nor my child was welcome in their home.

That's how I ended up here, at the homeless shelter. It wasn't my first choice, but I have a four-year-old and she needs to eat and have a bed to sleep in. So there I am feeling all sorry for myself and then he showed up. I called him my Miracle Man. I was too blind to see then, but he only had eyes for Jade.

At first, though, he was everything I wanted. He said his name was Howard and he was friends with Franklin. He leaned close, like he was going to tell me a secret and whispered that he knew that his friend always wanted a daughter. Then came the best part, he would let me stay at his house while we planned how to approach Franklin.

I knew something was off as soon as we moved in. It wasn't a typical house. I mean, it was a house, right in the historic district and everything. I guess what I mean is, it's not like a home. And there were all these strange men walking in and out at all hours. I asked him about it once and he just said they were business associates. I think he knew I didn't believe him.

But there were long stretches when he was gone, so one day when he was out and there wasn't anyone else walking around, I decided to snoop. And that's when I found out the truth. He goes by The Gentleman. And he is mean and awful, evil and vicious. I should have known something wasn't right when he kept brushing me off whenever I brought up Franklin, but it wasn't until he told me to shut the fuck up about Franklin that I knew he would never approach him and I got scared and started to snoop.

Now I wish I hadn't. I feel sick just thinking about the things he's done and what he's planning to do. I took what I dared, to have some proof if I ever got out of here, but that's looking less and less likely. I think his office has cameras and if that's the case, he knows I know. So I'm doing this for Jade now.

These papers are the confirmation that he plans on having Franklin killed. He's going to make it look like an airplane accident. He's still working out the how and when details, but trust me, the enclosed docs have what you need if you look hard enough. One is an email from Howard confirming Franklin's travel plans. Another is Howard sending that confirmation to an unknown third party telling him the plan to take out Franklin was to move forward.

The other thing you should know about him is that he is running several businesses. But not the kind you're thinking of. His are storefronts for people to shop for women. I don't think I need to expand on that.

I started this out by saying this was my letter to the world. I was wrong. My letter to the world is Jade.

"That's all," Alyssa whispered. She blinked the tears out of her eyes and tried not to think about how she'd failed both her sister and her niece. She wasn't sure what she had expected to find when she looked his way, but it most certainly was not the look of absolute horror she found. "Kipling?"

"Howard." He spoke the name through clenched teeth.

"What?" she asked, too caught up in memories of her sister to make sense of what he said.

"Howard Germain. He has to be the person who was appointed as Jade's guardian." He ran his fingers through his hair. "I can't believe I didn't see it until now. Especially after we discussed how odd it was Elise knew we had a sister."

One by one, several pieces of the puzzle that made up the case fell into place and yet, with each seemingly answered question, two more popped up in its place. And how much more must Kipling feel that same thing? Howard Germain was a longtime friend of the family.

God, what a mess.

"Why didn't your parents get custody of Jade?" Kipling asked. "They should have, right? Why didn't they?"

Alyssa shook her head. "I don't know. They never even mentioned a granddaughter." Her stomach twisted at the thought that her mom had rejected he own flesh and blood. She jumped up.

"What?" Kipling asked.

"There has to be paperwork somewhere, right? I'm going to rip this place apart until I find it."

He didn't say anything, but simply followed her. There were three possible places she thought the paperwork might be: their safe deposit box, her mother's bedside table, or the safe they kept their important papers in. She opted to try the safe first since it was closer and she didn't want to go into her mother's bedroom if she didn't have to.

She found them in the very bottom of the safe, buried under a handful of two dollar bills.

"Oh my, God." She passed the court documents to Kipling. "Part of me hoped they had nothing to do with it, but they did. They gave her to him."

"Bastard didn't even give her his name." Kipling read through the pages quickly. "Kaja Jade German. What an ass."

"No wonder she feels like she doesn't belong anywhere." Overwhelming sadness that she'd somehow failed both her sister and her niece washed over her. Next to her, Kipling reached for his phone, but his expression told her he felt the same.

"I'm going to fix this," he vowed. "No matter what."

She only hoped it wasn't too late.

"Knox," Kipling said into the phone. "Howard Germain."

He didn't need to explain, she heard the middle Benedict brother's curses through the phone. Kipling glanced over at Alyssa. "We're at Alyssa's parents' house. We just found some information that her sister had left hidden in a purse. It indicated he was the guardian and a lot more." He shuffled through the pages. "We believe she also has the evidence that we need to prove he was behind the airplane accident as well as some trafficking operations allegations, but nothing that would hold up in court. Of course, we won't know anything until we can get somewhere to look at it properly."

From the other end of the phone came a low whistle. "I can't believe he's into all that," said Knox.

"We can't, either. It's like the man we thought we knew never existed."

"There's something else," Knox said.

"More than what we've already learned?" Kipling asked. "I don't know if I can process much more. Hold on, let me put you on speaker."

"This is important. You two have been staying at the beach place?"

"Yes."

"I was getting ready to call you. Germain knows about it and he has bought all the surrounding property."

Alyssa was positive that her expression mirrored Kipling's. He had been so certain no one knew the place existed.

"How long has he owned them?" Kipling asked.

"It's hard to tell with any certainty." Knox was typing from the sound of it. "From the online records they appear to switch hands a few times but I can't determine if these are real businesses or are just more fabrications like Finition Noire. If we assume that they are, he's owned the land for over ten years. If it's just since he's been listed, maybe a handful."

"Either way it's not good," Kipling said.

"I agree," Knox said. "I don't think you two should go back there."

"I agree, we won't. I don't know where we can go that's safe. I'm not coming to the house. If he comes after us, I don't want us all together. I'm fairly certain he's after Alyssa and myself now so I'd like to keep the focus off you guys. Benedict House is the best place for all of you. I don't think you should split, but don't go out if you don't have to. Make sure Keaton and Tilly are adequately protected and don't let Bea out of your sight."

"Never doubt it."

"I'll call in and keep you updated when I can."

The brothers hung up after saying good-bye. Alyssa couldn't help looking over at Kipling. "What are we going to do?" she asked.

But he only shook his head. "I wish I knew what to tell you."

Kipling had never felt more worthless. If it had only been him, it would be okay. Well, maybe not okay, but at least he could handle it better. He stood up and walked to the window. But it wasn't only him, he wanted to support Alyssa. Not to mention ensure his younger brothers and Tilly and Bea were all safe. Most of all, Jade.

On that front he felt like a complete failure.

He looked out over the expanse of the neighborhood, watched people walking around with their normal lives. Looking as if nothing out of the ordinary was happening.

And for them, it probably wasn't. He'd never wanted so much to switch places so badly before in his entire life.

Alyssa came up behind him and placed her hands on his shoulders. He leaned back toward her and she wrapped his arms around him.

"I would say it'll be okay," she said. "But I don't know that it will. However, I do know that we're in it together."

He took her hand. "That means a lot more than you think it does. Thank you."

"I don't think we should stay here," she said.

"You're right," he said. "I don't want to put your parents in any danger."

"I guess we can't go to Benedict House, either."

"Correct."

"How do you think he knew about the beach place?"

"I'm not sure." he said. "It's possible Mom told him about it. I know they were all at the same college. I'm not sure how close Mom was to Howard." He sighed deeply. "And I don't know where we should go, either. Anywhere we go, we'll put people in danger. The other option is to sleep in my car." He raised an eyebrow at her. "How are you at camping?"

"Horrible," she said. "If I hadn't left the force, we could have asked for a safe house. Not that think one would be safe. I'm not sure the police department isn't in on this with him."

"Yes, I agree with you on that. Let's look at this rationally. What are our objectives?"

"Get Jade back."

"Yes," he said. "In order to do that, we have to know where she's being kept. Unfortunately, whoever is keeping her—Germain, I assume—hasn't contacted me lately. Knox is trying to track him down, but isn't having any luck so far."

"The other thing we need to do," she said, "is to bring

him down as well, but I don't think we have information to do that yet, either."

"Right."

"So what do you think we should do?"

"If you think you're up to it, I propose we go to the homeless shelter. The one your sister was at. Make it out to be like a little unannounced visit of Benedict Industries. We'll do a little bit of snooping, and see what we find."

"Let's go."

CHAPTER 11

As far as parties went, Howard Germain rated this one a solid six out of ten. Based on the time, he didn't think this one had any chance of redemption. He was ready to call it a night. Kappa Sigma had one planned tomorrow night. Maybe it would be better. He headed to the door.

"Howard."

He turned to his best friend and roommate, Franklin Benedict. It was highly unlikely Frank wanted to walk back to their apartment together since he'd broken up with his latest side piece of fluff. No, if he knew Frank, and he felt as if he did after living with him for two years, he'd be looking for a new bed to enjoy for an hour or two. Odds were in his favor he'd find it.

"Benedict." Howard nodded in the direction of his friend. "What are you still doing vertical?"

Frank laughed as if it was the funniest joke he'd ever heard. "I found her, man."

"Found who?"

"The future Mrs. Benedict, of course."

Howard simply played along. He'd been introduced to future Mrs. Benedicts for as long as he could remember.

It was almost a certainty there was nothing special about this one. But, to please his friend, he looked up when Franklin said she was over near the speakers.

He didn't say anything for several seconds. He wasn't sure he breathed.

The woman standing near the speakers took his breath away. It was more than her looks, though she was certainly beautiful. It was her entire being. The way she stood, the way she smiled; hell, even the way she tilted her head to the left a bit as she talked to the women around her.

He could see why she caught Frank's eye. He preferred blondes and hers looked completely natural. Nothing like those out-of-the-bottle jobs so many of the women he went out with had.

"Come on," Frank said. "Let's go introduce ourselves. I see Lisa just walked up to her."

Lisa being one of the women he'd dated for six hours and then left.

"You sure you want to go up to her while Lisa's up there? Aren't you afraid she'll tell her something so she won't go out with you?"

"Lisa and I parted on good terms."

"I get the feeling your definition of 'good terms' doesn't mesh so well with mine."

Frank punched him in the arm, but Howard wasn't joking.

The crowd wasn't as heavy as it'd been just an hour ago. Apparently, he wasn't the only one who thought the current party lacked something vital. But the small crowd only meant it took them less time to make their way to where the girls were.

"Ladies," Frank said as he approached the small group.

As it turned out, Frank did walk home with Howard that night and he would sleep alone. But he had a dinner date for the next weekend with Helen (or the future Mrs. Benedict as he kept calling her) and that was all he talked about as they made their way home.

"What do you think?" he asked Howard at one point in the conversation.

Howard knew he really didn't care one way or the other about what his roommate thought of his newest love interest. Likewise, Howard didn't feel like discussing his thoughts about Helen with the guy he knew would be over her in a matter of weeks.

So instead of agreeing with Frank that yes, she was gorgeous and no, he'd never seen bluer eyes on anyone, he answered truthfully.

"I think I hate you."

"I think we have a problem," Alyssa said about five minutes after they left her parents' house, as they drove along the highway to the homeless shelter.

Kipling glanced over at her. Every so often she was looking at the rearview mirror. When she wasn't looking there, she was looking at the passenger-side mirror. "What do you see?"

"I think we're being followed."

His heart started to pound, and he gripped the steering wheel tighter. His gaze flickered to the rearview mirror. He didn't see anything, but that didn't mean it wasn't there.

"Black SUV," she said. "He's a couple of cars behind us at the moment, but I'm sure he's there."

She was very calm, and even though he reminded himself that she did this for a living, he didn't see how it was possible for her to be so calm. "Have any suggestions as to what we should do?"

"Turn right up here at that light," she told him. "Then take the immediate left."

He followed her directions. "Still there?"

"Yes." She glanced over her shoulder. "But I didn't expect to lose them that quickly. Make a U-turn at that hotel up ahead and on your left. This is where we lose them."

He made a quick U-turn at the spot she indicated and couldn't help smiling as her plan started to become clear. As soon as they made the turn, the car was swarmed by tourists in such a way that they were the only car that made it through the light. Kipling forced himself not to look at the black SUV as they went past it.

"What now?" He asked when the crowd thinned and there was no longer anyone following them.

"Now we need to ditch your car."

"I was afraid you were going to say something like that. You know if we do that it also means we ditch our hotel room for the night."

"You didn't seriously see us sleeping in your car, did you?"

"No, but it was nice to have options."

"We need to leave it somewhere crowded," she said.

"I have an idea," he said. "What about the cruise terminal? I think there's some ships coming in today. It'll be very crowded and congested and there will be a good number of police officers around."

"Perfect."

"We should get on a bus," Kipling said without hesitation once they had parked his car in the large parking deck near the terminal. "We can blend in with the crowd better. And it's probably the last thing anyone would expect us to do."

Alyssa bit her bottom lip. "Sounds reasonable." She stepped out of the stairway and into a crowd of people. "Come on," she called to him. "Hurry up."

Kipling wasn't sure how well they fit in with the crowd, neither one of them looked like a tourist. But they made it to the bus station without anyone aiming a gun at them, so he chalked that up as a win.

"Do we need to figure out where we're going?" he asked Alyssa, who was purchasing two tickets.

"No, I'm getting us each a three-day pass. That way we can hop on the first bus we see and figure out where we're going once we're on. Right now, I just want out of this part of the city."

Kipling had to agree with her. He looked around. Nothing and no one looked suspicious or seemed to be paying them any mind. They waited with a large tourist group, hoping to blend in and hopped on the first bus that appeared. Kipling wove through the people standing, keeping a tight grip on Alyssa's hand. He half expected her to jerk her hand away and to tell him she was fine, but surprisingly enough, she didn't.

They found two empty seats and sat down. Alyssa immediately reached for her purse and Kipling glanced around. No one seemed to be paying them any attention and he relaxed a bit. They appeared to be free for the moment.

The bus came to a stop and they stayed seated while people loaded and unloaded. Kipling tried to look at everyone who got on. No one looked their way. He took that as a good sign.

A skinny young man, wearing baggy pants and completely bald, walked their way. Kipling glanced at him, but didn't pay him much attention. He had a massive headache and on top of that he hated the bus, or he had the few times he'd ridden one before today. He closed his eyes hoping to ease the pounding in his head.

"Mama," a young boy behind him said in a hushed voice. "That man with no hair has a gun."

Kipling's entire body tensed and his heart began to pound. Probably it was nothing, but he wasn't going to chalk anything up to coincidence. He raised his eyelids just a touch, just so he could see, but would still appear to be dozing to anyone who looked.

Bald Man sat across the aisle from Alyssa, head nodding as he supposedly listened to music through earbuds. If he'd heard the boy, nothing in his body language gave it away. Kipling was fairly certain Alyssa had heard as well, but she gave nothing away, either. He could feel her pressed against him and she hadn't tensed at all.

Trying to act casual, he rested his head on her shoulder and slipped a hand to her knee, and whispered, "Young man to your right has a gun. Not sure he's after us."

She kissed his cheek and murmured in his ear, "I heard. It'd be wise for us to get off at the next stop."

"Let's go," he said and they both stood and moved a bit closer to the doors. Alyssa stood to his side, but turned her body so she could keep the gunman in her line of sight.

The bus slowly pulled to a stop and when the doors opened, they sprinted outside. Neither one of them dared to look back, afraid it would be too obvious.

"If he was after us, I don't think he'd have had time to get back up here." Alyssa spoke under her breath as they jogged across the street to a shopping center. "Let's go to the second level."

"Which means he probably followed us out."

They'd made it to the top and Kipling took a second to look down. Sure enough, Bald Man was crossing the street, talking on his phone.

"Shit," Kipling said.

Alyssa knew she was going to crash as soon as the adrenaline dropped and she wasn't looking forward to it. If she was lucky, it wouldn't happen until they made it somewhere safe.

Kipling had amazed her with his clear head and quick thinking. He never seemed to panic.

"There's a taxi over there," Kipling said, pointing just a short distance away. Odds were good they could get to it before Bald Man saw them.

"Let's go," she said, and jogged toward the taxi with Kipling at her side.

She shivered.

"Where to?" the driver asked as they slipped into the backseat.

She looked over her shoulder as she shut the door. Thankfully, she didn't see anything.

"We should eat," Kipling said, slightly out of breath. "It's been a long time since breakfast."

"That's fine," she said. She wasn't hungry, but she knew he was right. "I'm fine with whatever you want."

While he gave the driver directions, she looked out the window. She spied their stalker reaching the top of the stairs right as they pulled away. Kipling had given the driver the name of a pizza joint on the other side of town and she closed her eyes and told herself to relax while she could.

But it wasn't until Kipling put his arm around her and pulled her so she rested against him, that she was able to.

Much too soon, the taxi pulled up to the pizzeria and she waited while Kipling paid the driver. He turned to her and smiled. "Let's eat. I'm famished."

Typical male, she thought. Being followed by a stranger with a gun did nothing to his appetite. She'd been hungry before, but now she was feeling more tired than anything and with the adrenaline coming down, the thought of food made her a touch queasy. But she needed to eat and knew she'd feel better after she did so.

"You go order," she told Kipling. "I'm going to grab a table outside by the window and be on the lookout."

"We're safe here," Kipling said. "At least for a while.

"Better to err on the side of caution."

She told him she didn't care what kind of pizza he got as long as he got her a big bottle of water to go along with it. She took a detour to the bathroom to freshen up and wash her hands before taking a seat at a table by the window.

Kipling was texting someone, but placed their order a few minutes later and headed her way with two bottles of water in hand.

"Knox called," he said, sliding into the seat across from her. "I just got a text. I told him we'd call tonight and that there were a few things we needed to talk to him about."

Alyssa nodded in between taking sips of water. "By talk about, you mean things he needs to hack into?"

"Yes," Kipling agreed. "I thought my way sounded a bit more legal."

She sighed. "I don't even care anymore."

"Hey." Kipling lifted a finger to raise her chin. "What's wrong?"

"Nothing," she said, but when he shook his head, she added, "I'm just tired is all. It's been sort of a crazy day. How can you be so calm?" It didn't mesh with her image of a shipping executive.

"Defense mechanism. I'm not thinking about it, therefore it doesn't exist."

She must have looked perplexed because he added, "It'll catch up to me later tonight and I'll crash."

She yawned. "I think it's already caught up with me."

Kipling stretched and leaned back in his seat, relaxing for the first time in hours. "Hopefully, we're in the clear now. We'll find somewhere safe and then we can both crash."

A waitress brought their pizza by and Alyssa didn't miss the way she smiled at Kipling. For his part, Kipling pretty much ignored her. His focus was on Alyssa. The heat in his stare warmed every part of her.

He must have noticed her staring because after the waitress walked away, he winked at Alyssa. "Eat up," he said, and reached for a slice.

She was on her second piece and Kipling was on his fourth when she felt a familiar tickle on the back of her neck. She'd been working as a cop long enough to know it couldn't be ignored. Someone was watching them. Her stomach turned and she put down the pizza slice she'd been eating. Her expression must have changed because Kipling's expression grew worried.

"What?" he asked.

"I'm not sure." She glanced around the immediate area. "Just a feeling."

"Shit."

"It may be nothing." She hoped it was nothing.

"Unfortunately, it's not," he said, dread filling his voice. "Our bald friend is back. Behind you."

The hair on the back of her neck stood up as she imagined the man staring at her. "How close?" She slipped her hand to her purse, ready to pull out her weapon.

"Not very."

She allowed herself a deep breath. "Should we get up and escape through the cafe's back door?"

"Does the cafe have a back door?"

"I don't know. Surely it leads to an alley or something."

"Is that a chance we should take?"

"It'll be easier to give him the slip if we go through the back door instead of doing it in front of him." If there wasn't a back door, she could potentially be putting innocent people in danger. But if they stayed here, people outside the cafe would still be in danger.

"Let's go." Kipling stood up, not moving toward the cafe until she got in front of him.

As she walked toward the entrance to the cafe, she

pulled out an old badge, and flashed it to the employees working inside. "Police. Is there a back entrance?"

The teenaged boy working the register looked like he was going to faint and the waitress standing next to him dropped her tray of drinks. Fortunately, she recovered quickly enough to nod and point toward the back.

Alyssa led the way, darting through the kitchen and out the back door. No sooner had the door closed behind them than they heard a commotion coming from the cafe.

Kipling cursed under his breath as he looked around the ally. "Damn it. It's a dead end."

Something inside the cafe crashed and Alyssa jumped. "There's a pet store next door. Come on."

She ran the few steps to the back door of the pet store and prayed it wouldn't be locked. The sweetest sound in the world was a bell ringing as she opened the door. She flashed the old badge again and, with Kipling behind her, ran out the main entrance and onto the street.

"This way," she said, dodging tourists and headed toward a church. Kipling stayed at her side and together they ducked under a barrier and into the lower level of the church. For several minutes they stayed near the doorway as they caught their breath and watched for anyone following them.

"How do they keep finding us?" Kipling asked right as his phone buzzed with an incoming text.

"Don't answer that." She held out her hand. "Give me the phone and your tablet."

His face paled in understanding. "They've been tracking us with our phones."

She nodded. "And probably your tablet. We're going to leave them here and then go hide in that school across the street and keep watch. Then we'll go to the shelter."

"How will I keep in touch with my family? What if Howard gets my number and calls about Jade?"

"We'll pick up burner phones so you can call home and if Howard wants to speak with you badly enough, he'll find a way."

"You don't think he'll take his frustration out on Jade?"

She wished she had the ability to give him the assurance he wanted, but she couldn't. "All I can say to that is that he's been her guardian for a long time. I wouldn't think he'd do anything too drastic at this point." She tried to sound confident, but she knew there was fear in her voice.

He gave her his phone and tablet. "I hope you're right."

"That makes two of us."

CHAPTER 12

"Your mother told me things are getting pretty serious be-tween that Benedict boy and that girl he's been dating. You're going to be a senior next year and it'll be time for you to think about settling down and getting married. Any chance we'll be hearing anything along those lines from you?"

Howard knew better than to curse at his father, so he bit back the string of words he wanted to say and instead replied with, "I'll make sure you're one of the first to know."

His dad thought that was funny for some reason and chuckled. Fortunately, after that, he patted him on the back and left him alone.

Damn it all. Like it wasn't enough that Frank and Helen were the talk of the entire fucking campus, but now he had to hear about it from his own parents over his Thanksgiving break? He knew his father and now that Franklin had an acceptable woman to marry, Howard would never hear the end about it being his time.

Unfortunately, he couldn't tell his father the truth. Couldn't tell him that he had found the girl he wanted to marry. That she was beautiful, smart, and perfect. Couldn't tell him because she was well on her way to marrying his best friend.

It didn't make sense to anyone, least of all Howard. Frank never dated anyone longer than two weeks. By his calculations, Frank should have broken up with Helen *months* ago. By now, if he'd followed his normal plan, Howard would have been able to swoop in and been the white knight that gave Helen both a friendly face for support and, when she was ready, the man who would love her the way she deserved.

But now, she only saw him as Frank's roommate. Someone to take her message that she called when he wasn't there. Like a damn secretary. And, now that he thought about it, Frank was out quite a bit lately and, since she was calling him, he obviously wasn't with her.

Was it possible Frank was cheating on her?

Was it wrong Howard hoped he was?

The doorbell downstairs rang. Probably more cousins. Since he had no desire to see his cousins before he had to spend over an hour with them at the dinner table, he decided to stay in his room.

Curiously, though, instead of the noise dying out as one would expect, it grew louder and louder. He tried to remember which cousins were arriving today, but he drew a blank. All he knew was that listening to them go and on was getting on his last nerve.

He paced in his room briefly, but doing so did nothing to ease the irritability of the ever increasing noise from downstairs. *Would they ever shut up?*

Right as he was getting ready to stomp down to the main level to find out what in the name of God had everyone in an uproar, his mother called for him.

"Howard!"

He rolled his eyes. He was going to have to see his cousins before dinner after all.

"What?" he yelled back.

"Do come down. It's the most fabulous news."

That was the moment some of the noise died down. Before Howard could be thankful for the brief respite, a very unexpected voice rang out above all the others.

Helen?

Helen was here. At his house. Why?

"Howard!" his mother called again.

He walked to the doorway of his room, still in awe that Helen was here, when he heard another voice.

Franklin?

Why would the golden couple be at his house? He started down the stairs, but not with as much excitement as he'd felt before. Helen. Frank. Fabulous news.

He froze halfway down the stairs and gripped the banister so tight he almost lost feeling in his fingers. He forced himself to breathe so he didn't fall headfirst down the stairs.

Oh, God. No.

No. It couldn't be. Anything but that. Because that would mean he was too late and it couldn't be too late.

"Howard, seriously," Frank said. "Get down here so I can ask you nice and proper to be my best man."

Too late.

Too late.

Two hours later, they headed to the shelter on foot. Though they were exposed that way, Alyssa thought they were safe since she assumed the general consensus was they were staying in the church. No one had entered in the hour and a half they'd kept guard across the street, but she knew better than to assume they weren't watching.

Once inside the shelter, the resident working the front office told them Jansen Miller, the shelter's overseer, was in his office and offered to walk them to it.

"It's okay," Alyssa said. "You don't have to go through all that trouble. Just point us in the right direction and we'll head that way."

Looking relieved she didn't have to be a tour guide, the young woman smiled and pointed down a side hall. "Mr. Miller's office is the second door on the right."

Alyssa thanked her and she walked with Kipling to the office that had been pointed out to her.

"Here goes nothing," she said, and knocked.

Within a few seconds, the door opened and a smallish man with balding hair stood in the doorway. He glanced at Kipling first. "Yes?" he asked, and shifted his gaze to her.

He turned so pale, she thought for a second he was going to pass out, but he quickly collected himself and, with a quick glance around the empty hallway, ushered them inside. He looked completely settled when he locked the door behind them and led them to a small office. He pointed to two chairs in front of his desk and took a seat on the opposite side.

"Hi, I'm—" Alyssa started, but stopped talking when Jansen held his hand up.

Jansen looked at Kipling. "I'm guessing you're one of the Benedict boys?" Kipling looked mildly shocked until Jansen continued. "It's the eye color. Very unique."

Alyssa was impressed he'd picked up on that. If she had done the same, everyone might have realized that Jade was related to the brothers.

"And I'm assuming since you are a Benedict, your visit has something to do with the funding request we submitted?"

"Yes," Kipling said. "We came by to look around and make sure your shelter was up to the minimum requirements. Especially since there have been several people disappearing from this facility over the last few months. We'd like to look into those files and see if perhaps there's any information that would help us find them."

Jansen leaned back in his seat. "I hate to be the bearer of bad news, but if that's the case, the missing people are probably dead."

"So you have heard of them?" she asked, surprised at his easy-go-lucky attitude about the entire thing.

"I never claimed not to have heard of them," Jansen said. "After all, I do work here. However, I'm not going to talk about them."

The man made no sense. Seriously. Could he be any more of a walking contradiction? "I'm not sure why you let us in your office if you knew who we were, but yet aren't going to give us any information."

Jansen templed his fingers. "Simple. I didn't know until I let you in that you were Allison Grant's sister."

Little he could have said would have shocked her more. She had numerous questions pop to her mind, but she couldn't get her brain to work well enough to pick one to ask.

"You knew Alyssa's sister?" Kipling asked, and she shot him a look of thanks.

"Not personally. I knew of her." He only spoke that much and didn't add anything further.

"And?" Kipling asked.

"There is no *and*. That's all there is."

He knew more. She knew he did. If he didn't, he wouldn't have reacted so strongly at the sight of her. "Please," she pleaded. "We came here at great risk."

"Not my problem. I didn't tell you to come."

"It's just," she took a deep breath, "I feel like I'm so close and for the first time ever, I believe I might have a chance to solve this case."

Jansen shook his head. "You won't. The only thing you'll do is draw unwanted attention to yourself. Trust me on this."

"I don't even know you. How do you expect me to trust you?"

Jansen pushed back from his chair and stood up. "Frankly, Officer Adams, that's not my problem. I hate to run you out, but I have a call starting soon."

"One last thing." Kipling stood up. "When you say you knew of her, what exactly did you mean?"

"Ms. Grant got involved with some shady people who attracted danger and trouble. Before she knew what had happened, she was in a lot deeper than she ever expected and couldn't find her way out. Now if you'll excuse me."

She wasn't happy about being kicked out of his office, she would have preferred to stay and ask question after question about her sister. But she knew a lost cause when she saw one.

Kipling looked just as confused as she felt. He waited until they heard the lock click behind them and shook his head. "If that wasn't the strangest meeting I've ever been in, it was definitely one of them."

"So it wasn't just me thinking that?"

"No," he said. "There's more going on here than what we're aware of." Kipling glanced around them as he talked.

She met his eyes. "So we have to come back. Tonight."

Jade wasn't sure she'd ever seen The Gentleman in such a foul and cantankerous mood. And that unwelcome thought scared her more than anything she'd seen in recent days.

He smashed his fist into the wall, not seeming to care or even realize that he was bleeding. "Tell me again how you let them get away," he said to whoever was on the phone he held in his good hand.

"I see," he said after some time. "And it never occurred

to you that this might happen if they discarded their phones?"

She obviously couldn't hear what the person on the other end said, but she did watch as The Gentleman's face grew red with rage. Yet, when he spoke again, his voice was calm. "I see. You didn't think that they would ever discard their phones. Where are the phones now?" There was a pause as the answer was given. "Good. Good. Very well."

He hung up and dialed another number. "Jackson. David is at the United Methodist Church. Inside. Lower level. Kill him and bring me all the electronics on his person." He turned around at her gasp, looking surprised that she was there. Though why that would be, she wasn't sure. She was tied up. It wasn't like she could go anywhere. But she wished she could so she could keep David safe. "On second thought, subdue him and bring him to me. I have someone here with me and I think a bit of sport would be just the thing to revive me."

He said nothing else, but hung up and walked toward her. She tried to hide the shiver he made run up and down her back, but she wasn't sure how successful she was. Not very, considering the evil grin he gave her. "David has failed me and as a result, he must die. You're the one who's going to kill him."

"Run that by me again?" Kipling knew she couldn't have said what he thought she did.

"We need to spend the night at the shelter."

He groaned. He had heard correctly. "When you said we had to come back, I didn't know you meant we'd have to spend the night. We can't go back there. We're too recognizable."

"I didn't say we were going to go as ourselves."

He lifted an eyebrow. "Who else would we go as?"

Forty-five minutes later, he made a note to never ask her that question again. She had managed to somehow find at the school, thanks to the drama department, materials that aged him considerably, but she couldn't find anything to mask his eyes. With a sigh, she finally handed him a pair of sunglasses. "Put these on."

He slipped them on and she leaned back against the countertop she had been working at. She'd done something to her face that added a few wrinkles and managed to make her look years older. As she studied him in return, she rubbed her hand on her much-too-realistic-looking pregnant stomach. He wasn't sure what she'd discovered that actually made her look pregnant. And he honestly didn't care to know. All he could focus on at the moment, was the way she looked pregnant and, even though he knew he shouldn't, he allowed himself to imagine for a second or two that it was his.

"Kipling?" she asked. "Are you ready to go?"

He glanced up from her fake baby belly. "What?"

She tilted her head. "Are you okay? I asked if you were ready to go."

"Yes, to both." The glasses she'd found for him slipped down his nose. "Do I keep these on?"

"I'm afraid so."

He sighed and held out his hand. "You should know if you were really the mother of my child, I'd drive. Or take a cab."

They walked to the shelter in silence. Kipling tried to keep his eyes on their surroundings, while at the same time taking care not to look as if he was doing so. He couldn't stop feeling like any second someone was going to jump out at them and say, "There they are," exposing them for all to see.

But nothing of the sort happened and they arrived at the shelter with no issues.

"Let me do the talking," Alyssa said as they walked up to the front door.

Kipling continued to be amazed by her. He'd yet to see her approach anything without the complete confidence that she would succeed. The only time he saw her falter was when they approached the front office. Fortunately, it was not manned by the same woman as earlier. And Alyssa was all smiles when the woman turned their way and asked, "Can I help you?"

"I hope so," Alyssa said, drawing out her vowels and making her normally subtle southern accent very intense. "I'm Lynda and this is my husband, Lloyd. We're on our way to Savannah and need a place to spend the night. Normally, I wouldn't mind being on the streets, you know, but we did that last night, and the little one didn't like it." She rubbed her hands over her belly.

"Of course," the shelter worker smiled sweetly at Alyssa and then turned her attention to him. "Would you mind taking the glasses off, Lloyd?"

Kipling looked at Alyssa. *Now what?*

But she seemed to have anticipated the question and stood in between them. "He has to keep the glasses on. He has this light sensitivity thing." She wrinkled her eyebrows. "Photo-something? I can't remember. All I know is that he can't take them off or he'll barf everywhere."

No more mention was made of his glasses, instead the worker flipped through a stack of papers. "Normally, we separate the men and women, but I don't think we'll do that in this case."

Alyssa and Kipling exchanged a *thank goodness* look.

"I have a private room I'm going to put you in since it's just for the night." She looked up with a grin. "Come with me, I'll show you around."

They followed her down a hallway they hadn't been in

before. Kipling couldn't help but notice that Alyssa looked more and more uneasy the deeper they went down the hall.

"Men's bathroom is right there." The guide pointed with her left hand. "And women's is right across the hall. Your room doesn't have a private bathroom and those are the closest to where you'll be staying."

They walked a few more steps and made it to an open door. "Here's your room. Everything you need should be in there, but come see me at the desk if it's not. Breakfast is at seven sharp." She didn't lead them inside, but bid them good night and turned and went back to the desk.

Kipling put his hand on Alyssa's lower back and walked with her inside. "Tell me what's wrong."

Alyssa took a deep breath and looked around the small room. It only contained a bed and two small chairs. "My sister was in a room like this. It never occurred to me to question why she had a private room."

Kipling didn't know how to respond to that, so he simply put his arms around her and held her close. "It's okay," he said, hoping it was the truth. "We're so close. We're going to find out what happened to your sister and get justice for her. And we're going to find Jade and the two of you are going to do all those aunt-and-niece things, like helping her get ready for a date and passing out ice cream when some jerk breaks up with her. I'll see to it that you catch up and become the best of friends."

She chuckled. He felt the vibrations up and down his chest. "I know you can't promise any such thing, but it does make me feel better to hear you say them."

"If I could give up my entire fortune to ensure it would happen, I'd do it in a second," he whispered in her ear.

They had decided to wait until just after midnight to go exploring. By then surely everyone would be in bed and asleep. They were certain someone was paid to keep watch overnight, but hopefully they would be able to keep out of that person's way.

However, just before midnight someone knocked on their door. Alyssa drew her gun and nodded to Kipling. He cracked open the door and they were surprised to see Jansen standing there.

He looked over his shoulder before addressing them. "The Gentleman knows you're here and he'll be here any second."

"How?" Alyssa asked.

"I'm not sure, but someone came by, shortly after you left, and took all the remaining files from that period of time."

"Shit," Kipling said,

"You need to leave. Now." He looked over his shoulder again, but this time, he lifted a hand in a half wave. When he turned back to them, his face was pale. "They're here. You can't leave through the door anymore." Another look over his shoulder. "Head out the window. Now!"

CHAPTER 13

Everyone was calling it the wedding of the century. If it had been anyone else getting married, Howard would have laughed at how pretentious it sounded. Sure, he'd agree, the bride's family had spent a small fortune on the event and damn near everyone was invited, and really, did there need to be ten bridesmaids? But the wedding of the century? Shouldn't that be reserved for royalty?

The real kind, that is. Not the kind that comes with a fake title given to you by the media to sell more papers.

But Howard wasn't in a laughing mood today. He was in a near panic because he was running out of time. This time tomorrow it would be too late. This time tomorrow, the only woman he'd ever loved would be married to his best friend.

Howard took most of the blame and laid it right on his own head. After all, the wedding hadn't snuck up on him. They'd been planning the thing for almost two years. So he had no room to say he didn't have the time to do anything. The truth was, he'd been chicken. He'd been afraid.

And it was so obvious to him, and therefore should be obvious to everyone, that Frank was seeing other women behind Helen's back. Howard would never forget the day he came home from class early and found Frank, naked and in the kitchen, with a woman who wasn't Helen.

He'd ignored the couple and went past them into his room, and slammed the door. Until that moment, he'd only suspected that Frank was cheating on his fiancée. Now he'd seen the truth with his own eyes.

Even now, months later, he still remembered feeling equal parts angry and bewildered.

Angry, because how could Frank cheat on Helen? Bewildered, because *why* would he cheat on Helen?

His first thought was that he needed to tell Helen, but the more he thought about it, he thought it would be so much easier for him to show up and be the knight-in-shining-armor who saved the day than to be the bastard who pointed out what an ass her fiancé was.

He risked a look at Helen. She looked radiant, but was it all an act? Sitting at the head table, sharing whispers and kisses with Frank, she looked happy and in love. Howard stood up and walked to the open bar to get a refill of his Scotch.

It no longer mattered if she was pretending or blissfully in love. He was running out of time. The years had become months had become weeks had become days. Now, he was down to mere hours.

Hours later, he was on a mission. This was it. Now or never. His last chance. He tried not to laugh at the thought that he had Frank to thank for it. If Frank had any idea what Howard planned to do, he'd never have asked his roommate to make sure his bride made it home okay.

But he had, and Howard was going to grab it and take it for all it was worth. Telling himself to settle down, he stepped outside.

His breath caught as it normally did when her beauty struck him. And beauty seemed almost common as a way to describe her. Especially in the moonlight the way she was now.

"Helen?"

She turned to him and smiled. "Howard, how are you? I feel as if I haven't seen or spoken to you all day."

He shoved his hands in his pockets. "You have been a bit busy. It's understandable. After all, it's not like you get married every day."

She laughed and as always when he heard that sound, his heart wanted to skip out of his chest. But tonight it was much more than that. Tonight, his heart not only skipped, it jumped and raced because this night was so much more important than any other night.

He wondered if Helen saw anything different about him tonight. Probably not, more than likely her head was going in fifteen thousand different directions and though he was getting ready to make it fifteen thousand and one, he didn't feel bad.

"Am I needed somewhere?" she asked, then frowned. "Surely not, it has to be after midnight. Do you have a watch?"

"It is after midnight. That's why I'm here. Frank asked me to make sure you got home safely." She still looked confused, so he explained. "It's your wedding day, so you can't see Frank until the big moment."

"Oh, right." She laughed again. "It is, isn't it? My wedding day." She looped her arm through his. "And you're here to see me home safely. What a gentleman you are."

He bet "gentleman" would be the last word she'd use when he told her what he was getting ready to do, but that couldn't be helped. He took a deep breath and said what he'd been trying to find the words to say for years.

"There's probably a better way to say this," he started. "I know there's a better time. Unfortunately, I find I'm out of time and this is my only opportunity. Or more aptly, my last opportunity."

"Howard." She pulled back. "You're confusing and scaring me. What in the world?"

"Just listen to me, Helen."

She nodded. "Go on then."

Fortunately, they were close enough to her apartment to walk. Also in their favor was the fact that there were very few other people out and about this time of night. A quick look around and he didn't see anyone else.

"Frank is cheating on you." The words rushed out and he felt so much lighter getting them off of his chest. But a quick glance at Helen showed the burden now fell on her and she found it too heavy to carry.

She stopped walking and, moving too fast for him to stop, slapped him harder than anyone ever had before. "How *dare* you!" She nearly spat the words at him. "And on my wedding day. I used to like you, Howard Germain. I thought you were a really nice guy and a good friend to Frank. Now I see that you're nothing but a miserable, sneaky snake. Go away. I'll make it home just fine."

"Helen." He'd known it wouldn't be easy. Had known she probably wouldn't believe him at first, but even knowing that wasn't enough to take away the sting of being called a liar. "You have to believe me. I wouldn't be saying this if it weren't true. You have to know me well enough to know I would never do anything to hurt you."

She was standing a short distance away from him, with her arms crossed and glaring at him like it was his fault her fiancé was a pig.

"I may have thought that before, but not now." It was too dark to see if she'd found any of what he'd said to be truthful. All he could make out was the glare. "Even if what you said was true, you'd have known about it long before now and you still waited until my wedding day to bring it up."

"That was wrong of me, but you have to believe me, I kept thinking you'd find out and that I wouldn't have to be the one to tell you." Desperation raced through him; she didn't believe him, and he didn't know what to do to make her believe. Not only that, but he was running out of time. Why hadn't he tried to tell her before now? An idea flashed through his mind. A foolhardy idea that would never work, but he knew he had to try. "Come with me."

"What?"

He held out his hand. "Come with me. Let's run away together. Just you and me. We won't tell anyone. I can love you like he can't." Something flashed in her eyes—yes—he was getting through! "There will never be anyone else for me, just you. Please, Helen. Just you and me, we can do it, all we need is each other."

But whatever he'd seen flash was gone and only contempt remained. "I hate you, Howard. Do us both a favor and stay as far away from me as possible tomorrow." She turned, as if to head to her apartment. "I'm walking home alone and if you try to follow me, I'll call the police."

He had no choice but to stand there and watch as his future, his love, and his life walked away and left him all alone.

It was never a good thing when The Gentleman paid you a visit at midnight. Jade had a feeling that went double when you were already his captive. He stood nearby, the perfect picture of lunacy, watching as she stirred. She hadn't gone to sleep, of course. Years of not only living, but also working with the man, taught her that early.

She dozed on occasion, but always lightly and never for any extended amount of time. Typically, she wouldn't have even closed her eyes if there had been a chance he'd stop by. That it had happened at all tonight only proved how weak she'd become.

"I remember a time when you could stay awake for forty-eight hours straight," he said. "Now look at you. Lazy. Weak. Although, I suspect you can't really expect much else from one of Franklin's brats. I thought at one time that if I trained you enough, I could work it out of you. I think we can both see how much of a colossal failure that was."

She didn't think it'd be in her best interest to talk to him, so she remained quiet.

He gave her a smile so dark and evil, she shivered. "It's not going to matter much longer anyway. So I should probably leave you alone, but we both know that's not my style."

Hell, did that mean he was going to stand there and throw insults at her? She needed to change the topic of conversation before he got started. All too frequently, she'd seen how he'd switch from insult throwing to throwing punches. She knew that in his current mood, if he hit her once, he wouldn't stop until she was dead.

"Why do you hate Franklin so much?" she asked. It was something she'd always wanted to ask, but never had.

But, of course, The Gentleman knew what she was doing. "Is it time for us to tell our life stories?" His voice sounded calm enough, but she could see the anger that rested just below the surface at the mention of Frank's name.

Again, she wasn't stupid enough to answer a question.

"I know your story," he continued, not seeming to care if she answered or not. "But you don't know all of mine." He looked at his watch. "And we have time before the man in charge of taking out your aunt and brother is due to check in. I suppose I could humor you for a bit."

She forced her face to remain neutral, but wasn't sure she was successful.

He glanced around the room and pulled a chair over toward her so he could sit down. "Your worthless father and I went to college together. He thought he was a god and the women on campus obviously thought so as well, because they were always all over him. I knew they were only using him and I didn't care because I was doing the same thing, using him, I wanted him for a job. Everything changed, though, our junior year. That was the year Helen transferred to our college. I remember the first time I saw her. I thought she was an angel, she was so beautiful, it was almost otherworldly."

He was looking beyond her, to something in the past, if she guessed correct. Whatever it was called to him and he was once more in its spell. She wished he could reside there.

"Of course, like everyone else, she only had eyes for Franklin. I didn't let that bother me. I knew how Franklin worked. Knew she'd be tossed aside as soon as someone new caught his eye. Except he didn't. Weeks turned into months. Everyone was in shock. Later, they would say that love changed him and made him a better man, but all it really did was force him to be discreet."

Jade couldn't stop the gasp that left her throat. Of course, he thought it was funny. "I can't believe that shocks you, his bastard daughter. Franklin was never faithful to Helen. It was the first thing that made me hate him, but it wasn't the last."

A flash of something that looked like rage simmered in his expression. She didn't want to know what her father did to earn that much anger. Fortunately, whatever it was disappeared quickly and he continued where he left off.

"A year later their engagement was announced and I

saw my chances with her start to disintegrate. I wasn't ready to give up, however, so the night before the wedding, I managed to get her alone and I told her everything. I'm not sure what I thought I was going to accomplish. All I got for it was a smack across my face. I never could figure out why she reacted the way she did."

"Did you ever find out why?" she couldn't help asking.

"Kipling was born six months after the wedding."

Jade nodded as if she understood everything, but in reality, she didn't. He fell in love with his friend's girl and that turned him into the monster he was today? But The Gentleman wasn't finished yet.

"Guess when I made my first human kill?" Without waiting for her to answer, he continued: "After the wedding, I was on my way home and there was a young girl hitchhiking on the side of the road."

She didn't want to hear about his first kill. The poor girl hitchhiking on the side of the road. But he wouldn't stop now. Not when he had that bloodthirsty look in eyes. She wondered if she could tune him out, if she focused really hard on something that was the opposite of killing and rape and everything else he was guilty of.

She had been trying so hard to tune him out, it took a few seconds for her to realize he was no longer talking, but had taken his phone out of his pocket and had answered it.

"Yes," he said, and that evil smile of his had once more returned. "Excellent."

Those were the only two words he spoke, but they were the only two he needed. He turned to her. "Story time is over. Our evening entertainment has just arrived."

Jade leaned her forehead against the cool stone wall and spit, wishing for some water to rinse her mouth. The Gentleman had let her go when she started vomiting and she'd fallen to her knees. Just thinking about her guardian made her stomach revolt and she took deep, even breaths to try to calm down.

"Worthless," he said from somewhere above her. She couldn't see him, but she felt this foot when he kicked her. "Stand up."

She slowly got to her feet, knowing it would only be worse if she stayed on her knees. But one look into The Gentleman's eyes and she knew it would be bad for her no matter what.

"You're weak. I've never seen you so weak. Even when you were a child, you were stronger than you are now."

He didn't say anything else for what seemed like a long time. He only stood there, looking at her with contempt.

"If I had ever thought you would be of use to me again, what just happened proved you never would be." He looked over her right shoulder. She supposed a guard was standing there. "Take her back to her cell and chain her."

And just like that, she was dismissed.

The guard didn't say anything to her as he took her back to her cell. She didn't want to be back in there because she knew once he'd left her alone, she'd replay the evening in her head.

From the moment David was rolled into the room, gagged and tied to the thick wooden board and propped up so he faced everyone, to the moment he realized what The Gentleman had planned for him, and finally that second when his worst fears were confirmed as one of the last remaining assassins, The Gentleman had stood before him and prepared to throw the first knife.

The Gentleman had laughed when the first knife stuck. "Just like those insects in Biology."

Jade hunched over and vomited on the guard's shoes. Even then, his sounds wouldn't stop. Her mind replayed the bloodcurdling screams slowly becoming groans as life drained away from the young man's body.

With nowhere else to go, Alyssa suggested to Kipling that they return to the school. It was a long, arduous trip back, but they took so many convoluted turns and doubled back an innumerable amount of times. So much so that they both questioned at different times if they even knew where they were going.

Though someone might have started out following them, they were both completely positive they arrived at the school alone. Earlier in the day, they had set up cots in a storage closet they felt certain no one would venture into. Especially considering the students and most of the faculty were still on break.

"Remember when I said I would crash later?" Alyssa dropped onto a cot. "This is me crashing."

Kipling took the cot next to her and reached out his hand for hers. "I'm right there with you. I think I could sleep for two days and not move the entire time I did so."

Alyssa gently squeezed his hand. "Do you think they got Jansen?" Though why she asked, she wasn't sure. Part of her could be happy forever being able to pretend he was safe.

"Do you really want to know what I think?" Kipling asked with a pointed look.

She thought through her response before giving it. "Yes, I think I do."

"There were gunshots fired right as we left the property. I'd be shocked if he survived."

"But it's possible, right?" she asked, surprised at how hoarse she sounded.

"Yes."

She sniffled. Damn, this case was getting to her. Either that or she was going soft. She didn't like either one of those options. She wished more than anything that they weren't sleeping on cots. But rather that they were sharing a bed.

If they were in a bed, he would pull her close to his side and tuck her head under his. It made her smile that they had shared a bed only two times and already she knew how they would position themselves. But not tonight. She sighed.

"Come here, Alyssa," he said, rolling to his side and scooting over to give her room on the cot.

She didn't stop to ask if he was sure or if he'd have enough room. He'd offered and she was going to take him up on it. Within seconds, she was in his arms and content. She guessed she was seconds away from sleep when his phone rang.

They were both immediately on high alert. As far as she knew, only his brothers, Lena, Tilly, and Bea had the number to his burner phone and no one had used it so far. She looked at her watch. For sure, there wasn't anything good going to come from a call this time of the morning.

"I don't know that number," he said, before putting it on speaker and answering. "Hello."

"Kipling Benedict," an unfamiliar voice said, but from the way his jaw tensed and the way he went from relaxed to rigid in two seconds, Alyssa could see that Kipling knew exactly who it was. Somehow she knew that this call was going to change everything.

"Howard Germain," Kipling replied, and Alyssa sucked in a breath. Damn, but she'd hoped she'd been wrong. "What can I do for you?"

"I was calling to see if you were interested in seeing your baby sister again?" Howard asked, and Alyssa decided he had the creepiest voice she'd ever heard.

"What kind of question is that?" Kipling demanded, and even though his voice was calm, she saw the anger in his expression and knew he was using all his self-control to remain calm. "Of course, I want to see her."

"Excellent," Howard, or The Gentleman, as she now knew he went by, said even as she worked to make sense of the fact that this man was not only the fiend she'd been chasing because of his involvement with the local missing women, but was also responsible for her sister's death. It was almost surreal. "That's exactly the response I wanted to hear. And in order to see her and get her back alive, you only have to do one thing."

"And what is that?"

"Bring me the police officer."

For a second, it felt as if her entire body shut down. She couldn't breathe. She couldn't move.

"Why?"

Howard only laughed. But it wasn't a normal laugh, it wasn't funny at all. It was scary as hell and she knew, after only hearing it once, that it would haunt her forever.

"What does it matter to you why I want her? You're getting your sister back. Or half-sister, that is."

"I'm not about to put my worst enemy in your hands, do you actually think I'm going to hand someone I care about to you?"

"Oh no, Kipling." Howard made a *tsk-tsk* sound. "Don't tell me you've grown close to the officer? The one who arrested you and made you into a laughingstock? You actually care what happens to her? It's a good thing your parents aren't here to see this. They would not approve of you dating someone in that profession. Honestly, between you and your brothers, you have managed to tie yourselves to the most worthless women."

"If you don't have anything else to say," Kipling said, with barely contained rage. "I think it's time to end this call."

"That's fine. You go and think about what you want

to do. As for me, I'll be in the backyard of your beach cottage tomorrow night at eight. You always talk about how important family is, all I'm doing is giving you a chance to prove it.'"

Kipling didn't say anything else, he simply hung up. One look at her must have been enough for him to guess what she was thinking. "No," he said, without even waiting for her to say anything. "It's out of the question. Don't even think of it."

She put her hands on her hips. "When you decide to knock off the annoying mind-reading trick, let me know and we can have a reasonable conversation like two adults."

"Are you implying that I'm not an adult or that I'm not reasonable?" he asked.

"I'm not implying anything. I'm saying that when you assume what I'm going to say or do and then tell me I'm not going to do, it's annoying. You need to stop using it and falling back on it when things don't go the way you think they should."

"Is that what I'm doing?" he asked.

"No. Not right this second. Right this second, you're just arguing with me and being a pain in the ass."

"Okay, fine. Stand there right where you are, look me in the eyes, and tell me you weren't thinking about offering yourself as a pawn to The Gentleman, in order for me to get Jade back."

"You make it sound so black and white, and it isn't. I'm a trained police officer, I know how to take care of myself, how to get out of certain situations, and when I can't, I know how to fight."

"Excuse me for pointing out the obvious, but Jade has been under his care for all of her life. Almost. Are you seriously going to stand there and tell me you think you know how to handle him better than she does?"

She couldn't believe that was his reasoning. "Frankly,

seeing the way she looked when she came by your house that night, add in a few more weeks on the streets, and now her guardian has kidnapped her. Yes. Actually I do think I'm better prepared and equipped to handle Howard Germain than she is." She cocked her eyebrow at him again. "Truth be told, I'm probably better equipped and prepared to handle him than you are."

"Don't be ridiculous."

"Oh, excuse me. Are you going to go macho on me now? Must protect the little lady from getting her hands dirty and all that? Seriously, I thought better of you." She turned to walk away, but Kipling was having no part in that.

"Don't walk away from me, I'm not finished with this conversation yet."

"Perhaps not, but until you can say something worthwhile or meaningful, I'm not going to listen to it."

"You are the most infuriating woman ever."

"At least you found that out early. Now you have time to look for a docile Southern belle who will abide by your every whim and command."

"I have no interest in that and you know that for a fact, Alyssa."

"Not based on this conversation I don't."

He took a step closer to her and she swore she felt his body hum the way it had at his family's beach cottage right before he'd taken her down the hall to his room. "I seem to remember you were very vocal with your own commands not so long ago, weren't you?"

She told herself she wasn't going to blush over anything she'd asked him for in bed. "Yes, I was and if I remember correctly, you liked it. A lot."

He had somehow completely crossed any remaining space between them. She could smell him and she bet if she moved her lips just slightly, she'd be able to taste him.

"I fucking loved it and you know it." His nostrils flared. "I don't know what bozo told you that you should keep quiet in bed and not ask for what you want, but he was wrong. And it's time you stopped listening to him and listened to me instead." He put a hand on both of her shoulders. "There is nothing sexier to me than a women who knows what she wants in bed and out of bed and is strong enough to not only ask for it, but to command it."

She almost didn't say it because she knew in saying it, she wouldn't be totally honest. It wasn't that she didn't want to have sex with him. Hell, she'd have to be comatose not to want to have sex with him. That wasn't it.

They'd been arguing about her giving herself up as a pawn to The Gentleman and Kipling had been very clear he did not want her to do it.

Even so, she closed her eyes and said it. "Prove it. Prove to me how sexy you think it is when a woman asks for what she wants in bed."

He dipped his head low, from all appearances, it seemed as if he was going to kiss her, but at the last moment, he turned just a tad and whispered. "For the record, I know exactly what you're doing."

She blinked her eyes and tried to look as innocent as possible. "I don't know what you're talking about."

"Don't play coy with me. You want to have sex, I'm pretty much down for it whenever. But don't think for a second that I'm led so much by my dick that I don't know what you're doing." She opened her mouth to speak, but he placed a finger over her lips, cutting her off. "I can't let you do it, Alyssa. You can't go to him. I'm petrified thinking that if you do, you'll never come back."

There was a time and a place to argue and or discuss how to best take The Gentleman down, along with the pros and cons over who would be the best pawn. Right now was not the best time. "I'm not saying I agree with you or that

I won't keep pushing for the role I think I'm best suited for. However, I'm willing to agree that this isn't the best time to make those decisions."

He chuckled. "Why do I feel as though you came out on top?"

"I don't know." She reached for the zipper of his pants. "But if you play your cards right, I'll let you be on top this time."

CHAPTER 14

Howard had experienced bad days before, but until he'd stood at the front of a church and watched his best friend marry the woman he loved, he'd never known just how bad a bad day could be. At times during the ceremony he had to hold himself back so he wouldn't interrupt the minister and tell Helen in front of her obscene amount of bridesmaids and ridiculous number of guests that she was minutes away from making the worst mistake of her life.

And then she had.

The same minister he had been seconds away from interrupting was introducing Mr. and Mrs. Franklin Benedict. The bridesmaids and guests clapped and Howard could only stand and wonder how he was going to live the rest of his life knowing that Helen had married Frank and he'd been helpless to stop it.

He made up his mind then and there that no matter what he had to do, he would never feel helpless again.

He did his best to abide by Helen's wish to stay away from her. It actually wasn't all that hard to do. Not only did she shoot him an icy glare that not only further froze his heart, but ensured nothing would ever make it thaw again. In addition, he found that anytime he got close to her, Frank was right there with her. At her side, holding her hand, holding onto her arm, or worse yet, kissing. For the first time in his life, he wanted nothing to do with Frank Benedict and he wasn't sure how that was going to work out for either of them because right before they graduated, Frank had asked Howard to come and work for him and his father at Benedict Industries. And Howard had accepted.

In his mind, he'd figured if Frank and Helen ended up getting married, and if he worked in the family business, meaning they would all spend a lot of time together, it'd be a good way for him to keep his eye on both of them. Make sure Frank didn't cheat on his wife the way he had his girlfriend. In other words, wait for their divorce.

The wedding director announced that the newlyweds were leaving and everyone stood to wish them well. But while everybody else was throwing rice at the tin can decorated car, he stood off to the side and fed rice to the birds. All the while, imagining their little bellies exploding. Later he would realize that while Frank and Helen were saying their goodbyes, he was ensuring a slight decrease in the pigeon population. It seemed only fitting in his mind. If nothing else, at least being busy with pigeons meant he was spared having to watch Helen leave him one more time.

He looked up and the newlyweds had thankfully left. The festive mood started to die. And just like that, the wedding of the century was over.

Thank goodness.

It didn't take too long for the remaining guests to start leaving and for the crowd to thin out. He wasn't sure why he was one of the last to leave. Perhaps he had some unreasonable hope that Helen would realize her mistake and come back. That on her way to whatever paradise Frank had picked out, she came to her senses and realized he'd been right the entire time.

But of course she didn't. No, of course not.

When he finally decided to leave the reception, he didn't feel like going back to the apartment he'd shared with Frank. Going back to his parents' house meant either twenty questions on why he was in such a piss poor mood or worse, when was he going to settle down. He could stomach neither.

For a while, he drove around. It was dark by then, and not a lot of people were out. Those that were, hurried along, as if driven by some outside force to make it to whatever place they were going as soon as possible.

That was what made it so easy for him to find her. While everybody else was running around, she was taking her time. Everyone else had somewhere they had to be and she was content with needing to go nowhere. It was her lack of hurriedness that first caught his attention. However what kept his attention was her blonde hair and blue eyes.

Yes, he thought as soon as she looked at him with those eyes that were almost the right shade, but not quite. And yet, the more he looked at her, the more he was able to convince himself it didn't matter. The hotel room would be dark. He'd see to it.

In the dark, she would probably remind him of Helen.

In the dark, he probably wouldn't be able to tell the difference.

In the dark, he could do whatever he wanted.

She didn't hesitate to come over to his car when he pulled it to a stop beside her on the road. Nor did she hesitate to get in his car when he opened the door for her and asked her where she was going.

She told him she was running away from home and he

could take her anywhere except back to where she came from. He told her that wouldn't be a problem.

She told him her name was Rachel. He asked if her middle name was Helen.

She was smart enough to say yes.

Or stupid enough.

He still didn't want to go back to his apartment, not with the memories of Helen and Frank being everywhere he looked. Especially those memories of Helen. He took Rachel Helen to a nearby hotel room. He opened the car door for her in the parking lot, and the door to hotel room. She laughed and called him a little gentleman.

She didn't laugh for much longer.

She didn't do much of anything for much longer.

As it turned out, Howard was wrong. There was no part of her that reminded him of Helen. None at all. Which is why he had to kill her.

But of course, that was Frank's fault.

Kipling reluctantly rented a car the next day to take them to the Edisto property they now knew belonged to Howard. He looked to his side where Alyssa appeared brave and confident, but he'd held her last night while she confessed to being scared. He told himself that if she could go through doing this, he could damn well find the strength to support her.

They didn't say anything as he drove to the beach property he'd thought only days before was so safe.

Safety, he was learning, was nothing but an illusion.

As they got closer to the beach, he couldn't stand the silence anymore. "Let's go through the plan one more time," he said.

"Must we?" she asked, sounding very tense.

He swallowed around the lump in his throat. He had a

bad feeling about this day. Something told him it wasn't going to run as smoothly as they'd hoped. Of course, he told himself, what did he expect when working with a diabolical serial killer?

"No," he said in answer to her question. "We don't have to go over it again. It's only that it makes me feel better the more we go over it. For some reason it makes me feel as though I have some control in the outcome. But the truth is I don't have any control over it, so I should just let it go."

"You may not have any control over the outcome," she spoke with the determination he admired so much. "But the one thing you can do is trust in me to do what I've been trained to."

Her words pierced his heart with guilt. "I didn't mean in any way to imply you weren't up to the task." They had almost made it to the long drive that led to the Benedicts' beach property and he pulled the car over because suddenly it became very important for him to say what he wanted to say before they reached where they were going.

Alyssa looked at him as if he were crazy. "Kipling, what are you doing? Why are we stopping? You know we need to get there and get everything set up before he does."

"Yes," he said, and he actually smiled, which he wouldn't have thought possible mere moments before. And even though he knew what they were getting ready to do was dangerous, he also knew that what he was doing was right.

"So why did you pull the car over?" She looked at him with a raised eyebrow. "I will kick your ass into next week if this is some sort of delay tactic or if you think for one moment you're going to talk me out of doing this."

"I love you." Three words. Three small words even, but while they'd felt so heavy on his tongue, now that he'd said them, he felt light and peaceful. "I love you," he said a second time because she was still looking at him like he'd lost every bit of sense he ever had and because it was so much easier to say the second time.

"Kipling." She shook her head, but before she could say anything else, he placed his finger on her lips.

"Shh," he said. "You don't need say them back. In fact I didn't say them so you'd say them back. I simply wanted you to know." He started the car back up. "Ready?"

She only nodded, but he saw the truth in her eyes. She loved him, too.

Alyssa looked at her watch. One in the afternoon. The Gentleman wasn't expecting them until eight, but he had to at least suspect they would show up earlier. She only hoped he wouldn't think they would be *this* early.

Even so, they had parked the car at the far edge of the property in order to scope the place out. There was a chance he'd see them, but as each second ticked along silently, she couldn't help but think that chance grew smaller and smaller.

She glanced up to find Kipling looking at her and she felt her cheeks heat and she hurriedly looked down. He loved her. Though it had seemed improbable the first time he said it, the more and more it resounded inside her head, the more and more she accepted.

He. Loved. Her.

She felt a stupid grin cover her face and she didn't even care. She turned to say something to him and ended up almost falling down because he was right there in front of her.

"Whoa," he said, placing his hands on her shoulders. "Careful there."

"I'm okay."

He kissed her cheek. "Guess what I just saw?"

"What?"

"Come here." He took her hand and led her to where

he'd stood moments before. "See that there, in between those two trees?"

She looked to where he pointed and squinted. "Is that a treehouse?"

"It is. My father had it put in when we were younger. We loved it, of course, and would spend hours there. It was the perfect location because you could see anyone approaching from the beach or street. Even better, they couldn't see you."

"Oh, no." She shook her head because she knew what he was going to say next.

"I'm going to go over there and see if I can see anything from it."

"That is such a bad idea."

"It's not. I might be able to see where he's keeping Jade."

"Or you might be walking into a trap and wind up dead."

He gave her an *are you kidding me* look, kissed her briefly, and whispered, "I'll be back before you know I'm gone."

He was going to go no matter what she said or how she felt, she knew it. All she could do was nod, tell him to be careful and pray she was wrong.

Each second he was gone seemed longer than the one before. She took her binoculars and watched as Kipling carefully entered the treehouse. Even then she stayed exactly where she was, unable to look away. And when two men followed Kipling inside, she didn't hesitate to go after them.

CHAPTER 15

FIFTEEN YEARS AGO
HOMELESS SHELTER
CHARLESTON, SC

He was going to have to kill Franklin's mistress. Or his ex-mistress to be more exact. And though he typically didn't have a problem killing people, it was a pity he was going to have to get rid of this one.

He'd certainly give it to Frank. He knew how to pick them. This one was young, and beautiful. Not only that, but she spoke with intelligence and he found her to be clever and witty. He'd thought about keeping her around. After all, he thought he could overlook the fact that she'd slept with Frank. It had been over five years. But then she'd done the unthinkable. She'd snooped around in his office.

Contrary to popular belief, he wasn't totally without a heart, and he could overlook certain things. Unfortunately, snooping was not one of those things. Snooping was born out of lack of trust and respect. For her to snoop showed she didn't trust him or respect him. And in the end, it meant he would have to kill her for it.

Of course, killing her brought to light even more issues. Namely, her daughter. Who just so happened to be Frank's daughter as well.

The irony of the situation was not lost on him. Franklin

had always wanted a daughter. Longed for a daughter. But the fates had not seen fit to give him one. Instead, they had given his mistress what he'd desperately wanted. That was what Howard called poetic justice.

He supposed it was also poetic justice that he would have to kill the woman.

But in killing the mistress, he would be the one who gained a daughter. He never put much stock in daughters. He had one, after all. For the most part, she was worthless. But if he were to become guardian to Frank's little girl . . .

He grew almost giddy thinking about how he would train her and the things he would teach the Benedict bastard. Oh, yes, yes, yes. Unknown to anyone other than him, he could single-handedly create the ultimate weapon to destroy the Benedicts. And what better way to destroy them than with their own flesh and blood?

He tightened his grip on the knife, suddenly ready to take care of the only thing standing in the way of all his dreams.

Brock was becoming a problem. Actually, the more he thought about it, Brock was already a problem—he was just quickly becoming a very big problem. Howard walked down the hall of the homeless shelter he'd set up as a stage for his real business of human trafficking. What had started as him wanting Helen look-a-likes had turned into a profitable business when he realized that he could help other men find their own Helens.

Brock, however, was happy with his wife Ann, and their daughter, Tilly. Last weekend, Brock had flown to Seattle with Howard and Frank. Brock had to go; Frank had told him when Howard questioned him on why. Having Brock in Seattle was going to put a kink in his plans. Frank wouldn't be a problem. As soon as they landed, he'd check into the hotel and then as quickly as possible, he'd be out trying to find female companionship for the duration of their stay.

Brock, however, was not only happily married, but had no interest in looking for anyone to sleep with. Normally, he spent time with Frank, but since Frank would be absent, that left Howard. He'd have to be careful and watch himself around Brock. Lately it seemed he had Frank's ear a lot more than Howard did.

Everything had been fine, right up until everything went to hell. Howard's Seattle contact had been able to set him up with what had to be the most perfect substitute for Helen he'd ever found. It had been that perfection that ultimately led to his current predicament. Namely, Brock had happened upon Howard at an inopportune time. To be exact, he'd shown up right as Howard was teaching Not-Helen what happened when she disobeyed him.

Howard had only seen Brock for a few seconds, but it had been enough. Enough for him to see the look of utter disgust in the other man's eyes. Enough for Howard to realize that Brock would never see how some women had to be treated in order to make them behave properly. But worst of all, Brock had seen that the woman looked like she could be Helen's twin.

Unfortunately, there was already talk around the office about Howard having a crush on the boss's wife. If Brock told Frank what he'd seen, Frank would do something drastic.

So Howard had to be drastic first.

Brock had to be terminated.

Jade knew she was in trouble when The Gentleman showed up at her cell in the middle of the afternoon. He never showed up then. Typically, he'd come by either first thing in the morning or late at night. Add in the fact that he was whistling and she knew nothing good was going to be headed her way. It seemed he'd always been the most cruel after he whistled.

He was alone. She bemoaned the fact that she was nowhere as strong as she used to be. Not even six months ago, had she been in this situation, she'd be able to take him down. But now, after months of living on the streets, she was so weak, she was of no use to anyone, especially herself. Which meant all she could do was go along with whatever he had planned.

"Today is a very exciting day for me," he said, coming into view and unlocking her door. "Although you may not feel the same way."

He opened the door and the first thing she noticed were his eyes. He looked a lot like the junkies she'd met on the streets when they were high. He had that same wild and dangerous look about him.

"Are you on drugs?" she couldn't help but ask.

He laughed again. "I'm high on life because today, finally, after years and years of planning is when I destroy the Benedicts."

That was why he was so happy? Why today?

"I see the questions in your eyes," he said. "You forgot I know you so well, didn't you? No worry. I'll tell you. Today is the day because they walked right into my trap. One of them anyway. But I'll start with one. Especially since he is the head."

Kipling? Did he mean Kipling was here?

He didn't elaborate and she didn't question him any further. There was no need, already she knew she was marching to whatever end he had planned. But even knowing that, her mind wouldn't stop trying to imagine what he had planned.

Then he led her to the room he'd killed David in and she felt sick because she was afraid she knew exactly what was going to happen. She actually turned to run, but he'd anticipated her move and a burly man she didn't know stepped out of the shadows to keep her in her place.

It wasn't until they stepped into that nightmarish torture chamber of a room and she saw Kipling gagged and tied the same way David had been that she realized how much she'd hoped she'd been wrong. Or how painful it was when that last strand of hope was snatched from you.

As soon as Kipling saw her, he pulled against the leather ties strapping him to the table. He tried to speak as well but, of course, he could do neither. It pained her to look at him, so instead she focused on the wall behind him.

"You'll never get away with this," she told The Gentleman. "Keaton and Knox will come after you with everything they have and you don't even want to see what the women will have planned for you."

"Do tell, Jade, please. I can't wait to hear about how a group of spoiled brats and their women will take me down. Have you forgotten all that I have done and all I have commanded with only a single sentence? I'm a god in this state and no Benedict will ever better me." He chuckled, which was somehow even worse than his laugh. "Besides, why would I be the one to get away with it? You're the one who's going to kill him."

It took several seconds for the full weight of what he said to make sense. She didn't think even Kipling had any idea what he meant until Howard pushed a rolling table of knives in front of her. His eyes grew unnaturally large.

"I'd originally planned for that police officer to kill him, but I think it'll be much more poetic for you to kill him and for your aunt to kill you."

Jade was finally able to breathe again. Just a little, but it was enough to ease the pain in her chest and and to clear her mind of the all-encompassing, internal "No" that threatened to drag her to her knees. "I won't do it."

She'd said it in a whisper, but even Kipling seemed to have heard from across the room and looked from her to The Gentleman. Jade knew better than to look at him, but she couldn't stop herself. Unfortunately, he wasn't looking at her half-brother, he was looking at her. And the rage she saw left her no doubt that she would not be leaving the room alive, but strangely enough, there was no fear associated with that realization. She felt oddly calm and at peace.

"You will," he said through clenched teeth.

"No." She lifted her chin and spoke the truest words she'd ever spoken, "I'm not afraid to die. I am, however, very, very afraid of living a life that doesn't matter."

The Gentleman slapped her face so hard, she almost fell to the ground, but she remained standing and faced his wrath. "Nothing about you matters," he seemed to delight in telling her. "Your father didn't want you. Your grandparents didn't want you. The best thing you can do is die and take a few people with you." He nodded toward Kipling. "End him. Now."

She crossed her arms. "No."

"Yes." The Gentleman grabbed a knife from the table and threw it toward Kipling. She wasn't sure she took a breath until she heard the *thunk* of the knife hitting wood, but thankfully missing Kipling.

What she didn't miss was the slight movement from behind Kipling. She wasn't sure, but she thought it was Alyssa. She looked wildly for something to divert The Gentleman's attention. Her gaze dropped down to find his hand, pressed flat against the table. and not hesitating, she picked up a knife and plunged it through his hand, pinning him to the table.

From the back of the room, Alyssa watched in awe at the way Jade handled the knife. She worked it like it was an extension of herself. Alyssa wasn't sure she'd ever seen anyone so graceful with a blade.

Of course, Alyssa realized in the second before it struck exactly what her target was. For some reason, Howard didn't notice until it was too late where the knife was headed. When it struck him, his scream was bloodcurdling. She got the impression he'd vastly underestimated Jade. Or perhaps she'd never physically attacked him before and he'd grown complacent around her.

She didn't care. All she cared about was that he was occupied. At the moment, she was worried about Kipling. Earlier when she saw him, she thought he was fine, but now she realized that was because she was at the back of the room and couldn't see him well. Up close he didn't look good at all. His eyes appeared somewhat glassy, though he seemed to have been alert enough to understand what was happening to him moments before.

She had to get Kipling out of whatever the hell kind of device Howard had him in. And quickly. She kept one eye on the back of the room where Jade and Howard were fighting, but tried to focus most of her attention on Kipling.

She called his name. Nothing. "Kipling," she tried again while keeping her voice low enough to not to get the attention of anybody else except him. It wasn't until the third time she said his name, he appeared to have heard. Even then she was only met with a slight groan.

Fumbling madly, she tried to figure out how to release him from the contraption Howard had him locked into.

"Oh," he said, looking at her and she didn't think she imagined that one of his pupils was larger than the other. Concussion? She needed to get him medical help soon.

"It's you," he said, though she was worried that he wasn't able to use her name. "I had the strangest dream. I was in a cage and one of dad's employees wanted to throw knives at me." His eyebrows wrinkled. "Actually, I think he did manage to throw one knife at me, but he missed. Or at least he missed in my dream." A shout from the back of the room captured his attention and he seemed to notice he was bound and he started to pull against his restraints. "It was a dream, wasn't it?"

"Shh." She'd found the buckle and straps used to keep him in the position Howard wanted. "Let me get this undone so I can see if you have any injuries I can't see. Then I'll prop you up and you can rest until help arrives."

He didn't say anything else and she feared what she'd find when she got him free. She already assumed he had a concussion. Would that be the least of his injuries?

The leather buckle proved more difficult than she'd thought it would be. She had just managed to get it undone and had carefully extracted Kipling away from it when a shout of distress from the back of the room caught her attention.

The Gentleman had managed to pull the knife out of his hand and held it in his uninjured one. That in and of itself wouldn't have been enough for Alyssa to be worried. Even as thin and weak as she was, Jade could certainly hold her own against an injured Howard. However, at the moment she was held tightly by a man Alyssa hadn't seen before.

Howard raised the knife. "I should have killed you when you were five."

FIFTEEN YEARS AGO
PRIVATE OFFICE ALONG THE BAY
CHARLESTON, SC

"Sir! Sir!" The nanny he'd hired to look after the Benedict bastard called after him. Howard gave serious thought to pretending like he hadn't heard her. But she was the third nanny he'd hired this week and the agency he'd been using told him that if this one didn't work out, they didn't have anyone else to send. He didn't have the time, inclination, or patience to deal with a new agency, so he took a deep breath and turned around.

"Yes?"

By the time she'd made it to him, she was panting heavily and he had to wait a few minutes for her to catch her breath. He plastered a frown on his face, but when she looked up, she appeared to be completely unaffected by his expression. "You have to do something about that child," she said.

"Funny," he said. "That's why I thought I hired you."

"I can't be everything that girl needs. She needs more. More of you. More stability. She needs a house. This half-office, half-residence place you have here is not adequate. And she needs—"

"Stop," he said, his anger growing. "I did not ask your opinion on matters concerning her environment or my house. Nor will I. That child is lucky she's not out on the street. Her mother is dead and her father doesn't want her. I'm all she has and she's damn lucky I was willing to take her in." He saw something move out of the corner of his eye. He gave the nanny some cash. "Here, take a break. Go get some coffee or something. I'll watch the child for a bit."

He waited until he was sure the nanny was gone before calling, "Jade, come on out now."

She appeared slowly, but she did come. As was her new habit, she was sucking her thumb.

He didn't know anything about little kids. He supposed it was rather funny he was so uncomfortable and rather intimated by such a small person.

He bent down to her level, placed his hands on his knees, and asked, "What kind of trouble have you been starting?"

She sucked her thumb harder and looked at him with those creepy Benedict eyes.

"Jade," he tried again. "When someone asks you a question, you need to answer."

Her thumb fell out of her mouth with a wet pop and she smiled. "I don't like you."

He was so shocked, he laughed. Oh, yes. Frank's bastard would work out great.

PRESENT DAY

Alyssa looked around, desperate to find some sort of weapon she could use. Anything. Hell, at this point, she'd take a rock. Her eyes fell on the knife Howard had thrown at Kipling and missed.

Yes!

She had never thrown a knife before, but it was all she had and she was damn well going to use it. Should she throw it at The Gentleman or the guy who had Jade?

The Gentleman. Always The Gentleman.

She reached for the handle of the knife, but right when she almost touched it, she was pulled away. Surprised, she felt herself rock back to land on her butt, and she gave a yelp of distress.

"Good job," The Gentleman told whoever had stopped

her. "Bring those two, and you, bring the bastard girl. I'm ready to end this once and for all."

With both of her arms pulled behind her back, there was no way for her to fight her captor. She tried kicking him, but he only laughed and told her she would have to try harder than that.

"I'll come back for the guy," he said. "From the looks of it, he isn't going to be causing anyone any trouble anytime soon."

A quick glance proved he was right. Kipling was curled up on his side, where she'd left him, but his eyes were closed and his breathing was labored. She hadn't had time to check him for injures after she'd released him. The only thing she could say with certainty was that he wasn't bleeding where she could see. She tried not to think of all the internal injuries he could have.

"I don't care what it looks like," The Gentleman countered. "He's a Benedict. Don't turn your back to him."

Alyssa and Jade were led to a small cell-like room down the hall where they were tied to the wall. There was only the one door and no windows, which meant little chance to escape. Alyssa was hopeful their legs wouldn't be tied, but as soon as Kipling was brought into the room, her ankles, as well as Jade's were tied together. She didn't spend too much time lamenting the loss of her feet, though; she was too busy focusing on Kipling. From what she could tell, he still hadn't opened his eyes.

The Gentleman's two hired men left and Howard stood in the middle of the room, looking at the three of them with uncontrolled glee. "Isn't this the strangest family reunion you've ever seen? You have the unwanted bastard, the unknown aunt, and the current head of the family. I tell you what, I have a few things to get set up. You three say your good-byes and I'll be back in few minutes."

Alyssa kept telling herself, this couldn't be it. She didn't feel like she was moments away from death. But the more she thought about it, the faster her heart went and she felt clammy. A glance at Jade offered her no insight as to what her niece was feeling.

Her niece.

Her chest felt tight. How could she lose her now when she'd just found her?

"Is he gone?" Kipling cracked one eye open after Howard left and Alyssa could have wept with relief at seeing him lucid.

"Kipling," Alyssa said. "Oh, thank goodness. How are you feeling?"

"Other than my head hurting so bad my teeth ache, I'm a bit pissed. I thought if I acted like I was unconscious, they wouldn't tie me up." He eyed the restraints with disgust. "So much for that." He turned his head toward Jade. "I know it probably doesn't mean much at this point, but I'm sorry, Jade. I wish I had known."

Jade shrugged.

Undeterred by her lack of emotion, he kept talking. "I always wanted a sister. Don't get me wrong, I love Keaton and Knox, and I can't imagine life without them, but I always felt like something was missing. I know now it was you."

Something that reminded Alyssa of regret flashed in Jade's eyes and she asked the young woman, "How long have you known?"

"That I was a Benedict? Since forever. He thought if I knew, it would make it easier for me to hate them. It did, for a while. But only until I saw that the Benedicts weren't at all evil like he said. The only evilness was in him." Jade dropped her head for a second before continuing. "I haven't known about you very long at all, but I knew before he did. He only found out recently."

"I can't believe I'm an aunt. I can't believe my mom

knew and never told me." Alyssa stopped; she didn't want to think about her anger at her parents. Instead she studied Jade. "I can see her in you, you know? My sister. Obviously, your most stunning feature is your Benedict eyes, but I see your mom in the shape of your nose and the way you hold your head."

Jade's eyes looked wet. "I don't remember her hardly at all."

"When we get out of here, I'll tell you anything you want to know about her."

"If you have a plan on how to get us out," Kipling said, "now would be a great time to fill us in. You didn't by chance happen to call the police or someone in the family before venturing onto Germain's property, did you?"

"I tried calling Knox and Keaton, but got voicemail from both of them. I didn't call anyone in law enforcement, because I wasn't sure how their loyalties lined up." In other words, she wanted to say, but didn't: We're screwed. "I wish I had a plan, but I've got nothing."

"Do you think you can reach inside my front pocket if we shift around a little?" Jade asked Alyssa. "I have some things that might be useful. If they're still in there."

Alyssa starting shifting, trying to get close enough.

"I swiped a key from one of the guards a few days ago," Jade said. "It might fit on these chains. It's in one pocket. I have a throwing star in my back pocket. I only got it a few minutes ago when I lifted it from the knife table without anyone seeing."

Alyssa worked harder. She had to get the key before Howard came back in. Had to. She pulled it out of Jade's pocket seconds before the door to the small room opened and Howard walked in, holding a gun.

"Time's up," he said. "I have a private jet on its way to take me out of the country. I hope you've all said your peace."

CHAPTER 16

Alyssa had never seen another person look so deranged and so completely devoid of anything resembling humanity. She hoped she had enough time to free her hands before he started shooting.

"I was down the hall, trying to decide who I wanted to shoot first, but I couldn't, so I thought I'd let you guys decide." He pointed the gun at Jade. "Should it be the lost little sister no one cared enough about to find?" He pressed the barrel of the gun against her forehead. "Guess who cares if I shoot you? No one. I could shoot you dead right here and now and I bet no one would even cry."

He held the gun still for a long moment. Alyssa was pretty sure no one dared breathe, though she worked as much as she could to unlock her arms, until he swung around and aimed the gun at her.

"Or should I shoot the unknown aunt? It's a sad story when you think about it. The young girl who loved history. Loved it so much and from such an early age that there was never any doubt in her mind about what she wanted to do with her life. She wanted to immerse herself in history. Read about it. Write about it. Study it. Learn all she could about it and then teach others about it."

Alyssa gasped. How did he know all that? It wasn't like it was public knowledge.

"But then your sister shows up dead and no one can figure out who killed her and you made a promise to yourself that not only would you never stop looking until you solved your sister's case, but that you wouldn't rest until there were no more cold cases. An admirable goal, but you had to let history go, didn't you?"

She lifted her chin, refusing to let him get to her. And yet the gun was still pointed at her.

"What a miserable life. Unable to do what you want because of a promise you made when you were a child? And of course, we can't forget your true shining moment. How for years you slept with a serial kidnapper and killer. I, for one, love the irony, but it's probably distressing to you. I'd probably be doing you a favor by shooting you."

Alyssa's body shook. She fully expected him to pull the trigger, which was why she was so shocked when he stepped away and took aim at Kipling.

"Then maybe, I tell myself, I should cut off the head first. The mighty Benedict firstborn and heir. But even I know that's not a good enough reason to kill someone. Surely, if I think hard enough, I can think of a reason to not only justify killing you, but also for shooting you first. And then I remember that you're the reason for everything, every life ruined, every life taken."

It was such a preposterous statement, Alyssa stopped working the key in order to hear how that was at all possible. Kipling didn't say anything, but she saw the confusion in his eyes. Even Jade looked surprised and Alyssa thought she knew just about everything pertaining to The Gentleman and his motives.

"You were conceived before your parents were married," Howard continued, but that still didn't make sense. What did that have to do with anything?

"Your mother, of course, knew she was expecting." Howard didn't stop, he was excited to tell this unknown detail to them. Alyssa could tell by the way his body trembled. "When I approached her the night before her wedding and begged her to run away with me, she wouldn't do it because of you. So you see, if it hadn't been for you, Helen would have been mine and none of this"—he swept his arm—"would have had to have happened. That means it's all your fault. You know, it's funny. I used to blame your dad, but he's not the real culprit. The real problem is you."

Howard looked from Kipling to her to Jade. "I don't care which one of you dies first, but I'm not going to decide. Jade, give me a number."

Jade didn't hesitate. "Fuck you."

Howard took aim at her. "Last warning."

Jade lifted her chin. "Fuck. You."

Howard shot her in her leg. "Give me a number."

Alyssa was shocked that the young girl hadn't cried out at all. There were only a few tears on her cheeks to show she was even hurt. "Jade," Alyssa said. "He's going to kill us all. Give him what he wants."

Howard actually smiled. "That might be the smartest thing I've ever heard you say."

"And no matter what," Alyssa said, doing her best to tune him out. "I'm thrilled to be your aunt. I want you in my family very much." She had rolled herself so Howard couldn't see her mouth, but Jade could. Hoping the young woman understood, she mouthed *I'm free. Go big,* and nodded.

Jade addressed Howard, "Nine hundred ninety-nine thousand."

Alyssa was willing to bet The Gentleman's face was priceless. As it was, he sounded totally out of character when he replied, "What was that?"

"That was my number," Jade explained.

It was the opening Alyssa was waiting for. "It's a ridiculous number, Jade," she said. "You should have picked something like three. You can count that. You can't count nine hundred ninety-nine thousand. I mean seriously, try it." This was it. Their only chance of escape. "One. Two. Three."

She had a slight jump on The Gentleman. It wasn't until she hit three, that he realized something was up and she wasn't only counting to show Jade what a ridiculous number she picked. But by that time, she had already acted. Having unlocked the lock seconds before, when she counted three, she rolled over and reached for Jade's back pocket. Jade shifted slightly, allowing her access. In one move, she grabbed a throwing star, hurled it at the hand The Gentleman held the gun with, and rolled them both out of the way of potential bullets.

She heard The Gentleman howl. Hoping against hope that she had struck him, she risked a glance at his hand. He no longer held the gun. It had dropped to the ground when the star hit his wrist.

Alyssa dove for the gun. Howard's face turned a brilliant shade of red right as he realized he could not reach the gun before she could. But that didn't stop him from kicking it out the way. Or at least trying to.

But Alyssa was faster and grabbed the gun before he could reach it with his foot. However, he did end up kicking her in the wrist. Gritting her teeth, she rolled the opposite direction from him, lifted the gun, and shot him between the eyes.

It seemed liked everything shifted to slow motion as his body first jerked backward and then fell forward. Alyssa thought he was dead, but she rose to her feet to check. Satisfied that no one would be alive following a gunshot to the brain, she dropped beside Jade and unchained her first.

"We need to get out of here, quickly, before those other two men show up." Alyssa didn't understand why Jade wasn't moving faster. Didn't she know they weren't out of danger yet?

Jade rubbed her wrist where the bindings had been while Alyssa went to work to unlock Kipling. "I'm almost positive we'll find their bodies somewhere in the building," Jade said.

"You think he killed them?" Alyssa asked.

"I'm almost positive," Jade said. "He told us he was planning to leave the country, right? If that's the case, he wasn't about to leave anyone behind. He'd never planned to leave anyone alive."

"How about the pilot?"

"Unless he's changed a lot in a short amount of time, he never had a personal pilot. I imagine it's the same charter service he's always used."

That was at least one thing to feel good about. She quickly unchained Kipling, growing more and more concerned with each second that passed. His eyes looked glassy again, worse yet, his speech was slurred when he spoke.

"Is he gone?" he asked. "Because all of a sudden I don't feel so good."

Alyssa called his name over and over as he lost consciousness.

CHAPTER 17

Alyssa paced back and forth across the floor of the hospital waiting room. Kipling had been in surgery for several hours. No one was telling her anything about his condition and she couldn't imagine anything worse. But then again they weren't telling his family anything, either. They had all showed up: Keaton and Tilly, Knox and Bea. Even Lena. Only to be told absolutely nothing, other than that Kipling had been alive when he arrived at the hospital.

Before leaving the beach, they called in officers from an adjoining county. As it turned out, Jade was right. On the way out they ran across two dead bodies. Both of the men who had restrained them earlier, both with their throats cut.

Jade herself had been relatively quiet since returning from having her leg looked at. She spoke to no one. Choosing instead to sit in the corner of the hospital waiting room. Alone. Just as Alyssa suspected she spent most of her life. That would change, and she hoped soon. Right now, of course, everybody was too worried about Kipling to think about much of anything else. Alyssa felt sick with the uncertainty of it all.

It was another two hours before anybody cracked open

the door to their waiting room. When the doctor entered the room, he looked tired, like he'd just fought in a mighty battle. And lost.

He looked around, quietly taking them all in.

"Benedict family?" he asked, with no emotion in his voice at all except for fatigue.

As the second oldest, Knox stood and took a step forward. "Yes," he said. "We're all Benedicts here."

The doctor nodded toward a group of chairs that looked like they could handle them all. "Let's have a seat."

There was nothing hopeful about anything that was happening, Alyssa thought.

She felt like crying. She couldn't lose him. Not now. Not after he told her he loved her. After they escaped everything. Tears prickled her eyes and the doctor hadn't even said a word yet.

"He's alive," the doctor finally said. "I'm afraid that's the only good news I have at the moment."

Tilly turned her head into Keaton's chest and sobbed softly. Keaton looked like he was in shock. Lena prayed.

Someone nudged her hand and she looked down to find it was Jade. Her niece gave her a careful smile, but for the most part looked unsure. Alyssa wanted nothing more than to pull her close in a tight hug, but was afraid that would scare her, so she settled for squeezing her hand.

"He has many severe internal injuries," the doctor continued. "The next twenty-four hours are going to be the most critical, but I have to be honest with you, it doesn't look good. You need to prepare for the worst."

No one had expected to hear that Kipling's condition was that critical and the doctor's prognosis left the group speechless. Knox finally coughed.

"Can we see him?" he asked, and his voice broke at the end. Bea sat at his side, holding his hand. Alyssa had never seen her look so pale.

The doctor sighed. "Typically, I'd say no, but to be honest, I don't think it's going to make a difference. Try to keep it to two at a time."

Knox nodded.

The doctor stood. "I'll let the nurse know to come get you when he's settled."

They moved as a group back to the other section of the waiting room. She kept holding on to Jade's hand since her niece didn't seem in a hurry to pull it away. She wasn't sure who was more surprised when Tilly walked over to them and took a seat beside Jade, her or her niece.

She knew Tilly was a sweetheart, but she also knew that out of all the Benedicts, Tilly had always had a major problem with Jade. Alyssa looked around to try and catch Keaton's eye and try to get a feel for what his fiancée was thinking. But at the moment, he was consoling Lena.

She told herself she didn't have to tell Tilly that now was not the time to have a long drawn-out discussion. Even Jade looked worried. But Tilly's smile was friendly and Alyssa felt herself relax.

"You know," Tilly said. "I don't think I've ever thanked you for helping Keaton with the secret passage. I might not be here today if it wasn't for you. Thank you."

Alyssa discovered at that moment that Jade had a beautiful smile.

They let Alyssa go by herself to see him. She knew the others had used their time to tell him good-bye. Though she had planned to do the same, as soon as she walked into his room and saw him, she knew she couldn't do it.

She pulled a chair over to his bed and sat down. His left hand was above the covers and was one of the few parts of him that wasn't either bruised or had a needle in it.

They'd been told he was in a medically induced coma and therefore would not be responsive. But she knew the brain was a curious thing and even though he might not be able to respond, there was a possibility that he could still hear. And right now she was counting on that.

She took hold of his left hand and studied it. Remembered how a few short nights ago, that same hand had loved her. The words hadn't been said between them, but their bodies knew. She stroked her fingers from the top of his wrist, across his knuckles, and down to his fingertips. She'd been told he wouldn't respond, but it still upset her.

She sniffled. "I'm supposed to be telling you good-bye, but I refuse. You don't get to leave me after telling me you love me. Do you hear me, Kipling? You can't leave me. So take as much time as you need to heal, but don't even think about cutting out early." She closed her eyes. "I love you, Kipling. Don't leave me."

But even as she said it, she wasn't sure if she was making things harder or easier. Maybe she should tell him good-bye, just in case she didn't have the opportunity to again. What if he died tonight? And she hadn't told him goodbye?

She dropped her head as the tears started to fall and if it hadn't been for that, she'd have missed it. His left hand twitched. They'd tell her later that it was an involuntary response, but she knew the truth. It probably wouldn't be days or weeks, but he was coming back to her.

And if she had to wait for years for him, she would.

CHAPTER 18

Two weeks later, there had been little, if any change. The medication used to keep him in a coma had been gradually reduced until there was nothing keeping him under. And even then, there was still no change.

At times, Alyssa would wonder if she made up seeing his fingers twitch. But she knew she had, even if she only ever saw it happen that one time. And even if no one else ever did.

The first few days, everyone stayed at the hospital. After that, especially when it became apparent that change would not happen quickly, only one of the two brothers stayed at a time. Alyssa supposed that was a negative about a family business, you had to do everything. Alyssa stayed at the hospital almost all the time.

She told them all she couldn't stand the thought of Kipling waking up and not being there. They understood, she knew they did, but that didn't mean they didn't keep trying to get her to leave for a while. The few times she attempted it, it was horrible. She kept wondering what was happening at the hospital and checking her phone to make sure no one had called or sent a text.

She hated her house. Hated that even though she knew

better, she still didn't feel safe in it. Ninety-nine percent of the time, she felt like a fish out of water. The only time she felt remotely normal was when she was in Kipling's room. It didn't matter that their conversations were one-sided or that no one was even sure if he could process or understand what was happening around him.

Jade stayed in the hospital with her and she truly enjoyed getting to know her niece. The young woman was unsurprisingly timid at first, but as they talked more, the timidity disappeared. At times, Jade would move in a certain way or she'd have an expression that looked so much like Allison, it took Alyssa's breath away.

Recognizing her niece was homeless, Alyssa offered her the keys to her place and told her to make herself at home. She thought she'd jump at the chance, but Jade seemed uninterested, choosing instead to stay in the hospital waiting room and keeping her company.

She grew to know the nurses who cared for Kipling, though she was quite sure she wasn't imagining the looks of sympathy they gave her. Being in the hospital gave her time to think. At times that was a double-edged sword because no matter what she thought, it always ended up circling back to Kipling.

After two weeks, it felt as if everyone was close to losing faith. Even Tilly, who had always been the most positive, stopped talking about how any second now he would wake up.

Of course they still really had no idea about what he had endured at Howard's hands before Jade and Alyssa saw him. What little they had pieced together from the doctor didn't quite tell the whole story. To be honest, Alyssa wasn't sure she wanted to know.

She was sitting in Kipling's room with Jade and though they spoke about what had happened that night with Howard, they'd never done so in Kipling's hospital room before. It only came up then because, crazy as it sounded, Jade had been told the day before that Howard had left her a sizable fortune in his will.

"I've decided I'm going to keep it," she told Alyssa. "But I'm going to use it to open a home or halfway house or something." She looked up with the smile that was coming easier and easier every day. "You know, something that he would have despised but that I could do a lot of good with."

"I think that's a great idea." Alyssa was working Kipling's arm the way the physical therapist had shown her. "In fact, you may want to speak with Keaton and Tilly. You might be able to start it under the Benedict Community Development Division."

"Yes!" Jade laughed. "That would have pissed him off even more."

"Is this something you want to do and not something you're just doing for spite? Opening that sort of property is a wonderful idea, but you don't want your life's work to be dictated by hate."

Jade didn't answer and she grew so quiet Alyssa glanced her way. Jade pointed to Kipling. His eyelids fluttered.

Alyssa turned and almost shouted. "Kipling! Can you hear me? Are you awake? Jade, get the nurse!"

She didn't dare breathe as she watched his eyes slowly open. "Alyssa," he whispered, his voice raspy and coarse from disuse. "I couldn't do it. I couldn't go. They wanted me to go and I almost did. But I couldn't leave you."

CHAPTER 19

His recovery was slow and oftentimes painful, but he was determined, and the hospital staff said that made all the difference. Even so, the air held a slight chill by the time he was finally able to go home.

"I'm never leaving this house again," he said once he walked inside. "Knox, can you ensure that happens?"

Knox shook his head. "Make you into a recluse? I don't think so."

"Damn. Keaton?"

"No can do, bro," his youngest brother replied.

Lena stepped into the hallway and appeared as if she wanted to say something but the words didn't make it out.

"Lena." Kipling walked the few steps to her and hugged her. "Something smells delicious. I hope you haven't overdone it cooking for me."

"There is no such thing as overdoing it on the day one of my boys comes home and you know it. You must be starving; that slop they call food in the hospital is disgusting."

"I can't disagree with you there." He put his arm around her and followed her into the kitchen where she promised his favorite chocolate chess pie waited.

Alyssa's spirits soared even higher watching the two of them disappear into the kitchen. She looked around for Jade but her niece wasn't there.

"She walked away from the house as soon as she got out of the car," Bea said. "I called after her, but she didn't stop. I'm almost positive she heard me."

Though she wished Jade had stayed, Alyssa understood why she left. In a way she felt the same. With Kipling home now, it was time for her to make the long-dreaded return to her own house. She looked toward the kitchen. Later. At the moment, she had a hot date with a hot man and some chocolate chess pie.

Kipling gave her a quick kiss after she sat down to eat pie. "Where's my sister?"

"Bea said she walked away as soon as she got out of the car. She has a phone; I can text her and see if she is coming over."

"Maybe in a little while. I don't want to come across as the older brother who always has to know where she is." But she thought he looked worried.

"What is it?" she asked.

"Do you think she wants to be here? I just assumed, but I think . . ."

She placed her hand over his. "I think she does, but I also think it might be difficult or at least more difficult than she thought it would be."

"Knox said she hasn't been over very much."

Alyssa knew she hadn't been. Jade had been spending most of her free time at Alyssa's. "No, but I'm sure that will change now that you're home."

"This house will be very quiet soon." Kipling looked around the kitchen. "Knox and Bea's house is almost ready for them to move into. And Keaton and Tilly will be getting married soon. I imagine they'll probably start looking for a new place to stay before long."

The doorbell rang and Alyssa watched to see if Kipling was going to get up to get it. He'd just taken a bite of pie. "I'm going to be lazy and let Lena get it. I don't feel like seeing anyone other than family today anyway."

But within seconds they heard footsteps coming down the hallway. They both turned to see who it was and were surprised to see Jade walking behind Lena. The housekeeper looked all out of sorts.

"If I've told this girl once, I've told her a thousand times, she doesn't have to ring the doorbell. Mr. Kipling, aren't you going to—"

"Not yet," he interrupted. "Have some pie, Jade."

"I will in just a minute. First I wanted to show you both what I've been working on for the center."

As suspected, Keaton and Tilly loved the idea of the center Jade proposed and had been helping her get it off the ground.

Jade pulled out her phone. "They sent a message telling me the sign was ready. I went by to get a picture so I could show you." She held the phone out so both her and Kipling could see.

Alyssa's hand flew to her mouth. "Jade . . ." she started, but got choked up. Kipling put an arm around her and gave her shoulder a squeeze. "I love it," she finished, looking over it again.

THE ALLISON GRANT SAFE HOUSE

"Perfect," Kipling added.

"You know that's why he didn't know you were my aunt. The different last names."

Alyssa nodded. "She kept our biological dad's name, but my mother had mine changed when my stepdad adopted me."

"Either way," Jade said, "I'll never forget standing there and hearing Howard say he'd never be bested by a Benedict. I can't believe he was actually right about something. He was brought down by an Adams."

"Semantics," Kipling surprised her by saying. "She'll be a Benedict. I was just waiting for the right time to ask."

Alyssa felt like she was in a dream as Kipling stood, turned to face her, and knelt on one knee. "I've been wanting to do this since I woke up in the hospital, but I made myself wait until I got home. Although I have to say I never pictured it taking place in the kitchen. I have, however, had this in my pocket all day, in case the perfect moment arrived." He reached into his pocket and pulled out a stunning solitaire diamond ring. "Alyssa Adams, will you make me the happiest man alive and marry me?"

She didn't hesitate. "Yes."

She barely got the word out before the ring was on her finger, she was in his arms, and his lips were on hers.

"About time," she heard from the next room, along with, "Do you know he had that jeweler come to the hospital *three* times while you were out?" She pulled away to see her soon-to-be brothers-in-law along with Tilly and Bea smiling and clapping. She wasn't able to return to the kiss because everyone wanted to hug and congratulate them.

But the biggest surprise came when Kipling addressed Jade.

"I've been talking with our family attorney and if you want—and I hope you do—he has the papers prepared to change your name to Benedict and at my request Lena has been supervising the renovation of some guest rooms for you. We want you as part of our family. Never doubt it."

Alyssa looked at Jade just in time to see her hands fly to cover her mouth and to hear her softly spoken, "Yes."

Kipling leaned over to whisper in Alyssa's ear, "You can do whatever you want with my room as long as you stay with me forever."

"I think that's a rather remarkable deal Mr. Benedict. I accept."

"Best one I've ever made or will make," he said before claiming her lips again.

Read on for an extra bonus scene

Kipling Benedict seemed to have lost his bride.

That itself was a bad enough problem, but add to the fact that today was his wedding day, and that his brothers had just started picking on him about losing his bride?

"Seriously, Kip?" Keaton asked, though the smile on his face was huge. "You already ran her off? It hasn't even been twenty-four hours yet. I thought for sure you'd at least make it forty-eight."

He seemed to be on the verge of saying more, but Tilly took his hand and told him to be nice.

Kipling discreetly excused himself from the small party of guests present at Benedict house. It had only been about three months since he had been released from the hospital. Neither he nor his missing bride, Alyssa, had wanted a big wedding. Instead, they wanted a day to focus on themselves and their love, not to be a big production.

As his best man, Knox had been the first to give a speech. He stood sheepishly, gave the bridal couple a big smile, and turned to face the crowd. "I almost turned him down when Kipling asked me to be his best man," he started. "Not because I wasn't honored or because I didn't want to do it. But because I was afraid of this very moment.

*Of giving a speech. Of trying to somehow convey to you
the love that this couple has for each other."*

The ceremony itself had been held in a local church, a
few hours before, and had been so emotional, very few of
those present had left with dry eyes. Even Jade, who had
been Alyssa's Maid of Honor, had cried. The reception
was being held at their house. It had been a wonderful
day. Except for his lost bride.

*"As you know, this has not been an easy year for the
Benedicts. And Kipling and Alyssa have faced even more.
Yet, here they are, more in love than ever, knowing they
can face what comes ahead, because they've already
faced the worst.*

*"But before I could turn my brother down, I heard
something. It was actually from my own wife. I'm not sure
what she was talking about, she wasn't talking to me, you
see. But she said, love is a verb. That stuck with me and I
thought about it for days. And I ended up accepting when
Kipling asked me to be his best man."*

He went around the house trying to find her. The thing
was, he knew Alyssa better than anybody, and he knew
she hadn't run out on him. Though truth be told, nobody
else believed that either. Not after the way she had refused to move from his side while he was in a coma or
during the months of intensive physical therapy after he
woke up.

No, if he had to guess, his wife had to go somewhere
quiet for a moment. To get away from the hustle and bus-
tle, and just breathe for minute. She was so very much
like him in that manner. He had learned out of necessity
how to ignore that part of himself, but she had not, nor
did he ever want her to.

Suddenly, he knew exactly where to find her.

*"I don't have a lot to say, but I want to tell you this.
Love is not a feeling. It is not an emotion. It is not that*

thing your stomach does when the person you like walks in the room. Love is a verb. Love is action. Love is doing.

The couple before you today has proven that over and over. Love is a verb. Love is sitting by a hospital bed refusing to believe the doctors when they say there is no hope.

Love is remaining by that hospital bed for months of physical therapy, when it appears that it's not doing any good.

Love is telling your brothers to guard the hallway and set an alarm if a certain someone comes by so you have time to get the jeweler out of your room before she sees him. All because you want to surprise her."

He walked down the stairs and down the hall to her favorite room. The sunroom. In the summer, it was his favorite place to rest, to think, and to just be quiet. In the winter, however, especially around Christmas, the room became magical. And since it was Christmas Eve, he had a feeling that was where she'd be.

She didn't hear him approaching. So he was able to stop for a few seconds and just watch her. She was, of course, beautiful. She still had her wedding gown on and she looked like the queen she now was. Sexy. Awe-inspiring. Regal. All those and more. That was his bride. His wife. His everything.

"Love is looking at a sister, and admitting you were wrong. It is both asking for forgiveness and giving it.

Love is putting aside the hate and the heartache and the disappointment that have been with you your entire life, and reaching out to accept the unknown, because for this one time, you believe the thing you never thought possible just might happen for you.

Love is letting nothing come between you. Not the bad things. Not the good things. Not anything. Because you know it is only together you can make it."

Currently she was looking out the window. The one

next to the Christmas tree she stood beside. The white lights on the tree gave everything a romantic glow, and he almost laughed. Ten minutes ago, he'd have made a vow the day could not have gotten more romantic. It appeared he was wrong.

"I stand before you today a lucky man. A lucky husband. A lucky brother. Because not only have I seen love, but I also live it. With my wife, and with my family.

No, the last year has not been easy for the Benedicts. Yet, oddly enough, it has been good, because it has shown us what's important and because it has given us so much. And I'm so delighted that from this horrible journey my brother and his new wife, Alyssa, have found each other.

So I ask you to raise your glass, to Kipling and Alyssa. May you always remember that love is a verb."

Before he could talk, she saw his reflection in the window and laughed softly. "Let me guess, Keaton is already bugging you about losing your wife?"

He shoved his hands in his pockets and moved to stand next to her. He reached out to brush away a piece of wayward hair from her face and kissed the spot just under her ear. The one that drove her wild. "Yes, even after I told him there was nothing you could've found out about me that would have made you leave."

Because she knew all his secrets and loved him anyway.

"His wedding with Tilly is next June. Let's think up ways to get him back," she said.

She turned to face him, and gave him that grin that she reserved only for him. The one he felt in his very soul. "I always knew you were my better half, now I know it for a fact. You're just as devious as I am. It's actually even worse from you because nobody expects it."

She would never agree with him on that. She claimed

she was not devious at all, even though truthfully he thought she knew better. No, in fact he was pretty much sure she knew the truth. She was much more devious than he was, she just didn't want to argue tonight.

He leaned down and gave her a soft kiss, whispering in her ear, "If you aren't running away from me, what are you doing all by yourself?"

"I would have thought you would've known," she said. "I was waiting for you."

He wrinkled his forehead. "You were? Whatever for?"

"It's our wedding day, right?"

"Yes," he said because she seemed to be waiting for an answer.

"And tomorrow's Christmas?"

"Yes," he said again.

"I need to give you your present."

"Now?" he asked.

She nodded. "I have one for you tomorrow, but this one is extra special and I needed to tell you tonight."

"Oh?"

"I went to the doctor yesterday."

He frowned. "You did?" He knew she had been tired lately. They had both chalked it up to wedding preparations, moving her stuff to Benedict House and the holidays. He hadn't known it was so bad she needed a doctor. Nor could he understand why she hadn't told him.

"Yes."

He cleared his throat. "I don't want to be overbearing or anything, but in the future, I need to know if you're so sick you have to go to the doctor."

She still wore that soft smile. "Absolutely. In fact, it just so happens there will be lots of doctor visits in my future."

His heart threatened to stop and he took hold of her shoulders, gently. "My God, Alyssa. Are you that sick?"

"I'm not sick at all." She must have recognized he had no clue what was going on because she added, "Daddy."

There was a strange buzzing sound in his ears and he felt himself smile as the word sunk in. "Run that by me again."

This time, she took his hand and placed it over her still flat stomach. "Daddy."

He didn't try to stop the tears as he took his wife in his arms and whispered how happy he was and how much he loved her.

It appeared he hadn't lost his wife after all. He had in fact, gained the world.

WANT MORE *SONS OF BROAD*?

Read on for the third novella
in this swoon-worthy series
by Tara Thomas

TWISTED END

CHAPTER ONE

This wasn't the way Janie Roberts had imagined dying.

Not that she thought about such things often, but when she did, she always envisioned it occurring much, much later in life. In her sleep and surrounded by family who would reminisce about her full and satisfying life. She definitely did not picture herself drugged, tied up, and tossed in the back of her best friend's almost-fiancé's truck, being driven to who-knows-where and to have who-knows-what happen to her.

Her mind was fuzzy. Damn it. He'd injected her with something. Mac. Alyssa's boyfriend. But even then, she found it hard to believe. Why would Mac do such a thing? He knew her. How was it possible he'd been the one who'd been threatening her?

It had to be him. Nothing else fit.

Her mind kept going back to *why* and she came up with nothing. She finally had to admit that no matter how crazy it seemed, Mac had been the man they'd been looking for. The one behind several kidnappings, and more recently, murders. The man she'd worked undercover to find. The figure in the shadows who never hesitated to tell her he would kill her.

That was the thought finally able to snap her out of the drug stupor. Mac was going to murder her.

No. That wasn't part of the plan at all and she'd be damned if she'd let it happen. Unfortunately, deciding that was a small comfort. What she really needed was a plan for how to keep it from happening.

She tipped her head so she could see the sky out of the window and tried to imagine how much time she'd been out of it in the truck. She felt herself drifting in space and shook her head. Whatever he gave her must also cause hallucinations. She couldn't let herself be caught up in them.

She closed her eyes and tried to concentrate on how much time had passed since he'd thrown her into his truck. Not too long, if she estimated correctly. Surely, no longer than thirty minutes. Knowing that, she tried to determine which direction they were traveling or where he might be taking her, but she eventually had to concede she had no idea.

She'd been at a police cookout with her boyfriend, Brent Taylor. He'd told her going was a bad idea, he didn't think she should be out in such a public place. He had been worried because of the threats she'd been receiving. Pointing out that the last one indicated he wouldn't do anything for at least a week didn't make Brent feel any better about them attending. But she'd insisted because she was moving to Washington, DC with Brent and wanted to tell her friends goodbye. And then she once again pointed out that the madman who had been stalking her wouldn't make a move for another week.

Right. Because deranged lunatics with homicidal tendencies are known to be people of their word.

She bit back a hysterical snort because at that second, her phone started to vibrate from her back pocket. Odds were it was Brent. She sucked in a deep breath and told herself to focus on reaching her back pocket. The deranged lunatic in question had tied her hands behind her back, but he hadn't taken her phone. If she wiggled just the right way, she should be able to reach the button that would answer. Granted, she'd have to hope that whoever it was could hear her with the phone in her back pocket, but it was better than nothing.

Her heart raced as she tried to hit the button before the phone stopped vibrating. She arched her back and held her breath. So close. She strained against the rope that bound her. Almost.

Success!

She hoped.

She couldn't hear anyone and though she assumed it would be Brent and he'd be looking for her, there was a possibility it wasn't. Her only hope was that whoever it was would hear what was happening and alert the police.

"Damn it, Mac!" she yelled. "Where are you taking me? Untie me!"

"Answer your phone. Answer your phone. Answer your phone." Brent closed his eyes as he chanted, almost as if she would obey if he focused hard enough.

He looked at the woman standing next to him. Alyssa Adams. Mac's girlfriend and Janie's best friend, and Charleston police officer. She looked positively green. He wanted to believe she knew nothing about this, but what were the odds of her really being that oblivious?

Though she had been the one to tell him about Mac's DNA being on the boxes that had been found in Janie's house.

Janie's phone stopped ringing and he braced himself for the recorded message of her voice-mail greeting, but instead he heard the rumble of a car engine.

"Janie!" he shouted into the phone, capturing the

attention of several people nearby. "Janie! Are you there? Are you okay? Talk to me!"

"Damn it, Mac! Where are you taking me? Untie me!" Janie's voice yelled, and he felt a small twinge of hope. She wasn't dead yet. But that was the only positive observation he could make at the moment. The fact remained, she was tied up and at the mercy of a man who'd promised to kill her in a week's time.

"Is that her?" Alyssa asked, concern etched into her features. "Is she okay? Where is she?"

Not wanting to waste time talking, he hit the speaker button. From the other side of the phone came a muted maniacal laugh. Then, as if a bit further away from Janie, Mac spoke, "You better shut the hell up if you know what's good for you. I'm not stupid enough to untie you and you'll find out where I'm taking you when we get there."

Alyssa wore an expression of such horror, Brent knew she had no idea what her boyfriend had been up to. "Oh God," she said. "I'm going to be sick." She staggered to a nearby tree and lost her supper.

"Your truck's a mess," Janie said. "Did you know that?"

"I told you to shut up," Mac replied. "Keep talking and I'll shoot you now."

"I have to pee."

"Hold it."

"I don't know if I can. Do you really want me to pee all over your truck?"

He strained his ears to try and hear something. Janie sounded more determined than frightened. And if she was acting like she had to pee in order to try and get away, she wasn't close to giving up. This time, there was nothing from Mac. In fact, there was nothing but the sound of the truck engine for several long seconds. Brent didn't move, but stood frozen, looking at his phone as if he could tell where she was if he looked hard enough. Alyssa, still pale, walked back to listen.

He was getting ready to accept that he wouldn't hear anything else, when a rustling sound came over the phone.

"Ugh, what did you drug me with? I can't even sit up." Janie groaned, and he heard a thump.

Brent's blood boiled. The asshole had drugged her? "I get my hands on him, I'll rip him from limb to limb."

"Hey!" Mac yelled. "What are you doing? Get back down!"

Mac's command was followed by squealing tires and a shout from Janie.

"Watch the road, you idiot!" she yelled back.

"Don't tell me what to do," Mac said. There was another squeal of tires and a loud thump and the line went dead.

"Janie!" Brent cried. "Janie!" But there was nothing other than dead air.

"It could have been anything that ended the call," Alyssa said. Brent knew she was only trying to help, but he was mad as hell and worried to death and even though he knew it wasn't fair, he could feel his rage begin to direct itself toward her.

"I don't need to talk to you right now," he retorted.

Surprisingly, she must have understood. She simply nodded and said, "I'm going to put an APB out on his truck."

She didn't say it, but they both knew that Mac was intelligent enough to know that's what would happen and that he would most likely ditch his truck. Brent checked his phone again, just to make sure Janie hadn't called or sent a text, but there was nothing.

He was at a loss as to what to do. Alyssa would start the investigation with the police. They wouldn't welcome his help, but he'd be damned if he was going to sit around and do nothing. At the minimum, he could get in his car and drive around. At least then he'd feel like he was doing something useful.

He took off in that direction. The night sky was still lit up with bright yellows, orange, and red as a result of whatever Mac had blown up as a diversion to get Janie. He swore under his breath. How could he not know that it was Mac who'd threatened Janie? Above all, how did Alyssa not know?

The person they'd been looking for was responsible for the abduction of several women from the club Janie had worked at undercover. A homeless man, Charlie, had been killed shortly after Janie had taken him to a homeless shelter. That item fit Mac nicely as he was pretty certain Janie had called Alyssa about Charlie before deciding where to take him.

Whoever it was had also left numerous roses for Janie. Even going so far as to break into her house to deliver them. But if it was actually Mac and Alyssa kept a spare key of Janie's, he wouldn't have to break in.

His thoughts were interrupted by a uniformed police office he didn't remember seeing at the cookout who stopped him. "Excuse me. Are you Brent Taylor?"

"Yes," he said, not wanting to let himself get too hopeful. "Do you have information on Janie?"

The young man wrinkled his forehead. "Uh, no. It's about your car."

With those words and a quick glance toward the brilliantly lit sky, Brent knew exactly what Mac had blown up.

CHAPTER TWO

He'd pulled the truck over.

Janie wasn't sure if it had been his plan all along or if he was reacting to her attempts at distraction. Either way, there was a very real possibility that this might be her only chance at escape and she was going to do everything in her power to get away. She only wished she'd had more time so she could have tried to untie her hands.

She went over her plan in her mind, willing her limbs to cooperate even though she still felt heavy as a result of whatever he'd drugged her with. The driver's side door slammed and she heard him walk to the back of the truck.

Straining her ears, she tried to pick up any sound that would give an indication of either where he was or what he was doing. From the metallic clanking, she assumed he was taking the license plate off the truck. Did that mean he was leaving the truck here or changing the plates?

Not that it really mattered; neither one was a guarantee that he'd be opening the door to reach her or that if he was, he'd be opening the door she wanted him to. So many variables. And she didn't have time to work through them all. She wouldn't let herself dwell on the fact that so many

things had to line up exactly right in order for her plan to
work. It had to work. That was that.

Mac threw something in the truck bed. Not a sound for
a long moment, but finally she heard the sound of gravel
crunching under his feet. He wasn't heading back to the
front seat, he was moving toward the door on her side of
the truck. Her feet faced the door and she prayed they'd
move when she needed them.

Mac's shadow came near her and he stopped at the door,
looking down on her. He gave an evil smile and her hopes
plummeted. He wasn't going to open the door after all. He
was just going to stand there. Hell, he could shoot her
through the window and be done with it all.

He reached for the door handle and she worked to keep
her expression void of any emotion.

That's it.

Open the door.

Come on.

The door to the truck cab swung open. "I knew you
weren't good enough to untie yourself."

Not yet.

"Had to come and double check, just to be certain. I've
come too far to let a worthless thing like you fuck up my
plan." He leaned closer. "But I can see I was right."

Little bit closer, asshole.

"You're not near the challenge I thought you'd be." He
took a step forward.

Almost.

"I'm slightly disappointed." He loomed over her, eyes
wild, and a maniacal expression that would scare her if she
thought about it too much.

She took a deep breath. His next step put him exactly
where she wanted him. Using all the strength she had, she
screamed and lifted her legs, kicking him in the groin as

hard as she could. He crumpled to the ground with a cry of agony.

Knowing she had only seconds, she forced herself to sit up and scramble out of the truck. Her legs threatened to give way as she landed on the gravel shoulder of the road, but one glance at Mac revealed the gun he had tucked in his waistband and she found the strength to stand.

"That enough of a challenge for you?" she asked, jumping past him. With one last glance over her shoulder to confirm he was still huddled on the ground clutching his balls, she took off.

She didn't recognize anything and a quick glance revealed no nearby houses or businesses. She could be anywhere and because she wasn't sure of what his plan in stopping the truck had been, she couldn't trust anyone she came across.

The one thing she knew with certainty was that Mac was going to get backup and when he did, he'd be enraged and hell-bent on finding her. She needed to be as far away as possible when that happened. So, even though the road was the easiest way to travel, she ran off the road and into the surrounding trees.

Her legs protested as she ran. Her body was probably still working through whatever drug he'd given her. She tripped over a tree stump and cursed as she went down on her knees. She struggled to get to stand, finding it harder than she thought it would be without the use of her hands.

In the far distance, she saw a light of some sort. It was too far away to tell if it was a house, a person, or a car. Whatever it was, she couldn't take the chance of finding out. There was too much of a possibility that it was connected to Mac. And yet she stood there, hesitating, because it was light—and light could mean help.

Something slithered across her feet and she bit the

inside of her cheek to keep from screaming. Damn, she hated snakes.

It was the kick in the ass she needed to get her moving forward, but in a path that ran parallel to the light, not toward it. She wasn't going to risk it. Once she'd moved safely away from the light and where she remembered Mac being, she'd work on getting her hands loose and call Brent.

Plan in place, she took off.

Brent was finished arguing with the cop standing in front of him. "Look," he said, surprising himself at how calm his voice was when what he really wanted to do was shout at the man. "I get that it's a big deal that someone blew my car up, but like I said, there are actually more important things going on right now."

"Brent."

He looked toward the sound of his name and saw Alyssa standing there. "I'll take care of this," she said. "Can I have someone take you somewhere?"

"Thank you, but I'll call a cab." He appreciated Alyssa stepping in to help, but the sight of her only served to remind him of the danger Janie was in. Not to mention, he wasn't totally convinced he could trust her. "Shouldn't you be looking for your boyfriend?"

"I heard Mac was here," the cop who been asking him questions said to Alyssa. "Is he nearby? I'd like to see him, after. It's been ages.'

"I swear to God." Brent ran his hand through his hair and bit back what he wanted to say.

"Go," Alyssa told him. "Janie needs you."

He didn't stand around to argue, but gave her a curt nod and headed toward the entrance of the park. Surely he would be able to catch a cab there. He'd have the driver drop him off at his house and he'd get another car.

A fair number of people still remained in the nearby

vicinity. Granted, most of them were either law enforcement or first responders. He also took note of the news vans stationed around the park's perimeter and groaned. He wasn't in the mood to be interviewed at the moment.

Ducking his head and walking faster, he moved with one goal: to exit the park without being stopped. He'd almost made it when a particularly pesky reporter who had interviewed him several times jumped in front of him and shoved a microphone in front of his face. This was the problem with being a well-know philanthropist.

"Mr. Taylor," she said, in that happy, plastic-sounding voice anyone with a brain knew was fake. "Local police are saying it was your car that was blown up. Do you have anything you'd like to say?"

He took a deep breath and pasted on his own fake smile."No comment, Maggie. Excuse me." He stepped to the side.

She moved to block him. "You don't have anything to say?" she asked. "Really?"

"Really. Now if you'll excuse me." He tried to sidestep her.

"Who do you think is responsible for blowing your car up?"

"I'm letting the police work that out. No more questions, either move out of my way or I'll move you myself."

Janie had no idea where she was. Of course, it would have been more surprising if she did. Having grown up in the Charleston area, she would've thought she at least knew some of the area nearby. Perhaps Mac had driven her farther than she thought he had.

Something crawled up her arm. She swatted it away. She also would've thought that the swamp would be less crowded with critters at night. But then again, what did she know? It's not like she went camping or anything.

Probably, she'd be doing better if she weren't so tired. She wondered again what Mac had given her. There was no telling what sort of drug he had knocked her out with.

Her arm itched. Damn bugs.

She looked at her foot; the ground seemed to glow in the moonlight. If she weren't running for her life, she might have thought it was pretty. She wished Brent was close so she could talk about it and show it to him.

She wondered if he'd gone camping when he was a boy. He mentioned spending summers in Greece while he was growing up, but never camping. Did people camp in Greece?

She shook herself. This is crazy. Must be the after-effects of the drug he gave her. She never felt so loopy before. And being loopy on the run from a madman in the swamp was a bad thing.

From her training, she tried to remember how to ensure she was walking in a straight line and not just circling around. Moss grew on the north side of trees. She checked several nearby and proceeded to do so every so often. She could also use the north star. She looked up, but that only made her dizzy.

There were lightning bugs everywhere. She thought that was funny for a swamp. Did swamps have lightning bugs? She shook herself and muttered that it was just the drugs again. Obviously, swamps had lightning bugs. She was standing in one. And she saw them.

She yawned. Looking around, she tried to discover where she might sit down and rest for a while. Nowhere. She couldn't stop.

The light she'd seen before had disappeared. There wasn't much of a light left anywhere, just the overall glow of the pond. Or swamp. Wherever she was.

She was slowly going crazy.

She needed a doctor. A hospital. Anything.

She took a tentative glance over her shoulder. She didn't turn all the way around, for fear of getting lost. Just a quick glance. Nothing but trees and swamp.

She wondered what time it was and if it was almost morning. Would it get really hot during the day?

Would she even be alive during the day? Or would some swamp animal come upon her and eat her at night?

She tried reminding herself that she was a police officer, and that she couldn't give up that easily. But it was getting harder and harder the further and further she walked through the swamp.

She wondered what Brent was doing. When was the last time she saw him?

There had been a party?

Yes, that was it. An outdoor party. A cookout.

He hadn't wanted her to go. Said something bad would happen.

Mac.

She screamed. Then stopped immediately.

He'd been right.

"I'm sorry," she whispered to the night sky.

She was cold all of a sudden, which was stupid because she was in the swamp, it was summer, and it should be hot. She told herself again it was the drugs.

How long would it take to get them out of her system?

She licked her lips. She was really thirsty.

The best things she could imagine, at that moment in time, were water and a place to sleep. She laughed, looking around. There was nowhere to sleep. And knowing she was in the swamp meant she couldn't drink. No water but the swamp water.

Something rustled in the trees nearby. She shifted her glance over that way, desperate to see. But of course it was night. And it was dark. She couldn't tell what it was. She squinted, hoping that would make it better. But of course it didn't.

She took a step forward and stumbled over something. Holding her arms out to catch herself, she realized they were untied. She couldn't remember when that happened. But then she looked down and saw that she had stumbled over a tree trunk. The best part of it was that the seat had been sawed off and provided the perfect seat for her. It was close enough to the nearest tree to provide a back.

Without even thinking, she sat down on the stump. Indeed, the back was perfect for leaning against. She would just sit here for a few minutes she thought. Rest her eyes a bit. She laughed, remembering how her father used to say that.

She opened her eyes again, just to make sure she was alone. But apart from the lightning bugs and whatever it was that was determined to make a snack of her, she was alone. Knowing she might not be when she woke up, she looked around for anything she could use as a weapon. She found a long sturdy looking branch, but she was afraid that if someone got close enough for her to use it, they could possibly take it away from her.

She leaned it against the stump she was sitting on and continued her search. Her fingers brushed a rock that fit perfectly in her hand. If anyone showed up, she'd throw the rock at them. Maybe she wouldn't even need the branch.

She placed the rock in her lap and took a deep breath. The swamp seemed to melt away. She was in her bed. She was sleeping. Nothing had ever felt so good before.

She dreamed of Brent.

CHAPTER THREE

Brent made it to the street where he knew it'd be easy to pick up a taxi, except he didn't see any. But he did find Alyssa waiting in her unmarked car. He wanted to ignore her, but he told himself he was being ridiculous. Alyssa hadn't done anything wrong, and he'd always thought she was a good friend to Janie.

"I thought everything would go faster if we paired up," Alyssa said.

He hesitated for a moment. Did he want to pair up with Alyssa? Could he deal with the constant reminder that it was her boyfriend who had taken Janie hostage?

The officer seemed to recognize his conflict. "You don't have to, of course. I just thought I would offer." She went to pull out, and in that second Brett knew he'd be stupid to pass on her offer.

"Wait," he said. "I'll go with you."

She stopped the car and waited for him to get in. Before they drove away, she looked over her shoulder, as if expecting someone might be following her.

"Are you allowed to do this?" he asked. The very last thing he needed was to get involved in some internal conflict with the police department. All that would do is slow the hunt to find Jamie.

"Probably not, but I didn't ask, so technically speaking, I wasn't told no," she said. He waited for her to say more, but she only added, "At the moment, I want to get away from here before I say more." Alyssa looked over her shoulder once again.

He didn't like it, but he knew he had no other choice but go along with it. At least this way, he'd be the first one to get the information, right along with Alyssa. There was something to be said about that. In the end, that was the important thing. Anything that would help them find Janie faster.

"Where are we going?" he asked. Had she already received news about Janie? It didn't seem possible but she was certainly driving with a purpose somewhere.

"I need to stop by my place. The police are going to Mac's office and apartment, but his laptop is at my place."

"And you think not only are you going to be able to hack into it, but that he just happened to leave his master plan on his laptop for anyone to find?" He knew he sounded sarcastic, but truthfully, that was her plan?

"Yes," was all she said.

Her apartment took less than five minutes to get to. Once there, she parked the car, but left it running.

"I'm going to run inside to get the laptop," she said. "I'm not expecting anything, but if you see anything suspicious, drive away and we'll catch up later."

It very well could be the most ludicrous plan he'd ever heard. But since he didn't have a better one at the moment, he nodded. She moved to get out, but at the last moment looked over her shoulder to him.

"Also," she said, "if I'm not back in five minutes, assume something's happened and get out."

He nodded, even though hell would freeze before he'd leave her alone and in danger.

"No." She reached inside and placed her hand on his. "I mean it. Leave. It'll be up to you to find Janie. Promise me."

"Okay," he managed to choke out. "I promise."

She gave him a small smile and left. After that, time seemed to crawl. He watched the people who were out and about, but didn't see anything suspicious. Then again, who could say what was suspicious?

Alyssa appeared after four minutes, holding a laptop case and a duffel bag slung over her shoulder. She glanced around the parking lot and then jumped in the car, placing the laptop in the backseat and handing him the other bag.

"Police are on their way," she said. "We need to hurry."

He noticed she drove out the back part of the lot and seconds after they pulled out, several patrol cars with flashing lights entered through the front.

She waited until they'd driven about ten miles before she spoke again. "There's a tablet in that duffel bag. Can you get it out?" He opened it, while she kept talking. "About eight months ago, the department put GPS tracking devices on all our mobile phones. As long as Janie keeps her phone on, we should be able to find it."

"Wouldn't they have disabled it when they fired her?"

"They should have, but I doubt they did. With all the department has on their plate at the moment. I can pretty much bet it's a low priority. In fact, I'd be willing to bet whoever is supposed to do it, probably doesn't even know."

He nodded, but his mind was playing over her earlier words. Find *it*. He noticed she didn't say they would find *her*. Even so, his heart pounded. He followed her instructions and found the app and punched in the code that would hopefully pull up Janie's phone. He beat down hope, trying his best to remain neutral. "And if Mac and whoever he's working with happen to know about the GPS, they'll throw her phone out the window and head one-eighty in the opposite direction."

"True, but we know she had the phone on her for a while at least. Besides, it's the most we can do at this point, short of driving around blind and waiting for a new clue to drop in our lap."

"You surprise me, you know that?" he told her.

Alyssa's grip tightened on the steering wheel. "How's that?"

"It appears as if there's an eternal optimist underneath that no-nonsense exterior of yours." He paused, but knew he had to finish his thought. "That's probably why you get along so well with Janie. She's like that." Though his voice had started out strong, the last sentence was only whispered.

Alyssa glanced over at him, a look of fierce determination on her face. "We're going to find her. I promise."

He simply nodded and turned to look out the side window.

Janie slowly woke to the sound of her name being whispered. She squinted against the light. Where was she? And why couldn't she remember anything?

"Janie?"

She sat upright. Someone *had* called her name. She hadn't imagined it.

She held her breath and glanced around the area, hoping against hope it was anyone other than Mac. At first she didn't see a soul, but once she'd looked over the area without any luck, she looked again. Slower this time. Straining to see if she saw anything that didn't look right or if any of the many shadows moved.

"To your left," the voice whispered and while it didn't sound like Mac, she couldn't say with any certainty that it was Brent.

But then he stepped out of the shadows and she nearly wept. "Brent," she managed to get out in a choked voice.

He smiled so big, it nearly covered his face. "Oh my God, Janie. Are you okay?"

Then neither one of them could talk because they were both on their feet, making their way through the muck, trying to get to each other. She tripped over rocks, sticks, and even her own feet to get to him. Finally, she collapsed in his arms with a sound that was a combination of a sob and a laugh, but he was making his own made-up noises, so somehow it didn't matter.

His lips found hers and he was kissing her as if they'd been apart for months instead of mere hours.

"How did you find me?" she asked. "How did you know where to look?" But he shook his head and held his finger against his lips.

Her blood chilled. Mac hadn't been caught yet. He was still around and quite possibly nearby if the way Brent was acting told her anything.

She tilted her head. Was it strange that it was only Brent who showed up and not a group of police? At the very least, wouldn't Alyssa be with him? And surely it was beyond strange that other than the one question about her being okay, she was the only one who had spoken.

"We have something," Brent told Alyssa fifteen minutes later when the GPS tracking app finally pulled enough data to show a red dot at the location it estimated Janie's phone to be.

"About damn time," she said. "I thought I was going to have to throw that piece of trash tablet out the window. So tell me, where are we going?"

Brent squinted at the tablet to make sure he was reading it right. "Somewhere in the Francis Marion National Forest."

"He could hear the frown in her voice. "Why would he take her there?"

"I'm thinking the couple of hundred thousand uninhabited acres is a good enough reason. He could hide for days." And he didn't want to go any further down that path. Likewise, he was glad when she didn't say anything else. The silence gave him the opportunity to focus on the red dot that was currently his only tie to the woman he loved.

The scanner Alyssa had turned on crackled to life and she reached down to turn it up.

"I'm in Officer Adams's apartment," a voice that sounded like her partner's said. "No sign of her or Mac, but the place has been ransacked."

"You trashed your apartment?" he asked her.

But when he turned to look at Alyssa, her knuckles were white and her face several shades paler. "No," she whispered.

She was in Brent's ridiculously large antique tub. He'd just drawn a bath for her and promised he'd be back in just a minute to join her. As she waited, she sank down into the bubbles to where a few tickled her nose. She couldn't name the scent he'd used, but it smelled like sunshine. Or summer back when she was a kid and out of school and having nothing to think about except where she was going to ride her bike that day.

"Is that smile for me?" Brent asked, walking into the bathroom.

She couldn't reply right away because instead of waiting for her to answer, he started taking his clothes off. First, he toed off his shoes, then he slid his socks off. He'd unbuttoned his shirt before lifting his head as he waited for her to reply. He smiled.

"I took that to be a rhetorical question," she said. "But I'll answer any way you want as long as you finish what you were doing with that shirt and move on to your pants."

This time his smile turned into a laugh. She loved his laugh. It was deep and rich and never failed to send shivers up her spine.

She still couldn't keep her eyes off him. Especially as he stripped his shirt off. And most especially as his fingers drifted to the button of his pants. But then they stopped again and she almost whined.

"Janie," he said, but his voice was all wrong.

Heart pounding, she looked up.

He smiled, but it wasn't the smile that made her all warm and happy inside. It wasn't Brent's smile at all. She blinked. Brent was gone and the man in his place was partially hidden in the shadows.

"Ready for some fun?" the man that wasn't Brent asked.

She tried to get out of the bathtub, but found she couldn't move. Looking down, she realized she wasn't in a bathtub at all. She was bound to some sort of table.

Her eyes watered because even as she tried to pull and jerk against the rope that held her to the table, she knew it was a lost cause. She tried anyway.

He stood in the shadows and laughed. "I'm glad you're finally awake enough. I thought maybe I gave you too much the second time and ruined the game for everyone." He took a step forward and her heart raced. The light fell across his face and she screamed.

Mac. She hadn't escaped after all.

CHAPTER FOUR

They stopped at a remote part of the park that Brent estimated was about two miles from the red dot that represented Janie. There were several roads through the forest, but they'd decided on this one because it got them the closest. Which was why he didn't understand why Alyssa told him they needed to stop where they were. He paced back and forth in front of the car as Alyssa turned on the computer.

"I don't understand why we aren't getting closer." He spun around in the dirt and looked at Alyssa.

She didn't even look up from what she was doing. "Because the dot hasn't moved. So either it's just her phone or they've stopped for the night."

But he knew there was one other possibility that could explain why the dot hadn't moved. He wasn't going to say it out loud. It was bad enough it had been a thought in his head. He stormed over to where Alyssa was.

"What are you doing?" he asked.

"I'm getting into Mac's computer." She didn't stop her actions, but at least she was explaining what she was doing. "I know his username, and if I remember correctly and he hasn't changed his password . . ."

He looked down the road that would take them to Janie. Or at least the red dot that symbolized her at the moment. "Let's go."

"Hold on." She didn't even look at him.

"I've been holding, and I'm going to find her myself. If you want to come—" The rest of the sentence left him as Alyssa lifted the laptop up and showed him the bottom.

"Holy shit." Brent couldn't believe what he was seeing. "He taped his password to the bottom of his laptop?"

"He made it too difficult to remember. He thought he was being clever." She talked while she typed. Her hands paused. And then she spoke with a huge grin. "I'm in. Trust me on this. We need to take a few minutes to plan."

He took a deep breath, mentally gave her sixty seconds, and watched as she went into Mac's e-mail.

"It looks like most of his correspondence is with a man named Mr. G. That could be anyone." She scrolled some more.

"Did you have access to his laptop?"

"No, why would I?"

He shrugged. "I know some couples share that kind of stuff."

"I never even thought about going into his laptop. After all, I never offered to let him use mine."

He was getting ready to tell her that of course she wouldn't, but that she was a police officer, when she said, "This is interesting."

"What?"

"The last e-mail is from tonight and it's unread." She pointed to it and read the part visible in the preview pane. 'Why aren't you answering your phone? Call me immediately. What the hell have you done?'"

"So Mac's gone rogue?"

Alyssa nodded. "From the looks of it. Unfortunately, we

still don't know what he's up to because we don't know what his plan or orders were to begin with."

Brent was getting ready to say more, but the silence was broken by a sharp scream.

"Janie," he whispered.

Mac laughed, but there was meanness in his eyes. "Scream all you want, no one's coming."

"I don't believe you." And just to prove her point, she screamed again.

He was by her side almost immediately and slapped her face. Hard. She was so shocked that he'd hit her, she stopped. She could tell he was shocked, too. It occurred to her that maybe he didn't have any problem dealing with the other women he'd kidnapped, but he might with her. After all, she wasn't a nobody, a stranger, to him. She was his girlfriend's best friend. They'd shared meals together. That was when it hit her that she'd finally accepted that he was the man they'd been looking for. Then she realized that in knowing her, he also knew what she was capable of and that made her feel even stronger.

She hoped to God the drug he'd used on her had run its course. She didn't think she could handle one more hallucination. Not if it had Brent in it. She closed her eyes to block out every thought of him. She would need her mind completely clear if she was going to be able to pull off an escape. And at the moment, she had to focus on Mac and not Brent.

Mac hadn't liked hitting her. She needed to do more to remind him that he knew her. Rule number one: make them see you as a real person.

"Why?" she asked him. "Why me?"

He narrowed his eyes. "Why not you? What makes you so special that you should be spared?"

She shrugged or she shrugged as much as she was able, being bound to the table. Anything to keep him talking and to not show fear. "I don't think Alyssa will be very happy."

His eyes blazed and she struggled to hide her shock. She'd never seen him that animated before. He bent low and in doing so, put his face right in front of hers. "I'm doing this for Alyssa. I'm doing it to keep her safe. He promised me she'd be safe. So you can drop the game of *let's keep him talking so he realizes I'm a real person*. I know you're a real person, but I'm never going to pick you over her. And if that means I have to take you out, I'll do it. For her."

He spun around and mumbled to himself as he walked away. Janie let out the breath she'd been holding and called to his back, "It won't work that way, you know." Hell, did he actually think he was being noble in his actions? Was he planning on Alyssa thanking him? Was he that delusional?

Mac didn't turn around but he did stop.

"There's no way he'll let you go now," she told his back. It had always been a theory that whoever they were looking for was not working alone. Nice of Mac to confirm that. But she still had to keep him talking. "Not that easily. Especially knowing how far you'll go for her. He'll always be there, between you."

He still didn't say anything. In fact, she wasn't sure he even heard her. But then she saw it, he balled his right fist and let it go so quickly. She'd have missed it if she hadn't been watching him so closely.

"Are you going to let him have that much power over you?" She might be pushing him too far, but she had to do it.

She wasn't sure how much time she had left.

He spun around and the rage she saw reflected in his expression took her breath away. He lifted a fist. "Not another word."

"Brent, no." Alyssa put her hand on his arm as he turned toward the sound. "You can't just run off like that."

He grit his teeth because he knew she was right. They were close to her. She was alive. The smartest thing to do would be to stay calm and plan. He knew that.

But there was another part of him, a rather big part he could admit, that whispered just because she screamed didn't mean she was still alive. That part of him urged him to run toward where the sound came from and make up a plan on the way.

He wouldn't be able to live with himself if anything happened to Janie because he didn't head to her immediately. Hell, he was smart enough to know that no matter what happened, he didn't want to face the future without her.

Rather than giving into either side, he picked the option in the middle. He didn't ignore Alyssa's advice, but he didn't allow her to take him back to the car, either.

"You're killing me," he said. "If something happens to her and it's because we didn't run off the second we heard her . . ." He couldn't finish his sentence. It hurt too much to think, much less say out loud. He'd never felt more defeated.

But one look at Alyssa showed him she was feeling the same. "I know," she whispered. "Trust me. I know. But I'm also a cop and experience has shown time and time again that if we take a few minutes to plan, it works out the best for everyone."

With a silent nod, he allowed himself to be led back to the car. The entire time, part of him screamed inside that they were wasting time and that they needed to find Janie *now* and to hell with a plan.

It tore him up inside that he'd heard her screams and he knew the sounds would haunt him for a long time to come. The worst part was, he felt helpless at the moment. There was nothing he could do to save her. He'd never been helpless. He'd worked hard his entire life to avoid that very thing. Yet when it mattered the most, all his hard work was good for nothing.

Alyssa took him to where she'd set up the laptop on the hood of the car. "I've skimmed through his read e-mails and from what I can piece together, he's definitely acting rogue."

"What? He wasn't supposed to kidnap Janie?"

She flinched. "No. Not exactly."

"How do you *not exactly* kidnap someone?" He watched her carefully, making sure she didn't hold anything back.

"He wasn't supposed to kidnap her. He was supposed to kill her next weekend."

The ground underneath him tipped and for a second, he thought he was going to throw up. Even though the threats Janie had received had stated as much, to hear them verified only intensified his desire to run toward where he'd heard her and not rest until she was safe in his arms.

"We have to find her," he repeated to Alyssa. "Now."

"We are, but we can't run off without a plan. Look at this rationally."

His fear for Janie was rapidly turning into anger at Alyssa. "Don't you dare stand there and tell me to be rational when the woman I love has been kidnapped. By the man you're fucking, I might add."

She surprised him by staying calm. "I get that you're worried. I even understand your anger and why it's directed at me. But I need you to understand a few things. One, every time we argue, we're wasting valuable time that could be spent on Janie. Two, Janie is like a sister to me and I will fucking take down anyone who hurts her." A knowing grin covered her face. "And let's not forget, I know Mac better than anyone." At his raised eyebrow, she typed something on the laptop. "For example, I know that he doesn't handle sudden change very well. It's borderline debilitating to him. So if we wanted to completely wreck his plan . . ."

As she detailed her ideas, something that felt a lot like hope made Brent smile for the first time in hours. *Hang in there, Janie. Just a little bit longer. I'm coming for you.*

Mac was worried about something.

He stood in a far corner of the room, looking anxiously at his phone and muttering under his breath. And even though she wasn't close to him, she could feel the sweat appear on his forehead. He eventually looked up and caught her staring.

Shoving his phone in his back pocket, he walked toward her. "What are you looking at?"

"I'm trying to decide how long you've been tangled up in this mess." No matter what he'd said, she felt she had to keep him talking. When he did, he couldn't hurt her or give her more of that drug. "I'm also trying to figure out why you got involved in the first place."

His phone buzzed and he pulled it out of his pocket while he talked. "That one's easy. I'm actually surprised Alyssa didn't tell you all about it. Gambling debt."

Alyssa had never mentioned anything like that to her, but more unsettling was his remark. She wasn't sure why, but the way he spoke it, so offhandedly, made her wonder again if her friend had been aware of everything from the beginning.

She felt like a traitor to even think such a thing, but the

investigative part of her knew she had to consider it. The profiler on the case had always held the belief that whoever their suspect was, he also had some sort of "in" with the Charleston PD. What would be better than to have a girlfriend who was not only on the force, but was also working the case?

Janie searched her mind, struggling to find any clue that would corroborate the hypothesis of Alyssa playing both sides since the beginning. No matter how far back or how deep she looked, she couldn't find one. Nothing. Janie hoped she wasn't letting her friendship blind her.

Just the thought of their friendship was enough to bring back everything they'd gone through as friends. And they'd been friends as well as coworkers for years before Mac even appeared on the scene. All the late night girl chats on the phone. The many times they commiserated about the sorry state of any man over thirty with a pint of double mint chocolate chip and two spoons.

No. Alyssa wasn't involved. No way.

"Why are you so quiet all of a sudden?" Mac asked.

"Just wondering if Alyssa knew about everything this entire time and was just playing me." She found it was hard to get the words out.

She didn't think she'd ever seen anyone's face get so red so fast. "No," Mac said. "Keep her out of this. She has nothing to do with it."

For a second she was touched by Mac's seemingly protective assertion that Alyssa was blameless. But then he opened his mouth and blew that all to hell.

"She's much too weak to be involved," he said. "Like all women. She couldn't handle it. Women are good for one thing and it's not what they have between their ears."

"Yup," Janie said. "I'm beginning to see why she always put off marrying you. That's disgusting. Tell me, is she fully aware of your view on womanhood?"

"Of course not. I'm not an idiot. I was planning to wait until our honeymoon before telling her she had to quit the police force."

"Oh my God, you're serious. If you knew her at all, you'd know she'd never quit."

"She wouldn't have a choice. Besides, being a cop is too masculine a profession."

How was it possible Alyssa had dated him for as long as she had and not seen or at least sensed the monster inside him? "You're a real piece of work, you know that?"

He laughed. "Yes. And I have you here all alone. Think about how that's going to turn out for you." He leaned in way too close for her comfort and whispered, "You here with me. All alone and no one having any idea where you are."

CHAPTER FIVE

Brent's phone buzzed with an incoming e-mail. He glanced down, planning on ignoring it as he had with all the other e-mails that had come through that night. Yet a look at the subject line changed his mind. This wasn't any ordinary e-mail. It was the report on Mac's financial records that he had requested weeks ago.

Alyssa looked at him like he was crazy for reading an e-mail. Too bad. Though it was small, there was a chance the e-mail might contain something that would help Janie. He opened the e-mail, scanned it, scanned it again a second time, and closed it, full of rage.

"Alyssa," he said.

She looked at him, her eyes growing large at his expression. "Yes?"

"Did you not think it was odd, or at least a little bit strange, that your boyfriend had one and a half million dollars in gambling debts?" It took all he had to say the words, he was so mad he could hit something.

Alyssa grew pale. "One and a half million?"

Brent didn't have time for this, he just looked at her. And waited.

"One and a half million," Alyssa mumbled to herself.

"Don't act like you didn't know." He was so tired of all the lies and deception and cover-ups. When would someone give him a straight answer? "Don't play me for a fool."

"I have never lied to you."

"Perhaps we need to define the word *lie*," he said. "Because in my book, keeping information that you know is pertinent to an investigation, is very much a lie."

"Did I know he had gambling debt? Yes, of course. But when I found out, it was only a quarter of a million. And he told me he would get help."

"And you just believed him, and never questioned him? Honestly, I thought you were smarter than that." He really didn't need to sit here arguing with her over this, he needed to be out looking for Janie. He took a step away.

"Wait." She put her hand up to stop him. "You have to believe me. He was getting help, going to counseling. I saw that. You have to believe I didn't know about the one and a half million."

Brent had always considered himself a very good judge of character, and for some reason, he didn't think Alyssa was lying. He still wasn't sure how she didn't know about the money Mac owed, but he was going to believe her. Because even more than he believed in his own instincts, he believed in Janie and Alyssa was her best friend.

"It's very obvious what he did to get out of bed with his debtors. He agreed to work for them and to do their dirty work," Brent said. "Unfortunately, he got involved with somebody who is very dangerous. And they have Janie. So for now, the conversation about money has to wait. For Janie's sake."

They hadn't heard another scream from Janie. It was growing darker, and the dot representing her phone still hadn't moved. He had a feeling they were running out of time. Finding her was more important. Finding her had to be the priority. He looked over his shoulder. "Let's get back to work."

Alyssa eyed him warily, but otherwise seemed anxious to change subjects. "I suggest that we split up. He'll be expecting us to show up together and, like I said, surprises can damn well debilitate him. Two years ago, I decided to throw him a surprise party for his birthday. I thought he'd like it. Something different, you know? But when we got to his place and everyone jumped out and said, 'Happy Birthday,' he totally freaked out. Ran to the bathroom and wouldn't come out. It was awful. Later, he apologized profusely and said he'd always been like that. Said he couldn't stand it when things didn't go they way he planned for them to."

Brent nodded. "Any luck pulling up a satellite view of the surrounding areas?"

"There was only one I could access without putting in my personal details. It's over ten years old."

Brent's stomach sank. "Ten years . . . that doesn't do us any good. Too much could have happened."

"It's the best I can do. If I pull up anything newer, it's possible Mac or whoever he's working with will know, the newer images show the information of who has accessed them recently and I can't imagine a scenario that works out well for Janie."

It was on the tip of his tongue to tell her it was a chance he'd risk when she continued. "Look at this,'" she said while her fingers flew over the computer keyboard.

He leaned over her shoulder to have a look and when he caught sight of what she had pulled up on the screen, he gasped. "Holy shit!"

"Right?" Alyssa agreed as they both looked at what appeared to be a gardener's shed. It was the only building to be found anywhere near where they were. "It must be used as a storage unit, workspace, or outpost structure."

"Or all three. Where was this structure ten years ago?" He tried to imagine what it would look like today, but quickly gave up. There were too many variables. Had the shed been taken care of or had it been left to rot? Were there any people nearby or inside? And if there were, how would they know if they were in cahoots with Mac.

Alyssa pulled up more info on the screen. "Ten years ago, it was almost a mile that way." She pointed in the direction the scream came from.

His heart pounded. "That's it. It has to be."

She nodded. "I think so, too. So here's my plan: Because there are two paths that lead directly to the shed, we should split up. The darkness will help keep us hidden." She pulled up a map of the area and pointed out the two paths. "You take this south one. It's more direct so you'll get there before I will, but wait for me to arrive before you go in. I'll take this path that approaches from the north. We'll meet in this small clearing here, off to the side of the building once we both arrive and regroup." She pulled out her phone. "I still have service, do you?"

He checked his phone. "Yes. You don't think we should stay together and both of us take the shorter path?"

"When he sees you, he'll think you followed him or something. He won't expect me to be involved because he thinks women are weak and have no business being in law enforcement." At his raised eyebrow, she added, "That's my suspicion based on recent conversations anyway. And the truth is, he can't keep an eye on both paths at the same time."

"Not unless the guy he's working with is here and they're both watching a path."

She shook her head. "From what I've seen, the person he's working with didn't know what he had planned tonight. Knowing that, I can't imagine him being here yet."

"Tell me this. If Mac hates surprises, why would he pull one off?"

"I'm not sure."

Which was bad news all around for Janie.

Mac was talking on the phone. Again. Since she'd woken up the last time, he'd made three phone calls. She didn't know if they were all to the same people or not. What she did know was that with each call, Mac grew more and more agitated. The call he was currently on was no exception. Whoever he was talking with, he was damn near yelling at.

Call her crazy, but she wasn't all that thrilled about being around him when he got off the call, not that she was overly excited to be around him period. The only thing was, she really had to pee badly. Before, in the truck, she'd told him the same thing and he'd told her to just go. He'd probably known she was just saying that and didn't really have to go. Surely, if he knew she really, really, really had to go, he'd let her.

The phone call he was on had ended and she heard his footsteps as he walked back toward her.

"Mac," she said. "Can you untie me? Please? Just for a minute? I really have to go bad."

"Do you think I'm stupid?" he asked.

"Of course not. I just assumed you'd think of a way to make it work. Like give me forty-five seconds only. Or something."

He thought about it. "Forty. And you leave the door open."

That would never work. "Thirty-five and you leave it cracked."

He leaned over her while he undid the ties. "Deal. But if I see you try anything, hell, if I even *think* you're trying anything, I'll put an end to you and not think twice."

She had no idea how she would make things work with that little amount of time. But maybe she could use the first time in the bathroom to gain information about how he worked and what he did. That way, the second time he let her go she could have thought about all the possibilities and decided on a plan of action. It wasn't the best idea; heck, she wasn't certain she'd get to use the bathroom a second time. She just didn't see any other viable alternatives at the moment.

He jerked her off the table. "Come on," he said." Let's go."

It had been far too long since she stood and she stumbled over her feet. Resulting in a slap from Mac.

"Hurry up," he said. "Damn klutz."

He shoved her to the bathroom, leaving the door open just a crack as they had agreed upon. "You have thirty-five seconds."

She just made it to the toilet when there was a knock on the back door. Hope blossomed in her chest. Though why exactly, she wasn't sure. It was doubtful anyone looking for her or Mac would knock on the door.

"Anybody in there," an unfamiliar voice said. "Park rangers. Open up now."

Mac cursed under his breath. "Give me just a minute."

"Open this door now or we bust in."

Mac opened the door on her and seemed to be satisfied that she was in fact going to the bathroom. "I'm getting rid of them, then I'll be back. You don't try anything. Remember, I'll kill you."

Maybe he would kill her, but the way she saw it, she was dead either way. She was going to run because this might be her only chance to try. There was a low window in the bathroom. She quickly relieved herself, pulled up her pants, and opened the window when she heard the front door open.

"This is private property, sir," the ranger said. "And not only are you not allowed on it, you are not allowed in here."

Mac couldn't risk looking back at her, not with the rangers standing with him in the doorway. There was far too great of a chance that he would be discovered and she would be as well. It was a chance, but one she was willing to take. Before Mac could answer the park ranger, she was out the back window.

She thought about running toward the car that the rangers had arrived in and hopping in the back. Unfortunately, it was too close to the front of the house. Which meant Mac would definitely see her. He definitely had a gun. She wasn't sure if park rangers carried one, but she didn't think they did. If she alerted them to her presence, all she'd do is get them all three killed.

Therefore, even though she hated to attempt to run away at night, on foot, and unsure as to where she was, she would do it. She found an overgrown path nearby and started running. She didn't slow down to look over her shoulder. If Mac was following her, she would find out eventually. Right now she had to get away as far as possible, and as quickly as possible. Surely by now people were looking for her.

She reached in her back pocket and grabbed her cell phone. Two rapid gunshots sounded behind her and she jumped, dropping her phone. She glanced around for it, but couldn't find it. Obviously, Mac wouldn't be far behind. She needed to keep moving, even if doing so meant leaving the phone.

Mac looked down at the two dead rangers in disgust. It had not been his plan to shoot them, but they wouldn't listen to reason and kept insisting he travel with them. He couldn't do that with Janie in the bathroom. Nor could he figure out how to explain her presence to them. He wasn't sure if she had been listed publicly as missing yet, but he wasn't going take a chance.

She had taken off, exactly like he'd predicted. That was okay. He would find her and when he did, he would make certain she paid for running out on him.

His phone rang right as he was getting ready to leave the shed. He sighed deeply, because he knew who it was.

"Sir," he answered.

"I've made a decision," the man on the other end of the phone said. "Kill the woman and bring me the body. I've decided I don't want her. She's too much trouble and will be better off to me dead."

"Are you sure, sir?"

"Would I have called you if I wasn't? Don't question me again, boy."

"Of course not, sir. I'm sorry, sir." Damn, damn, and triple damn. What was he going to do now?

"How soon should I expect her body?" The Gentleman asked.

He wasn't sure how to answer that. The Gentleman didn't know that he had lost Janie. He wasn't about to tell him that, either.

"Give me two hours, sir."

"You have forty-five minutes."

"Sir?" There was no way he could met that timeline.

"Forty-five minutes. You're here with a body. Or else you'll become the dead body." The Gentleman hung up, leaving Mac listening to dead air.

He had to find Janie and find her quickly.

CHAPTER SIX

"Move, move, move, move, move," Brent chanted over and over again. He kept his eyes cemented on the red dot on the tablet, willing it to move again. But it didn't.

He wanted to howl, throw the tablet, and punch a tree. Either of those. He had started to hope, like he had not hoped all night, because he had watched as the dot on the laptop began to move. It wasn't a lot, and it didn't go far, or fast. But it was moving. He knew, knew in the depths of his heart, that Janie had gotten away.

But then he heard those two shots ring out. And as soon as they had, the red dot stopped moving. Yes, Janie had gotten away. And then he was almost certain that Mac had found her and shot her.

How did you move on when the worst-case scenario came to pass? Even more, how did you move on when you'd been part of what brought that scenario to pass? He'd known it would be a bad idea for her to go to the cookout with the stalker situation unresolved. He'd known it. And yet, they went anyway, and now Janie was dead.

How would he live without her?

He couldn't think about that now. Now he had to find Alyssa. Surely she had heard the shots. He contemplated heading back to her car, but decided to continue on to the shed.

He checked the gun he took out of Alyssa's duffel bag without her knowing. Loaded and ready. The next time he saw Mac, he planned to shoot him as many times as possible. He walked down the overgrown path, imagining the scene.

Unfortunately, without fail, doing so brought to mind images of Janie. He choked back a sob. "Janie."

A twig to his right snapped. He swung around and pointed the gun in the direction the sound came from. "Come out slowly with your hands up and let me see you."

Another twig snapped, but he still couldn't see who or what was making the noise. "Come out now, or else I start shooting."

He thought he heard someone speak, but the sound was so low, he couldn't make it out. He aimed toward the ground, hoping he wouldn't actually hit anyone, but that whoever was out there would take him seriously.

"Brent?"

He froze. It couldn't be. It had to be his mind playing tricks on him. He shook his head. He couldn't start imagining voices now, he had too much to do.

"Brent."

He never thought figments of his imagination would sound so real. He squinted and looked toward where the sound came from. Out of the dark cover of trees, Janie appeared. For a second she looked at him as if he'd drift away.

"Oh my God," she said. "It *is* you! Brent!"

Then neither one of them said anything. He wasn't sure who made the first move and he didn't care because she was in his arms and the world made sense again. He held her to his chest tightly and never planned to let go. "Are you okay? Did he hurt you? I heard those shots and I thought. . . ." He couldn't bring himself to say the words.

She couldn't answer any of them the way her head was buried in his chest. She gripped his shirt in a death grip. He kissed the top of her head. "It's okay. I have you now."

"Can you get me out of here?" she asked.

"Alyssa!" he said. "She's headed to the shed. We need to get to her first."

He knew heading back to the place Mac had held her would be tough, but he also knew there was no way they could leave Alyssa behind.

"We need to get off the main trial. Mac may still be around somewhere." Janie pulled him back toward the trees. "We can get to the shed this way."

They held hands as they jogged. Brent wasn't about to let go of her. "We'll stay hidden in the tree line once we get to the shed. That way we can wait for Alyssa without Mac seeing us."

It didn't take long for them to reach the shed. Brent couldn't believe how close they had been. "Did he bring you here in that truck?" he asked, pointing to the vehicle in the drive.

"No, that must belong to the rangers who came by. I wonder. . . ." her voice trailed off as a look of horror covered her face.

"You wonder what? Here, have a seat." He cleared a place for her to sit; she still looked a bit too weak for his tastes. As he'd hoped, their location shouldn't be visible from the house, but gave them a view of the path Alyssa would be arriving on.

"There were two rangers who arrived right when I was escaping. And not long after I heard two gunshots."

"Probably too much to hope that the rangers shot Mac."

Janie looked straight ahead. "Mac has totally lost it. It didn't even sound like him."

Brent rubbed the top of her hand. "You're safe now. That's all that matters. We'll get Alyssa when she comes. For now, let's call for backup and they'll take care of Mac. You never have to see him again."

A gun clicked behind them. Brent squeezed Janie's hand, but stilled the rest of his body.

"I'm afraid that's not how this ends." Mac sounded entirely too calm. "Now, I need you both to go get in the rangers' truck. We're going on a little trip."

"I'll stay right here, thank you very much." Janie crossed her arms as if to tell him that was that and she wasn't discussing it.

"I've about had enough of your mouth. I just shot and killed two men. Trust me when I say I have no problem adding a mouthy ex-cop to the list."

"I don't care. I'm staying here."

"Get in the truck!" Mac yelled.

"No."

Mac aimed his gun and shot Janie in the foot. She yelled and crumpled to the ground.

"You son of a bitch." Brent dropped to his knees beside her, pulling her to his side. "It's okay, baby. I'll get you to a hospital."

"Shouldn't make promises you can't keep." Mac leveled his gun at Janie. "Now, get in the truck."

Brent grabbed his gun and aimed it at Mac. He'd expected the man to turn his gun away from Janie and toward him, but Mac kept the focus on Janie. "Nice try playing hero, but it won't work. Drop your gun and get in the truck or I shoot you and leave your body here."

"He's bluffing," Janie said through clenched teeth, her voice sharp with pain.

"Janie, Janie, Janie," Mac said. "This is what happens when you leave before you should. You missed so many things. Like me killing the rangers. I suggest you get in the truck now."

Janie looked over to Brent. He could see past the pain in her eyes to her need for the assurance that everything would be okay. He wished he could give her something. He whispered to her, "On three."

He took a step as if he was going toward the truck, imploring Janie silently to stay where she was. She raised an eyebrow and he shook his head. Her lips were pressed tightly together, but he wasn't sure if that was because she was in pain or disapproved.

"One. Two." Brent watched Janie as he mouthed the numbers, afraid that if he looked at Mac, he'd give himself away. On three, he meant to act as if he were putting the gun down, but to instead shoot Mac. Unfortunately, Mac must have been on to him, because no sooner did Brent lift the gun only the slightest bit in order to shoot at Mac, than a searing pain rippled across his left upper arm. Completely unprepared, he dropped the gun and grabbed his arm, only to see blood flowing from between his fingers.

"Brent? Oh my God, Brent," Janie cried. "Are you okay?"

"He shot me." Brent still couldn't believe it. Moving with one thought in mind, *shoot Mac,* he reached for the gun, only to see Mac standing above him, aiming the weapon he dropped at him. His heart plummeted to see he held Janie with his other hand.

Mac gave an evil laugh. "I should kill you, but I want you to live knowing just how worthless you really are. But I really don't want you following me, either."

Janie screamed. A ball of fire exploded in Brent's chest. And the world went dark.

CHAPTER SEVEN

Janie was so shocked by Mac shooting Brent, she wasn't able to move. "Brent?" she whispered, but he didn't move. She decided right then and there, she wasn't going to move, she wasn't going to do anything Mac told her to do. She wasn't going to move from this spot because that meant leaving Brent and she was never leaving him. She closed her eyes tightly, not wanting Mac to see her cry.

Unfortunately, Mac must've been onto her plan. He didn't tell her to do anything, instead he calmly picked her up as if she weighed nothing and tried to deposit her in the back of the rangers' truck. She refused to let him get his way. She yelled and tried to bite him, and when that didn't help, she punched and kicked with all her strength. He moved her so easily, she finally realized she still suffered from the effects of whatever drug he'd given her. All too soon, she was in the truck. No matter how hard she tried to climb out of the truck, Max once again was one step ahead of her, took some rope, and tied her hands and feet securely to the seat.

"You have been quite a nuisance this evening," Max said. "I need to have you somewhere in a very short amount time . . . well, have your body somewhere in a short amount of time. Can't have you jumping out of the truck now, can I?" He laughed at what she assumed was a look of pure horror on her face. "Don't tell me you actually thought you were going to get out of this alive?"

She turned away. She wasn't going to answer anything he asked. She sure as hell wasn't going to give up, either. As long as there was a breath in her body, she was going to plan for escape. She couldn't keep herself from looking over to where Brent slumped. Still unmoving.

"You did," Mac said, obviously taking her silence the wrong way. "I think that makes you the worst detective ever." He chuckled under his breath. "Frankly, it makes you look very naïve."

He pulled away from the shed and Janie turned to look over her shoulder, willing Brent to move. But there was nothing. Before she could turn back to the front, a movement from the back of the truck caught her eye. At first she thought she was seeing things, but as she watched, Alyssa appeared.

Their eyes caught and Alyssa shook her head. Janie kept her face neutral and turned back around. Mac didn't know where Alyssa was.

His next statement confirmed that. "I'm only keeping you alive for now because I think you might be useful in tracking down that worthless girlfriend of mine."

He drove only a bit further before stopping the truck. "This is where you die."

Janie found it hard to breathe, but managed to say, "That's what you think."

He smacked her cheek. "How stupid do you think I am? You don't think I saw her the second she climbed in the truck?" He lowered his voiced. "Maybe the two of you together will give me the challenge I've been looking for and that you haven't been able to provide." He untied Janie from the truck, but left her hands tied together.

"Here's what's going to happen," he said. "You and I are going to walk to that tree with the yellow ribbon on it, I'm going to tie you to it so your arms are wrapped around the trunk and then I'm going to count to five. I'll let you guess what happens next."

Between the pain in her foot and the fear she was breathing her last precious breaths, she felt as if she was going to be sick. Was Alyssa really unarmed?

Her body shook. He was going to kill her. Brent was already dead. Oh God, she didn't know what to do.

They were getting too close to the tree. She had to think of something, but the only thing she could think of was so simple, there was no way it could work.

But she had no other choice.

Mac was half holding her, half dragging her. She walked with him a few steps, waiting for the perfect moment. He shifted the gun slightly and at that second, she let her body drop into dead weight. As she'd hoped, he was totally unprepared and let out a stream of curses. But more importantly, he used both hands to try and pick her up and in doing so his grip on the gun slackened just a bit. It wasn't much, but it was all she needed.

She grabbed the gun and while he tried to reach it, she bit his arm, her teeth sinking into his skin. He yelped and pulled away. She rolled in the opposite direction. Ignoring the pain in her foot, she pushed herself to one knee and aimed.

Alyssa jumped out of the truck and with a yell, she took off toward him, knife raised in one hand. Mac looked from one of them to the other. His expression contorted into something inhuman and with a running leap, he took off as if to grab Janie.

Janie fired the gun the same second his body slammed into her. She fell backward, her head slamming into something hard. The edges of her vision grew blurry and suddenly, she was too tired to keep her eyes open any longer.

The Gentleman stepped deeper into the shadows from where he'd been watching the entire exchange between Mac, his girlfriend, and Janie. His gut had told him there was no way Mac would be showing up with Janie's body. The man had been a liability with his pride and lack of discernment. Lately, he'd also been lazy and the decision had already been made that even if he had brought the woman's body, The Gentleman would terminate him as well.

His only regret was that he didn't get to face Mac and have him realize his true identity. Although in all truthfulness, Mac may not have recognized him. With a grin, the thought hit him that the same could not be said for Alyssa. That one would know who he was.

Will know, he corrected himself.

With Mac dead, Janie and Brent would no longer be a threat. Especially when he finished his plans. He wasn't going to spend any more manpower to take them down. However, the same could not be said for Alyssa. She wasn't next on his list, but she was on it.

Her time would come.

The Gentleman knew they'd send the bottom of the barrel to respond to the call he placed. The two young police officers were not happy to have been called to the docks while everyone else was at the park and they had no problem telling whoever was willing to listen.

"The park is where all the excitement is," the blond officer said, kicking a pile of abandoned clothing to the side. "This assignment blows."

"This is what we get for being low man on the totem pole," his darker-haired partner agreed.

"Having to take the shit calls?"

"Something like that." He looked around. "I thought the caller said he'd be here waiting for us?"

And he was on. He loved this part of the job, and with a grin, stepped out of the shadows and into the pale light given off by the streetlights.

One of the officers, the one with dark hair, spun around and a surprised look crossed his face as he realized who stood before him. "I know who you are. You're—"

The words remained unspoken due to the bullet The Gentleman put through his forehead. He spun and aimed at the blond officer who was belatedly reaching for his weapon. "Lower your weapon."

The blond looked frantically from him to his fallen partner. "Who are you?"

"Lower your weapon." He waited and then added, "I'm about to make you more important than what's happening on that island. Lower it. Now."

He wasn't sure why he was so surprised when the young man actually did what he was told. God, he loved newbies. He walked the few steps to the stunned policeman and calmly took his weapon.

Disgusting. He wasn't sure why the Charleston PD hired these imbeciles. Without thinking about it, he lifted the officer's weapon and shot him. He looked around. There weren't people around, but he couldn't count on that lasting. Not with him firing a gun twice. That meant he had to work fast.

Moving quickly, he put both guns in the blond's hands. Carefully, he draped the hairs he'd picked up on the body of the blond officer as well.

Janie and Alyssa would be looking for the person Mac took orders from. He'd just ensured they found him.

CHAPTER EIGHT

Janie slowly became aware of the low hum sounding in the background, then the soft buzz of people whispering. She was in a hospital. But before she opened her eyes, she squeezed them tightly. Brent wouldn't be here, she realized with a sharp stab of pain in her chest. Had Alyssa told everyone where to find him? They had to be able to bury him. Properly.

Maybe she could stay in the hospital bed with her eyes closed forever and she'd never have to look upon a world without Brent.

"Janie?" Alyssa asked because, of course, she would be in the room.

As soon as the thought crossed her mind, she felt bad. Alyssa had stood by her for years and it was doubtless she'd be able to get through the foreseeable future without her best friend.

Janie opened her eyes and forced a smile. "Hey."

Alyssa dropped her head and whispered, "Everyone will be in shortly now that you're awake. I need you to go along with the story I've been telling."

"What are you talking about?"

"The official story is that I shot and killed Mac."

Janie struggled to sit up, but Alyssa put a hand on her shoulder to keep her in place. "Don't sit up. You might pull something."

Alyssa wasn't lying, Janie ached all over. She settled back down onto the uncomfortable mattress. "Why is that the official story? What happened after I blacked out?"

"You're not an employee of the police department any longer and when everyone showed up at the park, I overhead Martin say that since you weren't, he was going to look into pressing charges against you."

"Charges for what? That's the most absurd thing I ever heard of."

Alyssa looked over her shoulder, but the door remained closed. She shook her head. "There's something going in on in that department that's not sitting well with me. I'm afraid Martin is involved."

The fact that such an important figure in the city's law enforcement could be in the back pocket of whatever mastermind orchestrated this situation was almost too outlandish to be true. Janie wasn't sure what sort of magic he'd have to pull to charge her with anything, but she was too tired to fight it. If it would be easier for Alyssa to say she took out Mac, so be it. She nodded. "Okay."

Unknowingly, a tear ran down her face. She hadn't noticed it until she felt the wetness on her cheek.

"Janie?" Alyssa took a tissue and passed it to her.

"Sorry." Janie wiped her cheek. "It's just—"

Suddenly she heard a voice from the hallway.

"I don't care if she's sleeping. That way I can be in the room when she wakes up. Don't put a finger on this wheelchair and I swear to God, if you touch me again, I'm suing the entire damn hospital. Don't patronize me, I'll think of something."

It sounded like Brent, but there was no way that was possible; she'd seen his broken body on the ground. She wondered how long it would be before she stopped hearing his voice everywhere she went.

But then a voice that sounded a lot like his half sister, Bea, spoke. "I appreciate you trying to do your job, sir. Trust me that he'll be a lot easier to deal with if my brother can just peek in and see her."

Janie swung her head toward Alyssa, but her friend had already walked to the door and opened it.

"Come on in, guys." Alyssa was smiling at whoever stood on the other side the door. "She's awake."

"Go," Bea said with a half laugh. "Please. Before you threaten anyone else with a lawsuit and they actually take you seriously and send the hospital's legal team to chat with you."

Janie's eyes were glued to the door. First she saw a wheelchair, then legs, and then, the face she never thought to see again was in her room and smiling. Alyssa and Bea discreetly left.

"Janie," Brent said and with that one word, she lost it, breaking down and sobbing. She buried her face in her hands, and within seconds, he was beside her and she grabbed his hands, not wanting to ever let him go.

"Janie," he whispered and kissed her hands.

"You're alive. I thought he'd killed you. You weren't moving." She couldn't stand to return to that awful moment when Mac pulled her away and Brent was slumped in the dirt, bleeding.

"It'll take a lot more than Mac to bring me down. It helped that he was a poor shot. Had he been a bit over to the left, he would have hit a major artery and I wouldn't have been as lucky. My shoulder's a bit messed up and I somehow managed to hit my head, but I'm alive."

"I killed him." She held his gaze as she told him. She didn't care if the rest of the world thought Alyssa had killed him. She wanted Brent to know the truth.

"She told me," Brent said. "I'm so proud of you. Your courage amazes me. And probably saved my life."

"I've never killed anyone," she said. "I thought the first time, I'd feel regret. Or at least feel something. As it is, I don't feel anything."

"It might come later, but don't worry, I'll be with you if it does. We'll get through it together."

A knock on the door interrupted their conversation, and a doctor stuck his head into the room. "Ms. Roberts," he said. "I heard you were awake. I need to look over your injuries."

"I'm going to stay right here," Brent said, and the doctor didn't argue.

It didn't take long for the doctor to examine her. When he finished he stood up and wrote on his chart. "Everything appears to be healing well. You're very lucky. Now let's see if we can get you two out of here by tomorrow."

"Best news I've heard all week," Janie said.

Brent winked at her. "I bet I have better news."

"What's that?"

"They found the second party in these cases. The ringleader."

Hope spread a pleasant warmness across her chest. Was it true? Was she really free? "Tell me."

"An officer on the force was found this morning. He shot his partner and then himself. He had Mac's hair on him as well as that of a newly murdered club girl."

"It's really over," she said to Brent, amazed. "Finally."

"Yes, and I can't wait to get started on the rest of our lives."

One week later, Janie waited in the bedroom for Brent to join her. He'd been making a phone call while she got ready for bed. And was she ever ready for bed.

In the week since they'd been back home, they had

slowly grown accustomed to what it was like to have a normal life. She had no idea how much she'd changed her normal routine until she returned to it. It was freeing and wonderful. In fact, there was only one thing missing. They had not yet done anything physical other than good-night kisses and holding hands.

If all went according to her plan, that would change tonight.

A floorboard creaked outside the bedroom.

"Janie?" Brent called as if afraid he was going to wake her.

She adjusted the silver slip of the babydoll lingerie she had on so it showed a bit more upper thigh and pushed a spaghetti strap off her shoulder. "Come on in. I'm not asleep."

He entered with a big grin that seemed to freeze in place as he took in the sight of her on the bed. She'd been afraid he'd turn her down for fear he'd hurt her or make her injuries worse or if he didn't, that he'd ask her so many times if she was sure, that he'd kill the mood.

He did neither. Rather, he crossed the room quickly so he stood beside her, and lightly cupped her bare shoulder. "You have no idea what seeing you like this does to me."

"What do you mean?"

He teased the remaining strap off her shoulder. "I've been waiting for you to give me a sign that you were ready."

She slid her hands under his T-shirt, delighting in the feel of his skin, trying to be careful not to disturb the bandage that covered his gunshot wound. "Then why didn't you say something?"

"Because I knew you'd let me know when you were ready."

"Brent?"

"Yes."

"Shut up and kiss me."

"Yes, ma'am."

"And none of those kisses like you've been giving me. I want you to kiss me like you mean it. Like you'll die if you don't have me right now, this second."

Instead of replying with words, he pulled the neckline of her bodice all the way down, exposing her to him completely from the waist up. Crawling up on the bed to join her, he held himself above her. And right when she thought she'd go crazy if he didn't move or do something, he crushed his lips to hers.

He held nothing back with his kiss. She felt his love and desire and even the fear he'd had when their future lay in a madman's hands. He pulled back slightly and whispered coarsely in her ear, "I'm not going to be rough, but I'm going to be very thorough and by the time I'm finished and we're both too exhausted to move, you'll know exactly how much I mean it."

Then, true to his word, he showed her with his touch, his kiss, and his moans of pleasure how much he loved her. When at last he entered her, he had her keep her eyes on his. His touch finished her healing and she knew she did the same to him.

EPILOGUE

Brent stepped over half-filled boxes, rolls of packing tape, and a stack of old newspapers in his attempt to find Janie. He'd looked in the bedroom and the sunroom. Finally, he saw her on the front porch. She wore a thin sweater and was sipping a cup of coffee.

It wasn't cold enough for a sweater. If he had to guess, he'd say she wore it so she wouldn't have to look at the scar on her arm. It had been six weeks since he and Alyssa had rescued her. Six weeks since Mac had been shot. Six weeks with no threats of any kind.

She was safe, but they were both learning that some-times safety was more mental than it was physical and that sometimes mental safety took the longest to accept. The good news was, it had been eight days since her last night-mares. He wasn't naïve enough to think she wouldn't have them anymore, but that was the longest she'd gone with-out one and he couldn't help but find that encouraging.

She moved slightly and he saw that she was on the phone. Probably with Alyssa. At one point, he'd feared Mac's involvement would drive a wedge between the two friends, but if anything, it'd only brought them closer together.

He'd tried, unsuccessfully, to convince Alyssa to move to Washington with them. He'd requested and been granted an extension on his start date. Alyssa, on the other hand, had been placed on administrative leave. He'd been livid and tried explaining to the police how, without Alyssa, he and Janie would probably not be alive. But his pleas fell on deaf ears.

One day, when he'd been in a particularly foul mood, he'd asked Alyssa why the hell she'd want to waste her life working for a department that clearly didn't value her. She'd given him that same calm smile that had driven him mad when they had been working together to find Janie. The smile he now realized was just an extension of her deeply held sense of purpose.

She said she'd made a promise when she was younger. An impractical, fantastical promise, perhaps—the kind that only the young who knew no better would make. But it was a promise, nonetheless, and one she wasn't going to break. He'd asked Janie if she had any idea what promise Alyssa had made. She'd simply said she had no idea, but that it must be deeply personal for her friend to have never mentioned it.

He opened the door to the front porch, and Janie turned and smiled. Without taking her eyes off him, she said into the phone, "Let me call you back, Alyssa."

During those awful hours when Mac had held her hostage, he'd vowed to never take a moment they had together for granted. Today, he planned to expand on that vow. He held out his hand. "Go with me on a walk?"

"The movers are coming this evening. Shouldn't we finish packing?" But she took his hand anyway.

"We'll finish after our walk." He knew she was probably confused. After all, the night before, he'd complained to her about all the things they had to accomplish. Truthfully, though, the way he saw it, only one task absolutely had to be completed and for that to happen, she had to go with him.

Hand in hand, they walked in silence. For the first few weeks following everything, he'd questioned her constantly whenever he thought she'd been too quiet. It had only been when she'd told him she was fine and she'd never lied to him so she'd tell him if she wasn't okay, that he realized he himself hadn't come through everything as unscathed as he'd thought.

They didn't have to walk too far to make it to where his surprise waited. He thought it a bit funny when she mentioned it first.

"Wonder what that carriage is doing here?" she asked. "They don't normally pick people up on this street."

"I believe," he said, unable to hide his smile, "that it's waiting for us."

"What?"

"You didn't think I was going to let you move out of Charleston without ever taking a carriage ride, did you?"

"It's really for us?" she asked almost too softly for him to hear.

A lone tear made its way down her cheek and he wiped it away with his thumb. "Yes."

She wrapped her arms around his neck and lifted her head to give him a soft kiss. "Thank you."

He returned the kiss and by then the driver stood to the side. He shook Brent's hand, helped them inside, and they were off. Brent couldn't keep his eyes off Janie. She was always beautiful to him, but today she exuded joy, and it had been so long since she'd done so.

For the first part of their ride, Brent simply watched her and it was as if she were experiencing her home city for the first time. Every so often, she'd give his hand a squeeze or he'd point out something that caught his eye. Who'd have thought playing tourist would be so much fun?

"Is everything okay?" Janie asked as the driver pulled off to the side in a quiet secluded spot of the park about ten minutes into their ride.

Though a family of butterflies had taken up residence in Brent's belly, in this he was able to confirm that everything was fine. The driver tied the horse to a nearby post and came to the side of the carriage.

"Beg your pardon," he said. "I have an urgent matter to attend to, but I'll be back in about ten minutes."

Janie watched him walk away and frowned. "I don't think they're supposed to do that."

They do if you pay them enough. But Brent didn't voice that thought. After all, he only had ten minutes. "It's fine."

"How do you know?" Janie was still watching the path their driver had disappeared down. From the looks of it, she wasn't going to be satisfied simply because he said so.

"Janie," he said, and when she didn't move or turn his way, he tried again. "Janie, look at me." She shifted her gaze and the worried look in her eyes pained him. "Everything's fine. The driver took off like that because I asked him when I booked the carriage to give us some privacy."

The worried look had been replaced by confusion. "You did? Why?"

He hadn't planned a speech or anything, having decided that the direct approach was the best. Making sure she kept her attention on him, he slid off the bench seat and knelt before her on one knee. All traces of confusion and any lingering worry left her expression and her hands flew up to cover her mouth.

His own smile came easy now that she had an idea of what he was doing. He reached into his pocket and pulled out the pale blue box that had been burning a hole in his pants. "Janie," he started, opening the box. "It's true we haven't known each other long and while I've never been a man to rush into anything, I've also never been able to hold back when I know something is right. And, Janie, we're right. I have no doubts."

She nodded in agreement with every word he said and her eyes were wet with unshed tears.

"Janie Roberts," he said. "Will you marry me?"

"Yes," she answered in a near whisper. And then repeated louder, "Yes!" She dropped her eyes to look in the box and gasped. He, of course, knew exactly what she saw. He'd known the second he saw it that the ring was for her.

A simple solitaire, set in platinum. She wouldn't have liked anything fancy; that wouldn't have matched her personality. Instead, the unadorned setting allowed the brilliance of the diamond to be seen and admired. He realized he was grinning from ear to ear as he took the ring from the box and slipped it on her finger.

He didn't have time to take a seat on the bench before she hauled him to sit beside her. Her arms flew around him and his followed, pulling her close.

"I love you," she said.

He gave her a gentle kiss. "I love you."

There was no more time for words as his lips found hers again and this time, their kiss was neither gentle nor short. Rather, it was a kiss of passion that whispered of a future filled with love and joy and desire. They were so caught up in the other that the driver, upon his return, had to cough repeatedly to get their attention.

"Would you like to continue your ride?" he asked.

Janie lifted her head only slightly. "No, but we won't complain if you have something else you need to take care of."

Don't miss the other novels
in the Sons of Broad series by

TARA THOMAS

DARKEST NIGHT
DEADLY SECRET

And be sure to look for her e-novellas:

TWISTED END
HIDDEN FATE
SHATTERED FEAR

From St. Martin's Paperbacks
www.stmartins.com